THE KILLING GAME

Alex Robert

This is a work of fiction. Any similarities to real people, past or present, places, actual events or situations are purely coincidental. This book should not be copied, forwarded, resold or given away in any form or means without the express permission of the author.

Copyright © 2025 by Alex Robert

All rights reserved.

By Alex Robert

Detective Jack Husker Crime Thrillers

Death Sketches
The Dead Don't Talk
A Dish Served Cold
Time To Die
The Killing Game

Death came with a cruel smile

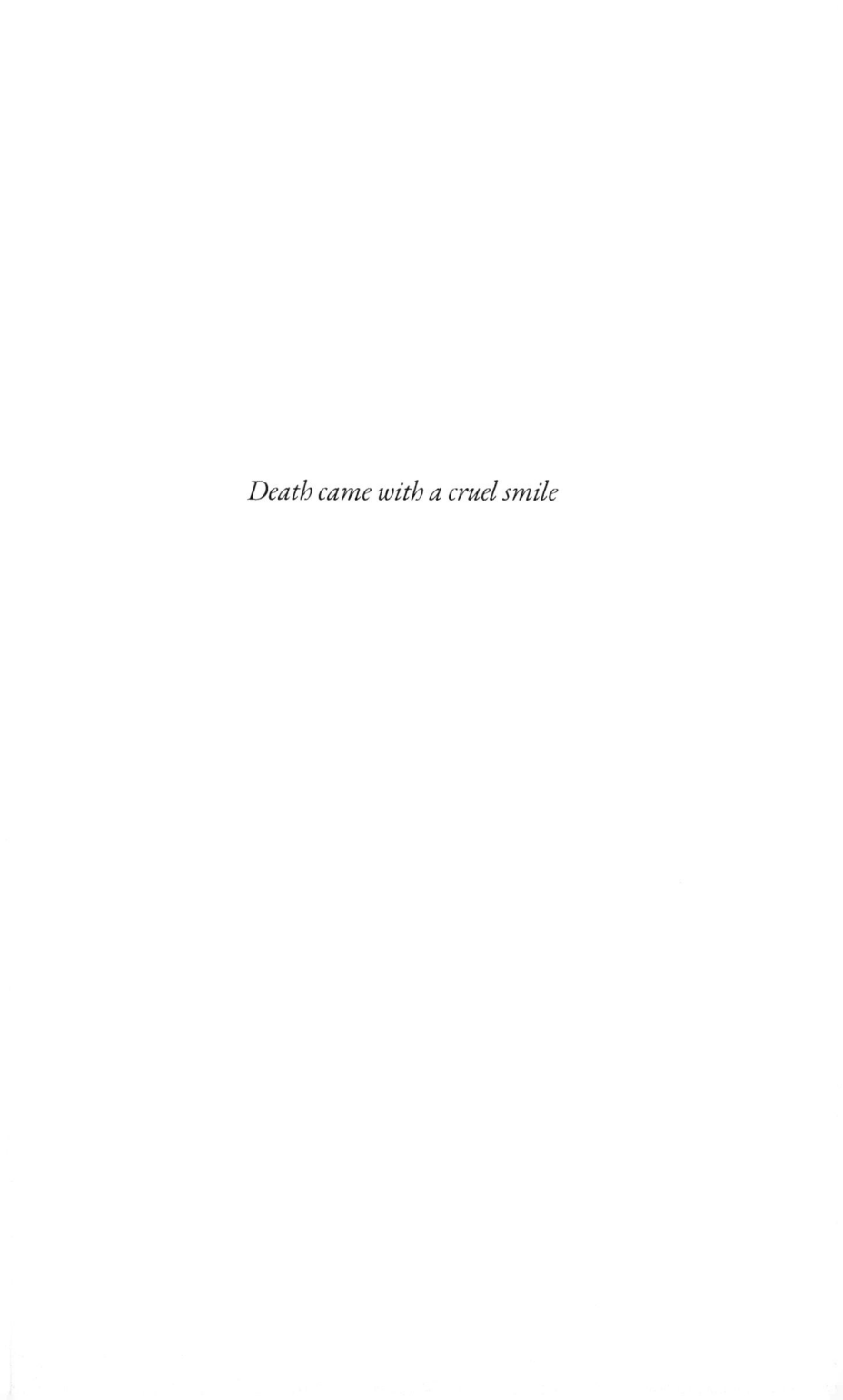

Chapter 1

Nervously, he stumbled down the dark narrow corridor. The drink had not helped, the four double vodkas the minimum he needed to calm his nerves. His hands reached up, searching for somewhere that might offer balance. There was nothing. The recently plastered walls were smooth, offering the hint they would wipe clean easily. Maybe he was just one of many who had trodden the very same path.

"What are you doing?" he mumbled to himself. His thoughts turned to his wife and children at home. He had let them down. For too long, he had not been there when they needed him. If it all went wrong, he would never be there for them again.

He had to fight the uncertainty that was in danger of overwhelming him. After all, this was for them. This would allow them to be free of the burden of debt. It was a debt which he had caused.

He moved to the end of the corridor and paused when he felt the metal handle. This was the most important decision of his life. He could turn and leave at any moment. After all, he was in charge. That was what they had told him. It was his choice to do it, not theirs. He stopped and allowed that thought to go through him. A shake of his head confirmed his feelings. Who were they kidding when they said he could walk away?

In one direction, there was the opportunity to have a life. The other meant nothing. The world he was running away from would only hunt him down. With a deep breath, he gripped the handle and closed his fingers around it. He gave it a heavy twist and stumbled forward into the room. Despite his fear, he would confront whatever was awaiting him.

Inside, his opponent sat quietly. On the opposite side of a table, eager hands played with the chips that were set out. They were turned over between confident fingers. There was no mistaking the expertise with which it was done. They were hands that were comfortable with the small plastic discs and the value they represented.

To the right, a symbolic stack of money was piled up on the green felt surface. Not all of it; the full amount would not fit on the table. It was enough to signify its presence as was the gun which lay beside it. No doubt, it was loaded and ready to be used. The barrel was pointed in the direction of the empty chair. The money and the gun offered the two potential outcomes. The reality of it could not be ignored.

"Mr Brand, please take a seat."

The voice was not as harsh as he was expecting. That made it worse. It should have been a threat or at least a barked order. It should have demanded that he sit at the table. To his opponent, he was a piece of dirt on a shoe, a creature barely worthy of being there. The politeness felt unnerving as was the smile. He wanted to hate his opponent. That was difficult when no ill feeling had been offered.

"It's Darren," he replied.

He eased himself onto the simple wooden chair and pulled it up to the table. In front of him was a pile of poker chips, all stacked neatly for the game. A closer inspection confirmed their value. Darren totted them up in his head. There was half a million sitting there. Never before had he played for such high stakes. Whatever the outcome, he never would again.

"It's all there."

"Sorry; force of habit. In my line of work, everyone is out to rip you off."

"What is it you do?"

"I'm in the recovery game. You know, breakdowns. I mainly do trucks."

"That sounds like a lucrative business if you don't mind me saying so."

"Not as much as it used to be."

"I guess that is what brings us here. Have the rules of the game been explained to you?"

"Not really."

"Then let me oblige. We are playing heads-up Texas Hold'em poker. There are two half-million stacks, with starting blinds of five and ten thousand. The blinds will double every ten hands. If you win, you take the million in cash. I guess you don't need me to explain what happens if you lose."

Darren Brand looked directly at the gun. He was shaking. His eyes focused on the trigger which could end his life. He tried to drag his stare across to the money. He was fighting a losing battle against the tide of realism ripping through him.

"Where's the million?"

"In the case over there, minus what you see on the table."

"Can I count it?"

"If you want. The combination is six-six-six on both sides."

"The number of the beast."

"Appropriate, don't you think?"

Darren shrugged. What did he care if they wanted a joke at his expense?

"I won't bother, thanks. I'll trust you."

"Are you sure?"

"Yes; you've got a kind face."

"That's good because it might be the last one you ever see. Do you want to deal or should I?"

"Haven't we got a dealer?"

"It's probably best to keep this game to ourselves, whichever way it turns out. It leaves one less witness to worry about."

"I guess," sighed Darren. "You can deal."

His opponent smiled and picked up the deck. The cards were spread face down around the table. Flat hands moved them before they were brought back to a pile. Darren indicated where he wanted the cut, an act the dealer completed with confidence. A card was discarded and then a brief exchange of looks preceded two cards being placed face-down in front of each player.

Darren flexed his fingers. He bent them backwards until they offered a sickening crack. His opponent grimaced and watched him reach for his cards. The corners were eased upwards, to reveal the identity to eager eyes. All the while, both players scanned the table, hoping for clues. There was nothing; not even a flicker. Instead, two sets of eyes stared down at what had been dealt.

"I'll call you," said his opponent. Five thousand was pushed in to even up the blinds.

Darren processed the information. He had an off-suit ace and a king. It was a hand to back heavily in a one-on-one game. He tried to remain calm to offer no clues to his opponent whose eyes tore into him. He kept the bet simple and pushed thirty thousand across the table.

"I'll raise you," confirmed Darren. As he stared at his opponent, his whole body felt more sober.

"And I'll call you," came the immediate reply. A matching bet was pushed into the middle without a blink.

A card was discarded from the top of the pack before three cards were dealt. The king of diamonds, the jack of hearts and the two of clubs were placed face up in the centre. Neither player offered a hint of what they were thinking and yet it was close to being the perfect scenario for Darren. It gave him the top pair with an over-card to go with it.

Darren took a moment to think and then counted out his chips. It was up to him to make his bet. Seventy thousand was assembled into a pile. Another glance towards his opponent brought no reaction. Nor did the act of pushing the bet into the middle of the table when he announced that he was raising the pot.

There was an initial moment of silence. A hand reached up and was dragged across his opponent's chin. Those steely eyes stared venomously at Darren. They were searching for any fragment of information.

"I'll call."

The ace which followed made Darren's heart race. It was time for him to make his move. His hand pushed a stack of chips into the centre without them being counted out. His excitement didn't allow it. The need to get his chips into the pot had overtaken any requirement to play things cool.

"I'll raise you," confirmed Darren.

"And I'll raise you all in," was the immediate reply.

Darren looked shocked and stared at his opponent. The temperature of the room felt like it had increased by a few degrees. The sweat on his forehead was dabbed away with a hand. He pulled on his shirt. It was clinging to his beating chest.

He watched his opponent's chips being pushed confidently into the middle. He looked down at his own pile and released a loud sigh. He was committed. There was too much in there for him to fold when he had the cards to back up his bet. With a deep breath, his trembling hands pushed everything he had to the centre of the table. It was his life, his family and everything he had ever worked for that was eased away from him.

"I'll call," he said nervously. The tone in his voice gave away his fear.

The cards were flipped over. Darren offered up his two pairs. They were no match for the set of three kings his opponent revealed. He was beaten unless the final card produced one of the remaining two aces.

Across from him, his opponent did not show any emotion. When the last card was dealt, there was still nothing and yet Darren knew it was over. The disappointment at seeing the four of hearts would be taken to his grave. He slumped back into his chair and forced out a nervous smile.

"What happens now?" he asked, the question punctuated by the sound of a soft whimpering groan.

His opponent picked up the gun, cocked back the hammer and fired a single bullet directly between his eyes. Darren Brand's lifeless body slumped back into the chair. His problems were over. His debts would be taken to his grave. Opposite him, a sense of satisfaction spread through his opponent.

Death came with a cruel smile.

Chapter 2

Lisa stood outside her flat with her arms folded. She watched the truck reversing towards her. The excruciating noise it made risked waking the dead. Her first thought was for her neighbours and what they might think about being disturbed at such an early hour. Those fears did nothing to dampen her excitement. She was staring at the first new car she had ever bought. It was on the back of the trailer, secured by a series of straps.

Once the truck was in position, a stocky lad jumped from the cab. Maybe thirty-five years of age, his tight t-shirt and tattoos were those of someone who worked out. His bulging biceps were displayed in a manner to ensure that everyone knew about his physique.

"Lisa, I take it," he offered.

"Yes, that's me," she replied, without taking her eyes off the car.

"Not a bad looking body, eh?" His smile presented his gleaming white teeth against his tanned skin. "I guess the car's not bad either."

It was too early in the morning for Lisa to make an effort to respond. It had been a late night, her limited hours of sleep already biting hard. She had shuddered when they had given her the early delivery time. Only the anticipation of seeing the car made her accept it.

"Where do you want me to stick it, love? I am talking about the car before you get excited. The name's Danny, in case you are asking."

"I wasn't but it is good to know. Have you got a surname, Danny?"

"Why?"

"When I file a police report, I like to have all the correct details."

"Police report? Are you a copper?" he asked, his expression turning to panic.

"Yes, I am. The name is DS Lisa Ramsey, in case you are asking."

"Oh shit, I'm sorry. I was only joking with you. I didn't mean anything by it."

"And I'm only joking with you. Not about being a copper but including you in a report."

"Really?"

"Yes, we only document the big fry, not the delivery boys. Shall we concentrate on sorting out my car?"

"Yes, sign here," he grunted.

"Not until it is safely off the truck. I'm not taking the risk of you backing that thing off there. You know what they say about men and reversing."

Danny's eager nod made Lisa smile. She loved watching him suffer. It ended his pointless flirting and allowed her to focus on her new toy. All sparkling in gun-metal grey, the paintwork glinted in the early morning light. The car was an extravagance but one which she could afford. She thought about her parents and how eager she would be to show them.

She could almost hear her father's voice, with his prudent tones echoing in her ears. Did she dare tell him about the finance or would that be a step too far for a man who had never taken a risk in his life?

She watched Danny lower the car off the truck. The winch eased it down with nothing more than a hand-held control. Stripped of his cheeky character, Danny looked timid and bored. It had become just another delivery job for him. His one opportunity to have fun had been taken away. Lisa's sympathy was minimal. The lad was good-looking enough to get his share of success. She would not be adding a notch to his bedpost.

"There you are. I'll let you park it in its space. I'm guessing you don't want a guided tour around it."

"No, it's fine, thanks. Where do you need a signature?"

"Here, here and here, when you are ready."

Lisa scribbled her name repeatedly on the sheets of paper. She took both sets of keys and a copy of the document with her name on it. She folded it twice and tucked it into her pocket. The mundane part of the deal was done. As she gazed at the car, Danny remained alongside her and stared wistfully in her direction. When Lisa said nothing, he scribbled on a piece of paper and handed it to her.

"What's that?"

"My number. If you change your mind, give me a shout. I wouldn't mind a ride with you."

"And don't tell me, you are not talking about the car," sighed Lisa. She stared at him with venom in her eyes. "You've tried that line and it was not funny the first time."

"You can't blame a lad for trying. You've got my number."

"Don't push it," replied Lisa. She walked straight to the car and left Danny to trudge dejectedly back to his truck.

Lisa got into the driver's seat and watched Danny drive off. Once the ignition was switched on, she drove into her parking space and allowed the engine to idle. She listened to it purring like a cat. For too long, she had made do with older cars or whatever she could borrow from the station's fleet. Despite the extravagance, there was no regret in her decision. Some trips out on a weekend would soon see it pay for itself as would the drive back up north to see her parents.

She took out her mobile and connected it to the car. Her contacts appeared on the screen, with Jack's number at the top. As soon as the list flashed up, her phone sprang to life. The loud ring of an incoming call echoed around the car. Every direction seemed to have a speaker to accompany DCI Eddie Louth's name being displayed. She accepted the call, hoping she had pressed the right button. The whole experience felt like she was learning a foreign language.

"Morning, sir."

"Good morning, Lisa. Where are you? It sounds like you are in a cave."

"I'm in my car."

"I take it your new car has been delivered."

"Yes, I'm just getting familiar with it."

"Hopefully, on hands-free?"

"I'm parked in my allotted space at the flat. That's as far as I have got."

"What did you go for in the end?"

"A VW Golf."

"Nice. I had a Golf at one point. That must put you in good company."

Lisa rolled her eyes and allowed herself to mutter a confirmation. It was no time to offer a put-down to her boss.

"It looks like I have caught you at the perfect time. How do you fancy a run out in it? It would make sure the engine is okay."

"What do you need me to do, sir?"

"Can you get out to Castle Howard?"

"I take it I'm not going sightseeing."

"Unfortunately not. Someone walking his dog has just turned up a body in the edge of the lake. We don't know the details but he says there is a hole in the corpse's head. He reckons it's murder. It seems like everyone is an expert these days."

"There are too many detective shows. My mother loves them even if she can't understand why I'm not on them. She seems to think that we cover the whole country."

"At times, it feels like we do. At least Midsomer is outside our territory. They turn up three or four bodies a week there."

"I'll get on my way, sir. We can't keep our budding detective in Midsomer Castle Howard waiting all day."

"Absolutely not. Keep me informed, Lisa."

"Will do."

"And take it easy. I don't want that shiny new car of yours getting dirty on its first trip."

"Thanks, sir. I thought it might be me that you were worried about."

"I am. I also don't want a claim coming in. Remember, I know how much those VW garages charge."

***

Lisa took a series of deep breaths to ease her nerves. She felt like she was a young girl taking her first drive alone after passing her test. That uncertainty was mixed in with a tingle of excitement. The odometer read three miles. Other than the delivery mileage, all the rest would be hers.

She slipped the car into reverse and eased out of her parking space. Lisa exited the car park and turned onto Malton Road. As she drove, she could sense a series of eyes upon her. The gleaming new car, with its new registration, was conspicuous on the open road. It put her on edge. She was not someone who liked to stand out from the crowd.

On the A64, she pressed her foot down to accelerate with the flow of traffic. It felt good when the car responded without the need to stamp down with her right foot. Already, she loved her purchase. Friends had warned her of its loss of value when it left the forecourt. She did not care. She had earned every ounce of pleasure it was giving her.

Lisa felt a pang of disappointment when she turned down a country lane. That changed when the car hugged the back roads as if it was born to be driven on them. Each bend was a joy to be savoured. She wished that she had taken the plunge sooner. She had made do for too long when she could afford something better.

At the side of Castle Howard Lake, she could see the police cordon in place. A large white tent had been put up and there was tape to halt her progress. An officer greeted her when she pulled up, his eyes narrowing as he gazed at her car. Lisa held out her warrant card. His cursory nod confirmed that he had not even looked at who she was. He had accepted her identity on trust.

"Nice car," he nodded.

"Thanks. Who's in charge here?"

"Good question. I guess Ben Hughes is probably the man to see."

She got out of the car and ducked under the tape. It left her car parked alongside the uniform. Not that he would do anything if something happened to it. His look was of envy rather than anything else.

Lisa walked down towards the lake. She cursed her footwear as she moved towards it. She had gone straight out without thinking about putting any boots in the car. Her town shoes were no match for the softness of the ground. With each step, her feet sunk further into the grass. Either she had put on weight or it was exceptionally soft. It did not take her long to blame it on the underfoot conditions.

By the time she arrived at the tent, her feet were soaked. The mud had oozed up over the top of her shoes. They would be ruined. Her bigger concern was how she would drive back. Her shiny new car would end up looking like a ploughed field.

"DS Lisa Ramsey coming in," she called out. She pushed the flap of the tent aside to allow her to enter.

Inside, the light was dim. Two white-suited figures were down on their knees. They were bent over a third person, whose feet stuck out from where they were crouched. Their faces turned to look up, the hoods on their suits covering all but the central oval of their faces. She recognised Ben Hughes. The lady beside him was not someone she had seen before.

"Hi, I'm DS Lisa Ramsey," she said, holding out a hand. "Call me Lisa."

"Deborah Reardon. I won't shake your hand if you don't mind," she replied while showing the state of her gloved palms.

"Hi, Deborah."

"Call me Debbie. We're not at Sunday school even if I am on my knees praying."

"Will do. Hi Ben; how are you?"

"I'm fine, Lisa. I'm getting too old to be on my knees in the cold. Other than that, I'm okay."

"You sound like an old man."

"I feel like one...not in that sense of the word before you say anything, Debbie," he laughed.

Lisa laughed with him as did Debbie. It was a moment of respite before their expressions reset. When silence returned, all three of them gazed down at the body. They nodded to confirm they understood what they were looking at.

"What do we know?" asked Lisa.

Ben offered his response. "The deceased is an adult white female, probably late twenties to early thirties. Approximately five and a half feet in height and weighing somewhere between nine and ten stone. It's difficult to be more precise because the body has been in there for some time. At this stage, I would estimate at least a week. I would not be surprised if it was longer."

"And the cause of death?"

"Give us a chance. You'll want her star sign next," laughed Ben.

"Yes, and what she had for breakfast on holiday last year," confirmed Lisa.

"That's easy; sangria," interrupted Debbie. Both Ben and Lisa looked confused when they turned in her direction. "Doesn't everyone have sangria for breakfast on holiday?"

"No," said Lisa.

"Nor me," confirmed Ben.

"Oh, then it is just me...sorry," blushed Debbie.

"We don't have a cause of death yet," continued Ben. "However, a bloody great hole in her head would give us a fair clue. It looks like she was shot in the temple from close range. If that didn't kill her, it would have sure given her a headache."

"Assuming it was done before she was killed," said Debbie, eager to contribute to the conversation.

"That's fair. We can't confirm that at this stage," agreed Ben.

"It would be unusual to shoot someone in the head after they had drowned in a lake, don't you think?" asked Lisa.

"We aren't ruling anything out," said Ben. "We've seen stranger sights in this job."

Lisa raised her eyebrows. She had heard the words and yet she knew what the answer would be. So did the others even if their professionalism meant they were not prepared to admit it.

"When will we know?"

"I am not sure. A fair bit of wildlife has had a go at the wound. It will take some looking at."

"Has she been out of the water for long?" enquired Lisa.

"Looking at the way the level of the lake has dropped recently, I would say that she has been above the water for a couple of days. It was just unlucky that nobody has seen her until now."

"Who did see her?"

"Someone walking a dog. One of the uniforms has spoken to him. He didn't have much to offer."

"I'll need to speak to him."

"That's fine, he's still there. He's a little bit shaken up."

"Just like Elvis," quipped Debbie, to which neither Ben nor Lisa responded.

Chapter 3

"Jack, couldn't you have put on something smarter? We are supposed to be going into the County Stand. They do have a dress code."

DI Jack Husker looked up towards his superior. The frown on DCI Eddie Louth's face confirmed that he was serious. Jack shrugged. His eyes glanced down at his appearance. It was hard to understand what was wrong. Yes, the grey jacket was ageing as were the blue trousers, which had not seen an iron in weeks. The scuffed brown shoes were relatively new or had seen some polish in the last couple of months. If he could have found some matching socks, the outfit would have been perfect.

"Would you like me to go home to see what else I've got?"

"And not come back? I don't think so. Do you own anything that would qualify as being smart and clean?"

"Do you mean clean or freshly washed?"

"They are the same thing to most people."

"Right, okay. That might prove difficult. I can probably find a pair of matching socks if that helps?"

With perfect timing, Jack lifted his trousers a few inches. One sock was blue; the other was grey. Louth's eyes rolled so far back that Jack wondered whether they were going to drop out through his neck.

"I despair of you, Jack."

"I'm sorry, sir. I'm just not a fashion icon. My only hope is to catch the fashion when it circles around for another go."

"I'm not sure you'll be ready for that. I sometimes wonder whether you should even be allowed out in public."

"So do I. That's why I didn't want to come. Tell me again; why are we going to the races? It will be bedlam."

"It's part of our policing in the community initiative. We have been invited as guests of Marcus and Laura Tummel."

"Great."

"You do know who the Tummels are, don't you?"

"I've no idea whatsoever but I'm sure it will be great."

"They are racehorse trainers based just outside of Malton. You have heard of Malton, haven't you?"

"Yes; they hold food festivals there."

"I'm impressed. Do you go?"

"No."

"What do you do in your spare time other than drink? No, wait, don't tell me. I don't want to know."

Jack sighed loudly. "And there goes my anecdote about the leotard, the feather boa and my wellington boots. I'll save that one for another day."

"How about you save it for another DCI? Better still, save it for another lifetime. Come on, let's go. We don't want your odd socks being late."

Jack followed Eddie Louth into a waiting car. Its door was held open by a junior officer. Jack doffed his imaginary cap, playing the role of importance to the limit. Jack rarely used a car other than a taxi, let alone one where a chauffeur was driving. For Louth, it was part of the normality of a DCI's world.

"Do I need to wave to the gathered crowds?"

"Just sit back and shut up. I want you on your best behaviour when we get there."

"And if I'm good, do I get an ice cream?"

"No, you earn the right to nominate someone else to take your place next time."

As the car drove through the streets, Jack fell silent. The incentive Louth had given him was the best he could have hoped for. He sat back and allowed the comfort of the leather seats to absorb him. He stared out at the growing numbers that were gathering in the city. It was York on a race day, which meant the drinkers and party-goers were out in force. It also meant there was guaranteed overtime for any uniform who wanted it. Every one of them would be needed. There was always plenty of trouble to deal with.

The last quarter of a mile to the racecourse took an age. The car inched along at a walking pace. Even the turn into the car park took a few minutes. Jack puffed out his cheeks and wondered why anyone would put themselves through such an experience voluntarily. There were far quieter racecourses if you wanted to see the horses. The truth was the majority would not even watch the races. They were there to be seen and to socialise. The horses felt like an unnecessary distraction.

Louth looked agitated throughout the delays. He checked his watch repeatedly while Jack remained silent beside him. He had nothing to say and was happy to let his eyes drift closed. The whole rigmarole of the races did nothing for him. The appearance of part-time drinkers only annoyed him more. It was like New Year's Eve all over again, with people emerging for a once-a-year session. They did not know how to behave in a pub and had even less of an idea with a bellyful of booze inside them.

It had been bad enough in his day when it was ale with the occasional chaser. Now, with shots in fashion, the behaviour was so much worse. There would be bodies slumped all over the city, with fights and sickness around every corner. Jack would avoid the front line of it. He would perform his community duties and then return home to hide away in his front room.

A wave of their warrant cards afforded them access to a side parking area for honorary guests. That allowed them to move out of the line of traffic and park up alongside a Bentley Continental GT. It was sparkling in the sun and came with a small crowd of admirers who had gathered around to be pictured alongside it.

"Why didn't we come in one of those?" asked Jack.

"Because our travel is paid for by the public purse as you well know."

"You're right, sir. It will be two return bus tickets for us next time."

Louth scowled and yet the point had been well made. Their car was excessive for the short trip they had undertaken. Louth spoke to the driver and asked him to hang around until he was called. When he looked up, Jack was already striding off towards the track.

"Steady on, Jack. What's the rush?"

"We don't want to miss any of the action."

"I thought you didn't like horse racing."

"I don't, but I quite like watching people. There is a fair chance of nabbing a couple of pick-pockets if we keep our eyes open."

"Jack, we are here as part of a community initiative, not to go chasing pick-pockets."

"If we see a crime, it is our responsibility to deal with it."

"Cut the clap-trap and follow me. We are going to meet the Tummels before you get distracted. And remember what I said about you behaving."

"Yes, Dad. I'll try my best."

***

Marcus and Laura Tummel were standing in the owners' enclosure. They were holding court with a crowd of people listening intently. Marcus looked smart if a little portly, his jacket unlikely to stand a chance of closing. In his late forties, he had the appearance of someone who had enjoyed a good life. His slightly reddening face and well-groomed hair gave him a healthy look.

To his right, Laura had her own group around her. They were fawning over her like over-eager puppies. Jack was not slow to notice her and nor did anyone else within viewing distance. Still in her early forties, she looked stunning in a distinctive figure-hugging red dress. It was overly tight in places and it had got the attention of the men around her.

As Jack moved closer, he noted her deep chestnut hair. Her locks were flowing onto a white pashmina thrown over her shoulders. It did nothing to hide her beauty, which was radiating around the owners' enclosure. The only person not staring at her was her husband.

DCI Louth hung back and put an arm across Jack's path. He was reluctant to move in with so many guests around them. He slowed their walk, hoping the crowd would dissipate. Jack had no such reservations and marched straight up to the group. He reached into his pocket, took out his warrant card and thrust it into the middle of the throng.

"DI Jack Husker; you are all under arrest," he said as Louth's face turned to thunder. "Sorry; force of habit. I meant to say, I'm DI Jack Husker and I'm here on a policing in the community initiative. I get the two so easily confused."

His words barely forced a reaction.

"And you must be DCI Louth," said Marcus with a smile. He blanked Jack and moved across to his superior.

"Call me Eddie. I do apologise for our local bull. The china shop is closed today."

"Don't worry; we all have them working for us. May I introduce Laura, my wife?"

She smiled and held out her hand as if expecting it to be kissed. Jack took it and shook it vigorously.

"Hi, Laura; I'm Jack."

"I sort of got that," she sneered. "You have managed to disperse the crowd."

Jack noted that her horde of admirers had moved on. None of them had any wish to associate with the police.

"They teach us that in basic riot training. I'm a dab hand with a baton and a shield if you need me at any time."

"I am surprised that you need anything to keep people away. What was your name again?"

"Jack Husker."

"Well, it is a pleasure to meet you, Jack. If you will excuse me, I have things I need to do."

"The pleasure was all mine," replied Jack.

"Marcus, come on, we have work to do," snarled Laura.

"Yes, walkies," muttered Jack under his breath.

Eddie Louth and Jack watched them walk away. Jack knew what was coming long before Louth turned towards him with venom.

"What on earth was that about?"

"I was just making their acquaintance. They seem very nice."

"Next time, don't," growled Louth. "And try to be more subtle if you are going to stare at her."

"I was just doing a bit of detective work, sir."

"Jack, you were practically undressing her with your eyes."

"I was trying to detect if Miss Frosty-Knickers had anything on under that dress."

"We are supposed to be making friends today, not alienating ourselves."

"I was only looking where everyone else was except for one person. Did you notice who was the exception?"

"I was," insisted Louth.

"Nice try, sir. The only one not interested in her was Marcus. Odd that."

"And that is the sum total of your detecting? You have worked out that some middle-aged husbands do not find their wives particularly alluring any more."

"That's not the only thing I have detected. Give me some credit."

"Go on; what other enlightenment can you offer?"

"I have detected where the ice cream van is," grinned Jack.

Eddie Louth shook his head in disbelief. Every part of him wanted to fight back against Jack's attitude. But why? What good would it do? Jack would just come back at him with something far more irritating.

"Fine, I'll buy you an ice cream," snarled Louth.

"Thanks, Dad," smiled Jack as he walked away from the DCI.

Chapter 4

Lisa spent an hour talking to the dog walker before concluding that she was wasting her time. He told her little other than he had seen the body while he was out walking. It was his first trip around the lake in nearly a year. He had noticed the wound to the head. After that, most of the time had been spent discussing his dog. The spaniel had a striking resemblance to one her aunt had kept. Its skittish behaviour was just as Lisa remembered from her childhood. It offered fond memories and put the man at ease.

The walker himself was an uninteresting man. He was a semi-retired rail worker who seemed to spend most of his free time doing voluntary work. She got his full life story and it left Lisa wondering why he did not continue to work full-time. His sole interests appeared to be his work and his dog. Lisa thanked him on several occasions before she finally managed to end the conversation.

Once free of his clutches, she walked back towards the scene. The body was already in the process of being taken to the morgue. It felt unusually swift. She spoke to Ben Hughes who was finishing off his work. Every detail was being documented meticulously by a man who was proving to be thorough in his work. Thankfully, Debbie was no longer there, allowing Lisa to have a proper chat with her colleague.

"Why are you moving the body so quickly?"

"We've got everything we can from here. It is due to rain. If it does, the body will get covered again. Plus, there is a slot free for the pathologist, so we decided to get her in. If you go straight there, you might get to see the post-mortem."

"I'm not that desperate for entertainment."

"You might get an early ID to work off."

"Are you trying to get rid of me?"

"Perish the thought, though I am tired."

"Is that from the job or have Debbie's jokes worn you out?"

"No comment."

"Thanks, Ben. I'll be in touch."

Lisa left him at the scene and returned to her car. She took great care to inspect her footwear and clothing. Every piece of mud was wiped off and then re-wiped to ensure it would not leave a mark on the interior. Once she was satisfied, she slipped back inside and allowed the smell of her new car to engulf her. It was all hers. She was not going to allow anyone else to enjoy it until the novelty had worn off.

The drive back was her first real opportunity to appreciate the car. The early nerves of being at the wheel had subsided though something was still nagging in her mind. Her GAP insurance was yet to be confirmed. That meant a hefty bill if she were to write off the car. She eased her right foot off the pedal as a natural reaction to her concern.

Her hands were in the ten-two position for the first time since her driving test. It felt like both her father and instructor were sitting there on her shoulders. They were identifying imaginary faults and shaking their heads towards one another. It spoiled things. Lisa knew that a time would come when she would be able to enjoy the car without such worries.

She arrived at the mortuary after an uneventful drive. Lisa pressed the intercom and was met with a gruff unwelcoming tone. It was a stern female voice that she did not recognise. Jack had warned her about the lady when she had phoned him to say that she was following the body on its journey.

"Hi, it's DS Lisa Ramsey. You are doing a post-mortem on a person of interest to me."

"Am I?" barked the response.

"I am interested in the body from Castle Howard Lake."

"I am afraid they are all bodies to me. Can this wait?"

"I was hoping to come and see you."

"You'll have to scrub up or come back in twenty minutes. That's your choice."

Lisa's stomach performed an unsettled dance. She checked her watch, knowing that Jack would march straight in. She was not Jack and nor did she have an iron stomach. Her avoidance of the mortuary for most of her career was not coincidental.

"How about you buzz me in and I'll wait in reception until you have finished?"

"That's fine but the term 'reception' might be an over-exaggeration. You'll be lucky to find a broken chair in there."

"That's okay; I'll stand."

The door sounded to allow Lisa to step inside. Immediately, she was hit by the smell. Her stomach tightened at the stale, sickly odour that she had no desire to know anything more about. She turned back towards the entrance and sucked in a last breath of fresh air. Once the door was closed, she was only yards away from experiencing the full gory detail of the work taking place inside.

The voice had been right about what was on offer. The space opened up into nothing more than a hallway. The threadbare carpet had a mountain of unopened post kicked to one side. There was nowhere to sit or drink a coffee. Not that Lisa would have been able to force it down. She checked her phone and then paced back and forth. Her patience was about to be tested.

It took nearly forty-five minutes for someone to appear. Not feeling her best, Lisa had resorted to leaning on the wall. Lisa half-smiled and pushed herself upright. She held out her hand. The appearance of the woman matched her voice. Mid-forties, with dyed blond hair and a weathered face, she looked like she had spent twenty years on a farm. Only her white coat offered any suggestion that she was a pathologist. Lisa offered another introduction. Her accompanying hand was left hanging in the air.

"Better not; I've only had a quick scrub," she replied, holding up hands that were encased in rubber gloves. "I'm Cathy Duggan, the on-call pathologist."

"Thanks for the warning," said Lisa. "I'm not too good in these places."

"You get used to it after a while. Now, if I remember correctly, I believe you were interested in the stiff from the lake."

"That's right," said Lisa, deciding it was not the right time to debate her terminology. "I just wondered whether you had any preliminaries for us."

"We are not miracle workers. We have only had the body for a short while."

"I know. It's just that Jack said you were very good."

"Jack…ah, Jack Husker. Is there anything or anyone that man isn't into? Oops, sorry, excuse the insinuation. I forgot that you two were involved."

Lisa blushed and chose to say as little as she dared.

"He speaks highly of you," she offered.

"I'm sure he does. Look, we are talking absolute preliminaries here, so don't go writing reports quoting me. Jack wouldn't, so I don't expect you to either. Is that understood?"

"Yes, that is understood."

"You are talking about a female in her late twenties to early thirties; an attractive girl or she was; maybe five foot seven with a good figure. Brown hair; brown eyes; she has a couple of discrete tattoos, which I can give you pictures of. I would say that she was probably single. If I was going for a cause of death at this stage, the safe money would be on the bullet hole in her head. It looks like a nine-millimetre gun from close range. I might be wrong given the state of the wound. We can follow up on that."

"That's impressive for a preliminary," nodded Lisa. "Any ideas who she might be?"

"That's the easy bit. She goes by the name of Josie Raynor."

"How do you know her name and why do you think she is single?"

"The name is easy, once you find her driving licence. It was hidden in a concealed pocket in her jacket. The single bit is a guess. There is no mark on her finger or ring of any description and let's be honest, not many men would want to lose a woman that attractive. There aren't too many of them to go around."

"I guess not," said Lisa.

"Having said that, the ring could have been stolen. I don't think it was. I am pretty sure this was no robbery."

"Do you think the motive was sexual?"

"That's the strange thing. There is no sign of that either. That is just a preliminary assessment, mind you."

"So why kill her?"

"That is where you come in, DS Ramsey. Remember, you're the detective. I'm just a pathologist even if I am considered a good one at that."

Lisa thanked her and left the building. She had never felt more desperate for the fresh air awaiting her outside.

***

Lisa called DC Kelly Knox as soon as she was back in her car. She sent the young detective to see Dan Millings. She had waited for a few minutes before she got back inside her spotless vehicle. The smell of the morgue was lingering on her and risked contaminating the interior. The last thing she wanted was a car with the aroma of a hearse.

Cathy Duggan's words troubled her. The lack of an obvious motive was hard to take in. Take away a relationship, a sexual urge or money and there would be little for the police to pursue. It had to be one of them. It was always one of the three. A person close to the deceased was normally the likely suspect. Nobody went around sticking bullets in the foreheads of random people, let alone someone as attractive as Josie Raynor.

Kelly Knox was delighted to get the call. Her day was dragging. She had been left without an active investigation to work on. It was hard enough to get opportunities as a newcomer to the team. When there was a lack of work, that became impossible. All the interesting tasks were retained by the more senior detectives who were keen to keep themselves busy.

In her short time in the station, she had heard about Dan Millings. He was making a name for himself as the head of the missing persons' team. Too young to have been put there willingly, his unfortunate incident at the wrong end of a murderer's gun had nearly ended his life. Since then, Dan had made something of his new job and had cleared the deadwood from the office. He had also secured funds to computerise the department, a process he was three-quarters of the way through.

When Kelly walked in, she was shocked by what she saw. It was the brightest room in the building and offered evidence of the money that had been spent. The contrast to the drudgery of where she worked was obvious. There was a team of three people working away at modern equipment, with a young man standing up to look over one of their shoulders. He smiled politely at Kelly without leering at her when she walked in. That alone was a welcome change to the reaction she normally received in the rest of the building.

"Hi, can I help you? I'm Dan Millings."

"Yes, I'm Kelly Knox. DS Ramsey sent me to see you."

"You mean, my replacement sent you," smiled Dan.

"I'm sorry; I don't understand."

"The Geordie lass. DS Ramsey, or Lisa, was brought in to replace me when I got shot."

"Oh, right, okay. Yes, that's her."

"How's she getting on?"

"Fine, I think."

"And do you see much of that grumpy old sod?"

"Are you talking about DI Husker?"

"See, you know him. I'm yet to meet anyone in this station who doesn't know what he is like. What can I do for you?"

"I've got a missing person to trace."

"What details have you got?"

"A name. I guess that is a good start," laughed Kelly.

"It's the best start there possibly is. Take a seat and I'll get some coffee. Is white, no sugar, okay for you?"

"Yes, that's fine. Do you want me to get them?"

"No, I'll go. There is no pecking order around here. You can sit yourself down. I got the top brass to stump up for a fancy machine, so it will take a minute."

Dan returned before Kelly had made herself comfortable. The pleasant atmosphere in the office was noticeable. Information was being readily exchanged between desks. Everyone was collaborating, offering a display of teamwork in action. There was none of the gnarly masculinity of an open office with too much testosterone in it. It felt like no one had anything to prove.

"Have this one," laughed Dan. "I tipped most of the other one over my hand. We have a fancy machine but no cups that are the right size."

"You can't have everything," said Kelly.

"Actually, we can. The new cups are coming tomorrow. I'm going to send the old ones up to you guys. Please don't tell anyone."

"I'll try not to. You can listen out for the screams."

Dan moved around the desk and sat down at his computer. He angled the screen so that Kelly could see what he was working on. He typed in his password and brought up the database he needed. Then he looked across at the young DC. He smiled. He could remember a time when he was that new to the station.

"What was the name you were looking for?"

Kelly checked her notes from her call with Lisa to make sure she had got it right.

"Josie Raynor."

Dan's fingers tapped the name into the database. Seven matches came up, all with a photo. Each offered a short profile beside the picture. He looked for a minute and eliminated two, leaving five options listed. One more was dispensed with before a series of faces came onto the screen along with their descriptions. He turned towards Kelly and shrugged to offer her the information.

"Wow, that was quick."

"It's hard to believe that less than a year ago we would have been heads down in dusty archives for hours. This is so much easier. Now, let's see if we can narrow her down. What else have you got?"

"It's her," said Kelly, pointing to a pretty girl with flowing brown hair.

"How can you tell?" asked Dan.

"The description indicates an attractive brunette. The other three are hags."

"Bitchy. Mind you, you've got a point," added Dan as he surveyed the greying features of three seventy-plus females. "Okay, Josie Raynor, what can you tell us?"

Dan clicked on the profile and scanned the information. Occasionally, he paused to digest the content. Kelly sat on the edge of her seat, waiting for the big revelation to come.

"What does it tell us?" she asked.

"It says that she is from York, which is a good start. Right, here we are. Josie Raynor is thirty-one and lives on her own in a rented flat. She is five feet seven inches tall and weighs approximately nine and a half stone. She did some modelling in her younger days. Nothing flash; just low-level stuff. More recently, she worked as a croupier in the city's casino. She was reported missing three weeks ago after failing to keep an appointment with her debt counsellor."

"She was in debt?" queried Kelly.

"She's young and good-looking," shrugged Dan. "Isn't everybody who fits that description in debt?"

"I guess so," replied Kelly. She blushed a little more than she wished to.

Chapter 5

"I've never been to a casino," announced Lisa suddenly. "I'm not quite sure what to expect." She fiddled with her neckline and then refolded her collar in a nervous manner that suggested she was awaiting an interview.

"You haven't missed much," grumbled Jack. His hands were deep inside his pockets, offering an appearance that was no different to a normal day at work.

"I take it, you have."

"Yes, it's full of people whose life is draining away from them."

"A bit like a pub," smiled Lisa.

"At a pub, you get something for your money. Here, you just get to wave it goodbye."

"There must be some winners."

"Just the casino," growled Jack.

They flashed their warrant cards at the doorman. It was the trigger for him to open the front door. Jack paused. He eyed the rugged shaven-headed man and the scars on the top of his head. He wondered whether their paths had crossed on a previous occasion. In front of him, the smartly dressed thug did not flinch. He was trying to offer the pretence of normality. He remembered Jack from his past.

Jack allowed Lisa to go in first. Her uncertainty saw her hesitate just inside the door. It was a foreign world where her knowledge was reliant on what friends and colleagues had told her. That was not much. The North East had been more about nightclubs than gambling.

A hostess met them by the reception desk. She cast her eyes towards Jack. Any pleasantness was tempered with her frown at his dishevelled appearance. For a few seconds, a stand-off ensued. Their two faces eyed one another. Professionalism finally took over. She offered a welcome, with her smile being directed at Lisa.

"Are you members?" she asked.

"No, we are with the police," said Jack. He pushed his warrant card towards her.

"You will need to sign in."

"What for?"

"Fire regulations. Once you have signed the sheet, you may go in. Is there anyone in particular you are here to see?"

"Yes, the manager."

"Rather than the owner?" she offered awkwardly.

"Just give me whoever is in charge," grumbled Jack. His patience was being tested.

"That will be Jordan."

"As in the glamour model?" asked Jack.

"As in Jordan Bilby. I will call him while you sign in."

When she walked away, Lisa leaned over and whispered in Jack's ear.

"No, you cannot strip search her," she hissed quietly.

"That's a relief. I would need a tin opener to get that dress off."

"I guess you've thought long and hard about that."

Jack allowed a moment of silence to confirm that he had no intention of responding. Anything he said was more than likely to be used against him as evidence.

As Lisa picked up the pen, she gazed at the names on the list. A quick scan offered nobody of interest on the hand-scribbled sheet. While she signed them both in, the hostess made a call. It only took seconds and then she smiled. Her hand pointed towards the casino entrance.

"Jordan says you can go straight in. He will see you in there."

"Thank you," offered Lisa before Jack could say anything to antagonise her.

The size of the casino shocked Lisa when she entered. She slowed her walk and gazed at the sea of tables. Over twenty roulette wheels were accompanied by more card tables than she could count. At the side, there were banks of machines offering up their flashing lights and alluring noises.

The casino was busy, with people buzzing around like bees. The whole place felt like a foreign land to Lisa. Through the crowd came a young man in a dinner suit, his immaculate appearance catching the eye. Mid-thirties, with slicked-back black hair, he had an angular jaw that was covered with stubble. He carried the tailored suit well, with his physique radiating through it. Lisa watched him move closer while Jack remained one step behind her. The man offered a glinting smile which lit up the room. His confidence was not lost on the pair.

"Remember, you cannot strip search him," whispered Jack, forcing a blush from his colleague.

"I wasn't thinking about it," she replied.

"Is that me you are trying to convince or yourself?"

"Ok, enough!" snapped Lisa. "It's one-all; okay?"

"Great," laughed Jack, "I'll see if I can get a winner or at least force extra time on the way out."

"Do you want a lift home?"

The question was never answered. The man was upon them and offered up a hand to Jack. After a quick shake, he placed a kiss on Lisa's cheek. Initially, she tried to refuse him, only to freeze under his stare. In that moment of hesitation, his stubbly chin brushed against her face. His distinctive after-shave left a pleasant aroma lingering in the air. He was everything Jack was not. And yet he would never be close to an ideal match.

"Hi, I'm Jordan. Welcome to my gaff."

"DS Lisa Ramsey," she smiled. "This is DI Jack Husker."

"What do I owe the honour to? Is this just a courtesy visit or have I done something wrong?"

"We're looking for information," said Jack as abruptly as he could manage.

"You have come to the right place. If you want a bit of inside knowledge, always bet on red." His smarmy smile had Jack's hackles rising.

"Let me put this another way. Do you want us to raid the place and shut you down?"

"Hang on; let's not get excitable. I pay my taxes and have every licence and certificate that I need. That is more than I can say about a lot of the establishments in this city."

"Then stop being a smart arse. We both know that it wouldn't take our guys long to find someone carrying something in here. Weapons, drugs, you name it; somebody will have something."

"Or you'll plant it."

Lisa shot a hand across Jack to prevent him from moving forward.

"Let's keep things simple. I think what DI Husker is trying to say is that it would be a lot easier if we could just have a friendly chat. Have you got somewhere we can go?"

"Of course," he smiled. "Let's take one of the booths. Would you like me to get Susie to bring some drinks? She's the girl you met on the way in."

"No, we wouldn't," said Lisa sternly. "We have seen enough of her already."

Jordan smiled and wetted his lips. He winked at Jack as he did it.

"Please, follow me."

They were beside the booth when a commotion broke out by one of the tables. Two large men descended on the noise in an instant. Strong arms grabbed a man by the shoulders and dragged him towards the door. Jack's instinct was to move towards it. This time, Jordan's arm went across him to request that he keep his distance.

"What's that about?" Lisa asked.

"He's a troublemaker," offered Jordan. "He'll have lost and kicked off. It's not the first time."

"So why let him in?" she asked, to which Jack was quick to interrupt.

"Because he loses too much money. It's people like him who keep places like this going."

"On the contrary. That is a very old-fashioned view. These days, it is the after-pub drinkers who pop in for one more that we rely on. They stake no more than twenty quid and have a round or two of drinks. They are our lifeblood because they keep coming back. To them, it is an end-of-night treat."

"And do they ever win?" asked Lisa.

"Of course they do," laughed Jordan. "Some are skilled punters."

"That's rubbish," barked Jack. "We both know it is pure luck."

"That's your view. All I'll say is the same winners generally crop up, as do, interestingly, the same losers. Shall we take a seat? If you want, you can have a few chips to give it a go when we are finished. We always get people started with a few freebies."

"I bet you do," muttered Jack. He slipped into the booth alongside Lisa.

It took Lisa a full minute to go through the details of who they were looking for. She stated the dates that Josie Raynor was supposed to have worked at the casino. Most of the time, Jordan Bilby shook his head. He had made up his mind without listening. Twice, he glanced at his phone. He showed little interest even when Josie's death was recounted. He shrugged as if he barely knew anything about the girl. And yet her employment record said otherwise.

"I can hardly remember her. I'm sorry," he confirmed.

"She worked here for three years," insisted Lisa.

"We have a lot of girls who pass through. They come and they go, so it is hard to keep track of them all."

"Not if you are a good employer, it isn't," said Jack. "When did you last see her?"

"No idea. I don't think she has worked here in the past few months."

"We will need to know the exact date that she left."

"We might have that."

"You will have that if you are keeping proper payroll records. Of course, I could get somebody from the HMRC to check that."

"Come on, don't be like that. We will get you the date she left, okay? Now, why don't I get you a drink and some free chips? Anything you win can go to charity if that gets past the issue of you being on duty."

"I'll pass, thanks," confirmed Jack.

"I think I had better pass too," added Lisa.

"Your loss. If you will excuse me, I have a business to run. Hopefully, we will see each other again under better circumstances."

Jack scowled. It was not seen by Jordan who had picked up Lisa's hand. He kissed the back of it and allowed his stare to linger on her before turning to leave the booth. Lisa blushed. His attention had caught her off-guard. It was not for the first time that day.

"I think it has just become two-one to you," she laughed.

Jack never heard her. His eyes were scanning the rest of the casino with an inquisitive stare which was looking past the shiny facade.

Chapter 6

AFTER A NIGHT OF excess, Jack and Lisa walked into DCI Louth's office. It felt like a ridiculously early hour and yet the time was nine o'clock. It had been Jack who had suggested they find a neighbouring bar. Lisa had left her car parked at the casino. Just one small drink, she had promised herself. She was not quite ready to abandon her new car overnight.

One had become two and then more than she could count when they got to The Cellars. Any thoughts of driving back to her flat were cast aside. It was all part of the ride if you chose to date an unreliable man. That was what she had told herself when she woke to a thumping head and an empty parking space outside her flat.

"Good morning, Mr and Mrs Husker. How are Hello magazine's favourite couple?" asked Louth.

Neither said anything in response. The energy in Louth's voice was enough to put them on edge. There would be a punchline. When it came, the outcome would not be positive.

"Did you have a good night at the casino?" he continued. "Any winnings to share?"

"We didn't gamble, sir," advised Jack. "We were on duty."

"Of course you were. Any word on our victim?"

"Yes and no," offered Lisa. "The owner knew the girl but that was about it. He did his best to put distance between them."

"How do you mean?"

"He played the card of her being just one of hundreds of girls who pass through."

"And was she?"

"It's hard to know. There were certainly a lot of girls running the tables in there. There were several more hostessing. Jack will tell you about the one that he noticed."

"Do I want to know?"

"What Lisa is trying to say is that there was a pretty girl. It's hardly my fault if I have to fight them off."

"Did you try?"

"Of course not," he laughed. "What sort of man do you think I am?"

"A dirty old one," interrupted Lisa.

"Can I suggest that we concentrate on the matter in hand?" said Louth. His eyes had narrowed to suggest a sense of irritation.

"Which is?"

"I have got two tickets to a black tie event the night after tomorrow…"

"Sorry, sir, you are not my type," interrupted Jack. "Lisa, you'll have to go."

"…which I cannot attend. I have therefore decided that you two should go."

"You said black tie…as in a penguin suit?" queried Jack.

"That's right."

"I don't have the gear."

"Then you can hire it. Don't worry; you will get the money reimbursed. It is official police business."

"I'm washing my hair."

"And you, Lisa? Are you washing Jack's hair as well?"

"I guess I can go, so long as someone comes with me."

"Then that's settled. Jack will go with you."

"But..."

"But nothing. You will have to get yourself smartened up. It's about time young Lisa had a proper date; heaven help her." Louth laughed at his quip before noticing that nobody was laughing with him.

Jack left the office mumbling under his breath. Two paces behind him, Lisa could hardly contain her laughter. It was undignified to snigger out loud and yet the situation demanded it. The thought of Jack in a dinner suit was a treat she could not wait for.

"Fancy a coffee?" barked Jack while doing nothing to hide his irritation.

"I would love one," said Lisa. She smiled and waited for Jack to explode.

He never did. He kept his feelings to himself, at least while there was an audience. Predictably, he marched out of the station, leaving behind the scene of his frustration. Lisa went with him. She followed Jack to a chain coffee shop two streets away.

"Are you alright, Jack?"

"Yes, I'm fine," he insisted. He ordered two coffees, carried them to the table and sat down opposite Lisa.

"You never go into the named coffee shops."

"I fancied a change."

"Is this as good as a relationship gets? Lying to each other about which coffee shop we like."

Jack allowed himself a reluctant grin. Her point had touched a raw nerve. The new Jack was not afraid to admit it. Two failed marriages had been built on a pack of lies from both sides. Lisa was now confronting him at the first hint of secrecy. It felt like a good sign in the early stages of their relationship.

"Okay, it's Louth," offered Jack reluctantly.

"Ignore him. That's what you normally do."

"It's not him specifically. It's this endless need to go into the community. Why can't we just go out there and nick the bad guys?"

"This is the modern way."

"As I keep saying, I'm not a modern type of guy. And no smart-arse comments."

"As if I would," smirked Lisa.

Any further exchanges were ended by a text on Lisa's phone. The handset reverberated across the top of the table and threatened to disappear over the edge. Lisa snatched it up from its position of danger and stared down at the screen. It was angled away from where Jack was looking.

"Can't keep your other man waiting," said Jack.

"I think you know this one better than me."

"Go on," said Jack with a frown.

"Dan Millings; the last partner you got shot."

"Careful," urged Jack. "I could always add another to the list."

"He's done a bit more digging on our mystery woman in the lake. It turns out that she had a bit of a gambling problem."

"Which is useful when you work in a casino," stated Jack.

"And even more useful if your boss is Jordan Bilby," noted Lisa.

"He seemed such a nice guy. I couldn't imagine him taking advantage of a girl if he had something on her, could you?"

Lisa shuddered at the thought. "I would rather not."

"And I thought you might fancy a night out at the casino with him."

"I've already got a big night out planned," smiled Lisa. "When do you fancy getting kitted out?"

"In about thirty years; just in time for my funeral. Drink your coffee and if you are lucky, I'll buy you a drink tonight."

"The Cellars?"

"Of course. See you there at about seven."

Lisa smiled. She reached over and squeezed Jack's hand to confirm it.

***

Jack spent the afternoon going through everything he could find on Josie Raynor. It was slow progress when the girl had little by way of a criminal record. A court appearance in her youth for a car accident was her only blemish. After that, there were only minor traffic offences. Then came the financial checks and her sorry tale of debt. There was a list of county court judgements against her which seemed to go on forever. She was in deep. So deep, that she had been declared bankrupt by the time she had reached the age of twenty-five.

Jack broke the monotony by making a trip to see Dan Millings. It had been a while since he had taken the time to visit him. Their paths were crossing less now that Dan had been confirmed as the permanent head of his department. It always felt good to catch up with him even if a small pang of guilt struck Jack every time they spoke. Dan had been his junior partner when he had taken that bullet. It felt wrong. And yet Dan's fitness and fight had seen him pull through. Would Jack have had the strength and will to recover? Jack knew the answer to that question though would never admit it to anyone.

Jack stopped in the doorway when he entered the office. It was the first time he had been in there since the major reorganisation. The place was unrecognisable. Jack remembered the sleepy space he had spent a few miserable weeks working in. He nodded his head in admiration. Nobody would complain about being part of Dan's new team.

"Come in, Jack. You are making the place look untidy," laughed Dan. "I'll get you a coffee."

Jack walked in and sat down on the first chair he came to. He swivelled back and forth while acknowledging the greetings from others around him. He exchanged a few words with a middle-aged officer working to his left. Jack recognised him but could not remember where he had seen him before.

Dan returned with two cups of coffee. The aroma was a welcome change from the other machines in the station. Jack eyed his cup suspiciously and then took a sip. It was like something which had been delivered from heaven.

"Wow, this coffee is good. How did you get one of these machines?"

"You've got to have contacts in the right places."

"Tell me who I need to ask."

Dan smiled. "Do you promise to keep quiet if I tell you?"

"Of course."

"I just ordered it. I signed the authorisation box and the next thing I knew, the coffee machine turned up."

"I must try that. I'll get one for my desk."

"Just don't tell anyone what I did."

"What do you think I am? No, don't answer that. I don't want to know."

Jack took another sip from his coffee. As he drank it, he allowed his eyes to wander across the space. It was a pleasant environment and it confirmed that Dan was doing well. Everybody around him seemed content with their work. That was not how he remembered the department. The old place had given him an urge to tunnel out of the building.

"Are you impressed?" asked Dan.

"I am. What happened?"

"We had a revamp."

"What did you do with the old-timers who were waiting in here to die?"

"They've gone."

"Even Dick Foster?"

"He was the first to go. That guy hadn't done a day's work since he came in here."

"How did you persuade him to leave? He was here for life."

"We gave him a choice. Either he went back on the front line or he would have to retire. Funnily enough, he assessed his options and decided that he could afford to go."

"You mean, he could afford to claim benefits."

"Probably."

"And the others?"

"Once he went, the others followed soon after."

"What about that young lad, Will?"

"He went off to university. He is studying criminology. He says that you motivated him to do something with his life." As Jack raised his eyebrows, Dan continued. "Yes, I found that hard to believe too."

Jack laughed. It was the first time he had ever been a positive influence on anyone.

"Anyway, how's the murder case going?" asked Dan. "Have you solved it?"

"Slow down. So far, we only have a former bankrupt who was up to her arse in debt and a smug employer who claims to barely know her. You could do me a favour by having a look to see whether you have anything on Jordan Bilby."

"Is he missing?"

"Unfortunately not."

"I can look but I won't have anything that you don't have. We don't really specialise in the living and the present."

"True enough. Here, you don't fancy a free night out, do you? It's a chance to get tarted up. That would be right up your street."

"No chance," laughed Dan. "I heard about your black tie date. You're not fobbing that one off on me."

"A man has to try. How about I buy you a pint instead?"

"Thanks, but I'll give it a miss. I have never got back into drinking after the incident."

"Lucky you. You are getting out, though, aren't you?"

"Of course. I'm currently dating a nurse from the hospital."

"Good, I'm pleased."

"For me, or are you just glad that Lisa is safe from my charm?"

"Both," laughed Jack. He finished his coffee and shook Dan's hand on the way out.

***

Jack checked his watch and decided that he was finished for the day. Though early, he felt in need of clearing his head. He set off from the station, determined to go for a walk. The route took him directly towards The Cellars. It offered the chance for a couple of pints before Lisa arrived. She would want to go for food, which would turn it into a full night out. Not that he minded. He was pleased to have got over that hurdle of awkwardness. For the first time in his life, he was in danger of feeling relaxed in the presence of a partner.

"You're early," commented Alf from behind the bar.

"That's because I've missed you, Alf. I thought I would come and see you before I had to share you with others."

"You were in last night, Jack. Or were you too drunk to remember? Mind you, that lass of yours was in a worse state than you were. She was steaming. I reckon you're made for each other."

"Thanks. Do you fancy joining me for a pint?"

"Go on, I'll have a half. I don't normally indulge at this hour but I'll make an exception for you."

"That's good of you, Alf. Rack them up."

Jack checked his phone and smiled when he saw the lack of messages. Once pushed into his pocket, he accepted the cold glass Alf handed across the bar. He took a sip and then drained the top third. He emerged with foam on his top lip, which he cuffed away with minimal effort.

Alf sipped his drink more slowly. He knew that if he finished it, Jack would be back with the offer of a second. It was better to keep a clear head, particularly when Jack appeared to have his drinking boots on. That meant a long night ahead. The last thing that was needed was a landlord with a fuzzy head.

Jack was well into his second pint by the time he retreated to his favourite seat. Tucked away in the corner, you could almost see where he had worn away the cushion. He always sat in the same place, in a position where he could watch the rest of the bar. He glanced across the pub and nodded at a couple of regulars who had nowhere else to go. They were clutching halves which had lasted them since opening time. Jack settled back and savoured the taste in his mouth until an unwelcome interruption came his way. A scruffy figure was looming over him, holding two pints of what Jack was drinking.

"Can I join you for one? I come with a peace offering."

Jack's recognition and distrust were instant. Andy Hutton was a journalist with whom he had locked horns on previous occasions. Still unkempt, his stomach was now pushing out over his trousers and the tail of one side of his shirt was hanging loose. Jack hated the man and everything he stood for. He looked at him and thought through his options. If he stayed, he was offering a free beer. To send him away might prove more problematic in the long run.

"Yes, I guess. Take a seat."

The offer was not needed. As soon as the word 'yes' was heard, Andy Hutton eased down onto a stool opposite Jack. He sighed when he lowered his body as if the burden of age and weight was taking its toll. The bead of sweat on his forehead confirmed that he was not a physical specimen with stamina. Jack watched him make himself comfortable. It would not take long for the true purpose of his apparent kindness to be shown.

"It's good to see you, Jack. I got you a beer."

A glass was pushed over in Jack's direction. It slopped over the rim and flooded the table. Andy Hutton shrugged at his error.

"I'll just drink what's in the glass if you don't mind," sighed Jack.

"Suit yourself," grinned Hutton before his repulsive lips engulfed his glass. He swallowed loudly before belching and proclaiming his verdict, with enough volume to ensure that Alf heard him clearly. "The beer's a bit shit in here, isn't it?"

Jack said nothing. He would humour the man while he thought about how many ways he could hurt him with a beer mat.

"So, Jack, you were just about to give me something juicy," sneered Hutton.

"No, I wasn't," Jack corrected.

"Come on, you must have something. How about that stiff in the lake? Any sexual deviance at play?"

"Is that being asked in a professional capacity or as something to get off on later?"

"Why do you always have to be so hostile?"

"You just seem to bring out the worst in me."

"Come on," urged Hutton. "What can you tell me about her?"

"She's dead."

"I sort of guessed that. Do you know who it is yet?"

"I'm afraid not. Rest assured, when we do find out, you'll be the…"

"Last to know," interrupted Hutton. "What about that girl of yours? You're punching above your weight with that one, aren't you?"

"Says who?"

"Says everyone who sees you with her," laughed Hutton who was enjoying his joke a little too much. "I think I'll hang around for a chat with her. It might be time to advise her of the error of her ways."

"She won't listen to you."

"Why not?"

"Because she has a brain."

"I'll still hang around. Free world and all that."

"Suit yourself. She's not coming in tonight."

"We'll see."

Jack waited until Andy Hutton slipped off to the gents before typing the warning text to Lisa.

Problem with a journo at The Cellars. Best stay away.

That's a new excuse from the Jack Husker book of them! It's fine, I need to speak to my parents tonight. If you don't mind, I'll see you tomorrow. Lx

Breakfast?

We'll see...night night x

Jack slipped the phone back into his pocket before Andy Hutton reappeared. When he emerged, Hutton grinned inanely. The look on his smug face gave Jack a sense that Lisa could have done much worse. Jack could picture himself ramming his fist down Hutton's throat. It was not worth the risk of breaking his hand.

"Ruddy hell, those bogs are rank!" Hutton exclaimed.

"Why did you come in here if you hate it so much?"

"To see you, Jack. I've missed you."

"I'm touched."

"Not by me, you aren't," he laughed out loud. "I just thought it might be time for us to bury the hatchet and I don't mean in my chest."

"As if I would," shrugged Jack. "You know we can't work together."

"Maybe not, but I'm sure we could help each other out from time to time. You scratch my back and all that."

Jack cringed. He was unable to rid his mind of the thought of Hutton's sweaty back. His hand would be going nowhere near it.

"We'll see."

"Look, Jack, I'm not looking for guarantees or anything like that. I just thought it was about time we stopped worrying about the past."

"In that case, I'll have a pint," said Jack.

"But I just bought you one."

"That was in the past," shrugged Jack. "I thought we weren't worrying about that."

He smiled as Andy Hutton dragged himself to his feet while muttering a few well-chosen expletives under his unpleasant breath.

Chapter 7

It was eight-thirty in the morning when Tina Brand finally picked up the phone to report her husband missing. He had been absent for six days. Their two children were asking where their father was. At first, she had laughed it off. A short disappearance was not out of character. When days were nearing a full week, she knew that something was wrong.

She had checked their bank account for any unusual transactions. His normal pattern was to withdraw large sums of cash. She knew where it went. His usual excuse of needing it for the business had long since worn thin. It was drinking and gambling money and would soon be lost.

Despite his failings, her love for him still ran deep even if it gnawed away at her to see the children without a father for long passages of time. She had tried to change him. That had only caused arguments. For the sake of peace, she had left him to work it out for himself.

A call from one of his drivers had confirmed that it was serious. The wages were unpaid and jobs were piling up in the office. Suppliers were growing impatient with the lack of response. His mobile was dead and his usual haunts had not been visited for days. It was a far more impressive vanishing act than anything he had managed before. Fearing the worst, Tina had called the police. She passed on as many details as she could before the tears began to flow.

Within five minutes, DCI Louth called Lisa. She was finishing her breakfast and was about to drive to the station. When she saw it was Louth, she put on her best professional voice. She was thankful she had a clear head from missing her date. Spending time with Jack was exhilarating though the mornings were often a tale of regret.

"Good morning, sir."

"Morning, Lisa. What have you got on today?"

"I suspect whatever you are about to tell me to do," she replied.

"That's perceptive of you. Are you able to drop what you are working on?"

"Yes, that's fine. What do you need me to do?"

"We've just had a call from a Tina Brand over in Strensall. She has reported her husband missing. He's been gone for six days."

"And she is only just reporting it? That's a bit odd, isn't it?"

"That's what I thought."

"Did she say why?"

"It sounds like it is not out of character for him."

"So why is she worried this time?"

"Their bank account hasn't been touched. Normally, when he goes off, he empties the account and only comes back when the money is gone."

"Maybe he has another account."

"I think we need to find out."

"On my way, sir. Send me the address."

"I've just sent it. Keep me informed."

Lisa read the address on her phone as soon as she had hung up. It was a residential road on an estate in Strensall. Had she been there before? It was hard to know when the roads were so similar. It was a mid-eighties development where most of the houses looked the same.

She was pleased to have another opportunity to drive her car. Better still, she had a satnav to direct her through the streets. Once inside, she turned on radio one and then wondered whether it was becoming too young for her tastes. She turned it off rather than waste time finding something else to listen to on a journey which would only take a few minutes.

She stopped the car exactly where the satnav told her. Just after nine, the street enjoyed the quiet of the day. Few cars were parked up to signal it was a working area. Only the bark of a dog heralded her arrival. She saw the paws of a golden retriever on the front window of the house three doors away. Lisa locked her car and walked down the driveway to number twelve. It was a house that looked like all the others.

Lisa never got the opportunity to knock on the door. It opened when she was halfway towards it. She was greeted by a woman who appeared racked with worry. Dishevelled and in need of some rest, the black bags beneath her eyes gave away her lack of sleep. Lisa forced a polite smile and offered her warrant card while noting that the lady was not yet dressed. A simple pink dressing gown was all that was wrapped around her. It was a covering which had seen better days.

"DS Lisa Ramsey."

"I'm Tina; Tina Brand. I was the one who called you. He's still not back."

"Is there somewhere we can talk?" asked Lisa.

"Yes, of course. I'm sorry; do come in."

"Are your children here?"

"No, they are with my Mum. I've got permission for them to be off school, in case you are wondering."

"I'm not here to check up on that. I just want to make sure we can talk freely," confirmed Lisa.

"Sorry, please come in."

A fresh smell greeted Lisa the moment she stepped over the threshold. The place was immaculate, from the shining laminate floor in the hallway through to the cream carpet in the living room. Lisa went to kick off her shoes, only for Tina to insist there was no need. Lisa smiled. She could only admire how perfect the house looked. Barely anything appeared out of place.

"This is a very nice place you have got."

"Thank you. In case you are wondering why it is so clean, I always scrub things when I am stressed. It's all I have done for the past three days."

"I'm not here to judge you, Tina. I'm here to help."

Tina tried to force out a smile. She couldn't. She slumped down into a chair and released a flow of tears. They continued long after Lisa had placed a reassuring hand on her arm.

"I'm scared," Tina sobbed as she placed her face into her hands.

Lisa allowed herself to sit down on the nearest chair. She gave Tina time to express her emotions. She felt for her, knowing the battle she faced. She knew the game too well. The length of time someone was missing was directly linked to their chances of coming home. She hoped that she was wrong. Something told her that Tina would be left to raise their children alone.

"I love him," she wept. It was a signal for the cries to grow louder. "I'm sorry."

"There is no need to be. Take your time. When you are ready, we can speak."

"You're very kind."

"I'm just doing my job. We will do our best to find him. I can promise you that."

It was the first bit of reassurance that Lisa had offered. It seemed to help and allowed Tina to control her tears. As she quietened, her head rose to reveal her sodden eyes. Her face said there was plenty more emotion to come.

Tina began to talk about Darren. They had been married for twelve years. Their paths had crossed when she worked for his company. He had done well for himself and had built up a fleet of breakdown trucks. It was a successful business before his drinking and gambling problems had hit him. After that, the money troubles started to bite hard.

"We moved here when we had to sell the big house. To be honest, we could never afford it. Darren won a couple of contracts and we thought we were millionaires. He said it would be alright. Then he started disappearing on business trips. They were normally forty-eight-hour benders. At first, I thought he had another woman. That was stupid. When you saw the state of him when he came back, you knew that nobody would have touched him. Nobody other than me, of course."

"Who does he gamble with?"

"Anybody and everybody. He would bet on two flies on a window if someone wanted to."

"Are you sure he doesn't have somebody else? I'm sorry but I have to ask."

"No, I don't think so. Darren doesn't have much of a sex drive. Believe me, I've tried. You know, dressing up and all that stuff." Tina blushed with shame as she said the words.

"Whatever you say is in confidence. We want to find Darren just as much as you do. When did you last see him?"

"Six days ago. He went to work and never came back."

"Why didn't you report it earlier?"

"He is away so often. I just treat it as being normal. I was so busy with the kids, I never even thought about it."

"What age are your children?"

"Seven and five. We have two girls. They adore him."

"I can imagine. You said they are with your mother."

"That's right. They keep asking when Daddy is coming back. What am I supposed to tell them?" The tears flowed when she said it.

"When did you think that something was wrong?" continued Lisa.

"It was when a couple of the lads started chasing for unpaid wages. Darren would never fail to pay them even if that means we go without. He has a moral code about things like that."

"Do you think something has happened to him?"

"I know something has happened," sobbed Tina. "I know he is dead."

"Let's not jump to conclusions. Can I ask one last question?"

"Of course; what is it?"

"Is he a member of the city's casino?"

"He is a member of pretty much every casino in Yorkshire. I can't see the attraction myself."

"And does the name Jordan Bilby mean anything to you?"

"No, should it?"

"Not necessarily. He is the owner of the casino in York. I just wondered if he knows him."

"Not that I know of. Mind you, Darren wouldn't tell me anything that he thought might worry me."

Lisa smiled politely. She wondered whether Tina's words were an echo of those she might say about Jack.

***

Jack was pleased when the call came through from Lisa. Her pleasant tone confirmed there were no grudges following his cancellation of their date. It had been for her own good. Facing Andy Hutton as a couple was not likely to be a positive experience. If they made one mistake on a case, he would parade their relationship across his pages as the reason the investigation had failed.

It was far better to sit back and let him fish for a story. Jack felt good about relieving his wallet of a couple of beers in the process. They tasted better for it and left him feeling like he had got one over on his foe. Their conversation had ended with a non-committal nod to look out for one another. Neither meant it. It was just something to say. Andy Hutton was a parasite. Jack would happily spray him like an insect if such a repellent existed for creatures like him.

He listened carefully while Lisa gave him all the details. It sounded familiar and the type of story he had heard so many times before. Darren had been a good father until the pressure of his business had become too much. Then came the outlet which offered the chance to let off some steam. Before he knew it, the thing which had saved him was sucking the life from his body.

"Any idea where he has gone?" he asked.

"I would say a trawl through the gambling institutions of the city might be the way forward."

"Are you thinking of the casino?" asked Jack.

"That would be one place to start," said Lisa.

"Do you fancy coming?"

"No, I can't. I'm already playing catch-up, thanks to the DCI. You'll have to go on your own. That's if I can trust you to behave."

"You're fine. I've never been the gambling type."

"It isn't the gambling I am worried about. Just keep your eyeballs in their sockets."

"How about I wear a blindfold? I'll do everything by touch," he laughed.

"Don't even think about it."

"Too late; I have."

"Jack, seriously, be sensible. I have got a nasty feeling our man Jordan might be neck deep in this."

"I think you might be right. I'll keep you posted."

"Thanks, and don't forget, you still owe me a drink from last night."

"How could I forget?"

"You can't; I won't let you."

"I know you won't."

Jack ended the call, aware of the smile painted across his face. He admonished himself for offering a moment of weakness. His reaction was akin to a lovestruck teenager. Lisa did that to him. She had a way of making him feel good, no matter the banter between them. To even think that she might be jealous was enough to give him a warm feeling inside.

Jack grabbed his jacket from the back of his chair. He slipped it over his shoulders and began to walk across the city towards the casino. During a lunchtime session, he expected it to be empty. And yet nothing about human behaviour ever surprised him. Gamblers did not operate by normal hours. Their addiction was able to eat away at them at any hour of the day. When the urge came, it was a craving which had to be satisfied. They would change their plans to feed that need when it arose.

At the door, Jack showed his warrant card and walked in. It was notably quiet in the reception. There was no sign of the hostess, just a lady sitting behind the counter. Anything more would be considered a waste when there were limited punters to pull in. He idled over to the desk to sign himself in.

A woman bumped into him on her way past. In a hurry, she moved at a double-quick pace. Jack caught sight of the back of her head, her hair rich with colour. He waited for her to turn around. She marched out of the door, leaving him to wonder whether he had seen her before.

"DI Jack Husker; it's good to see you again. Are you back for those free chips that I offered you?"

He turned to see Jordan Bilby's smiling face looking towards him. Still suave, with his slicked-back appearance, the guy oozed with smarm. Jack could imagine himself punching his smug face even if he had no reason to do so. He just riled him. Nothing the guy did would change that.

"Who was that?" asked Jack.

"Who?"

"That lady who just left."

"I don't know. I didn't see her."

"She walked out of that room just before you."

"Sorry, I think you must be mistaken. I was in the office with our accounts lady. I suppose it could have been her. I doubt that she caught your eye."

"Are you sure?"

"Eve is sixty-seven and not, how shall I put it, the most alluring proposition. Of course, if you like an older lady…"

Jordan's words tailed off when Jack threw out a venomous stare.

"You could check the CCTV for me."

"It's switched off. We're doing routine maintenance at the moment."

"That's convenient. Do you mind if I check?"

"Yes, I do, unless you have a search warrant. I'm guessing you don't or you wouldn't ask."

"You've got it all worked out, haven't you?"

"There is nothing to work out. Mine is a very simple business. Now, what can I do for you? I'm guessing this is not a social call."

"Darren Brand," said Jack.

"Darren Brand to you too."

"Don't be a smart arse. What do you know about him?"

"I can't say that I know the name," shrugged Jordan.

"He was a member here."

"So are half of the city. I don't know most of them either."

"They don't fund your business quite like he does."

"Are you suggesting something?"

"Actually, I am. He's a problem gambler. I think you might like his type."

"I hope you are not implying that we are the sort of establishment which takes advantage of such people. We have plenty of warnings displayed about gambling responsibility and setting limits. It is in our interests to have happy customers who come back again and again. A quick win for us only costs us in the longer term."

"It's good to hear that you have such ethics. Do you follow the advice you offer?"

"DI Husker, we are a reputable business. As I have said, we have nothing to gain from short-term opportunism. It would just give us a bad reputation."

"I'm sure you don't. Now, if you don't mind, what do you know about Darren Brand?"

"As I said…"

"Yes, I heard all that. How about you come up with a proper answer?"

Jordan Bilby did not attempt to hide his irritation. He puffed out his cheeks. It was loud enough to cause heads to turn. With a shake of his head, he walked over to the reception. A wafted hand moved the receptionist away from her terminal. Jack walked behind him and stood over Jordan Bilby like a shadow. His eyes were on the screen.

"Do you mind?" asked Jordan.

"No, I don't."

"I do. If you want any help, go and stand on the other side of the desk. This is confidential information and, as we have established, you do not have a warrant."

"I could get one."

"Then go and get one. Or you could just be polite and recognise that I am doing my best to help you."

Biting his lip, Jack moved away. He exchanged looks with the receptionist. The roll of her eyes confirmed their common thoughts. For now, Jack played along. He stood patiently, anticipating the revelation which was never going to come. There was little point waiting for Jordan Bilby to respond.

"Just give me the name again."

"Darren Brand," Jack repeated firmly.

"Brand...Darren Brand...we have two Darren Brands."

"Is that so he can hit his limit twice?" asked Jack.

"Not unless he can become thirty years older in doing so. It is a common enough name."

"How about you give me the one that I am interested in?"

"I am guessing it is this one. He is forty-four and lives in Strensall."

"That's him."

"He is a member and has been for four years."

"And yet you don't know him?" pondered Jack.

"We have a lot of members."

"What was his record?"

"I don't know."

"How much did he lose?"

"Again, I don't know."

"I thought you guys tracked everything."

"If he had an account with us, we would know his position. Darren did not have an account. He used cash. Sorry, I cannot help you any more than that."

"Can I have a printout of his record?"

"No; that is confidential."

"Mr Bilby, I am rapidly losing my patience."

"And so am I, DI Husker."

***

After a day which had not offered much, Jack was pleased to meet up with Lisa. She was waiting for him when he reached the restaurant on Goodramgate. It was her insistence that they went for dinner. The promise of a drink the previous day had been replaced by an Italian meal. Jack had not been allowed to refuse. Lisa's text advised him of a time and a location. All he had to do was turn up.

Lisa was sitting with a glass of wine in front of her when he walked in. Jack was quick to gesture to the barman as he approached her. He made sure Lisa's glass was refilled and ordered a beer. No matter that it would be some fizzy bottled lager. It was wet and alcoholic and a welcome relief after his day.

"I'm impressed," said Lisa, half-standing up when Jack approached. "On time, for once."

"Naturally," insisted Jack.

"You say that as if it is normal," she laughed.

"It is normal. Just not very often," he grinned. "How was your day?"

"Grim, followed by dull, followed by grim. Yours?"

"Not much better. That Jordan Bilby character is some piece."

"I take it you talked to him."

"Of sorts. It was more that I talked and he sneered. I could have swung for him."

"Please tell me you didn't."

"No, I didn't. I was close though. That smarmy little git thinks he owns the place."

"He does."

"Not the casino. I mean the whole city."

"Did he tell you anything?"

"Not really. There was enough evasiveness to tell me that he knows Darren Brand. I reckon he also knew Josie Raynor more than he is letting on. Then there was the other woman that I saw."

"What other woman? Do I want to hear this?"

"It's nothing like that. As I arrived, she left hurriedly. I'm sure she came out of the back office with him. He says she didn't and then claimed not to have noticed her."

"Who was she?"

"I don't know. I couldn't place her. I only saw her from behind."

"Jack, you are slipping. I would have thought you would recognise every girl in the city from behind."

"I was looking at her head."

"I am sure you were. How about the CCTV?"

"Not working. Trust me; I got all the excuses."

"So what did you do?"

"After he had gone, I settled down in the corner of the casino with a tonic water and watched."

"A tonic water?"

"Don't worry, I never touched it. I just wanted to see who came and went."

"And?"

"Let's just say that he isn't short of problem gamblers in there and he doesn't do a lot to stop them."

"Why would he? They are his profit."

"That's not the story he likes to tell. Do you know the strangest thing?"

"What?"

"The majority were female and I'm not talking about down and outs. It looked like a day out for bored housewives."

"You must have been in your element."

"Most of them were too old for me. I like a younger lady who can appreciate the faults of an older man. Have you ordered?"

"I was waiting for you. I thought I might get the pensioners' special once you got here."

"Careful, or I won't let you use my free bus pass home."

"Yes, Grandad."

Jack settled back and smiled. A contented feeling bubbled through him. It was good to have found his match with someone who could stand their ground. The only thing that could spoil his day was the waiter. And he did by bringing the worst-looking beer Jack had ever set eyes on in his life.

Chapter 8

Jack left Lisa's flat at six o'clock in the morning. It felt like he was conducting the morning-after walk of shame. Not since he was a student had he felt such guilt. His first instinct was to look around, fearful of who might see him. It was stupid when the streets were so quiet and he had not done anything wrong.

Lisa had offered him a lift back to his house. Her gleaming car was parked proudly outside the block of flats. It looked pristine as if it had been polished every day since she had got it. She had washed it twice; first by hand and then on a visit to the supermarket. With barely a couple of buckets of water and an army of Eastern European workers, her car had been made to look like it was new. Jack smiled when he passed it. As nice as it was, he needed the early morning air to clear his head.

Walking under the city walls, Jack looked up. He eyed the familiar roofline above him. Some early morning commuters were skirting the inner ring road. Jack ignored their noise and headed in the vague direction of home.

In Goodramgate, he passed the restaurant they had dined in. The whole evening had taken place without the hint of an argument. When had he ever spent time with a woman and not exchanged a few heated words? Despite his reluctance to accept it, the whole experience felt good.

As he walked, Jack checked the messages on his phone. One was from DCI Louth. A summons to a nine o'clock briefing was enough to spoil his mood. He wished that he had not seen it. Such an oversight would have allowed him to turn up late without a hint of guilt.

Jack now felt obliged to turn up. He dreaded the larger gatherings Louth insisted on having. First, he would head home for a shave and a shower. If the mood got to him, he might even search for some fresh clothes in the wardrobe.

On the way back, he stopped at a cafe. A bacon roll and a cup of black coffee were bought to take away. Lisa had changed him. A wallet now had a permanent presence in his pocket. More importantly, there was money inside it to pay for whatever he wanted. Six months ago, he would have been searching through his jacket to retrieve a crumpled note which had slipped into the lining. Now he had cash with him wherever he went. It felt so much better not to be embarrassed when the time came to pay.

He savoured the smell of the bacon with each step he took. He succumbed to temptation long before he had made it home. He sat down on a bench and placed his coffee on the floor beside him. Nothing was quite the same as an early morning bacon roll enjoyed in the open air. For a moment, his eyes dipped closed to allow the flavours to soak into his taste buds. Those precious drops of grease were a welcome invasion into his mouth. He took a swig of coffee and just sat there. He wished his perfect day would come to an end rather than be spoiled by work.

***

After his early start, Jack walked into the station long before he was required to. It meant that he arrived early for DCI Louth's briefing. Heads turned towards him. A series of puzzled looks were exchanged while comments were made behind hands. Eight people were already present despite Louth being yet to appear. His timing would be to the minute. He would expect an audience to have gathered ahead of his arrival.

Lisa made it in just before nine o'clock. She walked in looking far more bright-eyed than when Jack had left her. She looked around and noted the empty seat beside him. Her common sense made her turn and sit on the opposite side of the room. That deliberate act brought a series of mumbled comments.

Eyes flicked between Lisa and Jack to assess whether they had fallen out. Jack stared back, daring somebody to say something. It made for an uneasy atmosphere, which only subsided when DCI Louth entered the room. He was not alone. He came with a surprising companion who looked thrilled to be there.

Alongside him, was DC Kelly Knox. All the eyes in the male-dominated room were trained upon her. Kelly had been a popular addition to the team since she had been brought in six months ago. Still attracting too many wandering eyes, she had now begun to dress more conservatively. That was Lisa's influence after a quiet word in her ear.

"Right, let's get started," announced Louth. "There aren't too many of us this morning."

If Jack had known that the briefing was not compulsory, there would have been one less in attendance.

With everybody facing forward, he took the opportunity to look across at Lisa. He mimed the actions to enquire as to what Kelly was doing. The young DC looked nervous and excited. Her face was beaming with a feeling of importance. Her position next to the DCI was one that she was proud of.

"If anyone is wondering why DC Knox is at the front of the room, I will explain," said Louth.

The eyes that had moved briefly to the DCI returned to Kelly. Lisa scowled at the uniform on her right. His leering had been noticed. He smiled back and licked his lips once in Lisa's direction. His eyes caught sight of Jack's venom aimed directly at him. He nodded at Jack with a smile.

"As you know, we are investigating the probable murder of Josie Raynor and the more recent disappearance of Darren Brand. Preliminary investigations have offered a link, being the city's casino. At this stage, the link is tenuous though there has been enough work performed by our officers to tell us that something is not right. If we add in some recent allegations relating to other offences taking place there, I think there is enough for us to investigate further."

"What other offences, sir?" asked one of the uniforms who had finally averted his eyes away from Kelly.

"I am not at liberty to say at the moment. I can confirm that they are secondary to our potential murder case."

"Why are you saying it is a potential murder?"

"As you know, nothing has been proven," advised Louth.

"Sir, the victim had a bullet hole in her head."

"That does not prove murder as I am sure you understand. Shall I continue?"

No one dared offer a response to confirm or reject the question. A couple of muttered acknowledgements were all that came.

"It is clear from our dealings with the casino owner, Jordan Bilby, that he sees the police as part of an elaborate game. Put simply, he is unlikely to cooperate, which means that we are going to have to put somebody on the inside. That is where DC Knox comes in. She has kindly agreed to go undercover as a customer to see what knowledge she can gain."

"You mean she is going in there to gamble away police funds," laughed a brave uniform at the front.

"She will be there as an observer. Her role will be to watch who comes and goes."

"Sir, she is going to look a bit of a prawn if she just sits there doing nothing."

"Rest assured, there will be some expenses available to blend in."

"Great; can I go with her?" said an excited voice. All heads turned to PC Mark Langton whose rosy round face smiled enthusiastically in Kelly's direction.

"DC Knox will be going on her own. The whole point is that she is an unknown face. The rest of the team will be available on call when she needs support. Is that clear?"

A series of murmured nods filled the room.

"Good; now get to it."

Jack and Lisa waited for the room to file out. Once they were left alone with Louth and Kelly Knox, they both approached the DCI. He was expecting it from the moment he had made his announcement. He smiled and folded his arms in preparation for the battle ahead. Alongside him, Kelly was still high on the emotion of being selected. She was hardly able to contain her excitement.

"Sir, can we have a word?" asked Jack.

"Of course, what is it?"

"It's about Kelly going undercover."

"It's a great idea, isn't it?"

"No, sir, it isn't," said Jack, before adding, "with all due respect."

"Jack, people normally offer 'with all due respect' before telling me I am an arse, not after. Kelly and I have spoken about this and it is the right thing to do. She fits the role perfectly."

"You mean Jordan Bilby will be all over her," replied Jack, to which Kelly blushed a bright shade of red.

"She is there to observe; that is all. It puts somebody on the inside. She will not be engaging with the enemy in any shape or form."

"Look, sir, it is your call. For the record, I think it is a bad idea. She is too inexperienced."

"It has to be someone new or he would know them," insisted Louth.

"Kelly is not ready," stated Jack.

"Lisa, what do you think?"

"With all due respect, sir..."

"Enough! Kelly will be fine, won't you?"

Kelly nodded in a manner which told Jack and Lisa that she was trying to convince herself.

"Anyway, let's talk about more important matters. How is the suit hire going?"

"What suit hire?" queried Jack.

"You are representing us at the charity dinner tonight. If you tell me you have forgotten about it, you are fired."

"We haven't forgotten, sir," interrupted Lisa. "We are getting kitted out this afternoon."

"You've left it a bit late, haven't you?"

"Not at all. We are both fairly standard sizes, so it won't be a problem."

"Just promise me one thing, will you?"

"Which is?"

"Send me a picture of Jack in his suit. I haven't had a good laugh in weeks."

"Then you should get out more," growled Jack. He marched out of the room before he said something that he would regret.

***

"This is bloody ridiculous!" snapped Jack as he stared into the window of the hire shop. In front of him, dummies were dressed in the finest wedding outfits, with their top hats and tails akin to a period drama. To their right, two female mannequins displayed colourful dresses. They were simple but elegant outfits that hung perfectly around their shape.

As Lisa lost herself in her thoughts, one in particular caught her eye. She loved the flowing burgundy satin on the left. That fabric would cling in all the right places while affording her some comfort where she might need it. All she had to do was persuade Jack to go inside.

"Come on; deep breath," she offered along with a reassuring arm.

"We are going to look like a right pair of idiots."

Lisa had done well to get Jack to go to the shop. All morning had been spent with him threatening to resign. Work had played second fiddle to the continuous rant he let out. Jack's ability to allow things to flow over his head had been discarded. Now he could not let the issue go. Everyone in the station had noticed it, with one or two taking great delight in the discomfort he felt.

"Make sure you are back by four o'clock," was the barb from Frank Campbell, to which Jack had made the mistake of asking why. "Because that's when feeding time is for the penguins and you don't want to miss out on the best herrings."

All of the station had seen the funny side. Jack hadn't and, in support of her partner, Lisa had pretended not to either.

"You'll be fine. We don't have to stay long," said Lisa, staring wistfully at the dress behind the glass.

"Is that at the shop or the do?"

"Which do you want it to be?"

"Both!" snarled Jack.

"You know the answer. The sooner we go in; the sooner we can come out." She beckoned towards the door.

"Do we have to?"

"I am afraid so. Do you want me to do the talking?"

"You'll have to. I will have no idea what they will be talking about in there."

"Don't worry; I'll look after you. Seriously, I will. You'll be fine," assured Lisa.

Jack puffed out his cheeks with enough force to make his lips reverberate. He felt light-headed. His dry lips were yearning for the coldness of a pint. And yet it was barely one o'clock. Lisa had insisted on going at lunchtime rather than delay it any longer.

Lisa pushed the door open. She paused to make sure that Jack was going to follow her. Once inside, the full impact of the place hit Jack like a freight train. They were three steps through the door when they were descended upon by two over-eager assistants. One was a balding man in his early fifties. He had a tape measure slung around his neck and his glasses on a cord. A slightly younger lady was by his side.

"Welcome to the world of being dressed properly," the man beamed, with a tone that made both Jack and Lisa cringe.

Lisa looked over towards him and noted his pinstripe waistcoat and trousers. There was a triangle of a bright yellow handkerchief poking out of his breast pocket. He looked immaculate, offering an indication that he was the model for the shop. The lady's choice of clothes was far simpler. She wore a white blouse and a black skirt. Lisa noted that she was a little larger than when she had first chosen the size of her skirt. The strain on the side button suggested that it might burst if she leant over.

"Hi," said Lisa. "I wonder if you can help us."

"That is what we are here for," beamed the gentleman while eyeing the pair up and down.

At any other time, it would have felt like an intrusion. His eyes appeared to be mentally undressing them, with Jack his main focus. All he was doing was going about his work and making an initial assessment. He was peeling away their street clothes, ready to adorn them with his choice of finery. It felt like their money had already been spent, such was the thoroughness of his stare.

"We are going to a charity dinner tonight and we need to dress for the occasion," said Lisa.

"Don't tell me; you are going to the event organised by Marcus and Laura Tummel. They are lovely people."

"That's right. I'm guessing you've done a bit of business from it."

"We always do. I reckon we dress two-thirds of the attendees."

"Do people not buy their clothes?" interjected Jack. It was his first opportunity to contribute anything.

"Not these days. Who wants to dress the same twice?"

"I can't imagine," Jack replied. He fought to avoid looking down at his own clothes.

"So, who's first for a makeover?" smiled the gentleman.

"Can we do both at once?" asked Lisa. She knew there would be limited time until Jack walked out.

"As you like, madam. What do you have in mind?"

"I like the dress in the window but I don't want to have the same dress on as someone else."

"There is no chance of that here, madam. All our pieces are unique. Let me get it for you. And for you, sir?"

"I don't care if I dress the same as someone else. Let's keep it simple."

"Simple it is, sir. Shall we get you measured up?"

"I'd prefer trial and error," said Jack. His scowl was not one to be argued with.

It sent the assistant over to the rails while the lady slipped behind the screen to the window. Lisa smiled to reassure Jack that everything would be alright. His mind had already drifted elsewhere. Trying on clothes was about as enticing as a tooth extraction at the dentist.

He had watched the way he had been eyed up. The eagerness of the man with the tape measure was not something he found comfortable. It was far better to take the trousers into a changing room and select the first pair which fitted.

"Which way do you normally dress, sir?" came the question from the rail.

"Always facing the neighbours," replied Jack. "Just give me the trousers."

"And does sir want to take the matching jacket into the fitting room with him?"

"No, I thought I would put it in the car and try it on in there."

Lisa's scowl came as a warning. Jack shrugged and took the clothes from the assistant. He was in no mood for making concessions, no matter how rude it made him appear.

The assistant waited for Jack to disappear behind the curtain and then smiled politely towards Lisa. Not for the first time, Jack had embarrassed her. Her uncertainty made the feeling worse. She loved the dress but insecurity filled her. She feared that she did not have the figure to do it justice. Something about her weight always nagged away deep inside her.

"Here you are, madam. Let's get it on you and then we'll look at any nips and tucks."

"Thank you," she whispered. "Sorry about my colleague. He's not a clothes person."

"That's fine. We get all types of customers in here. If you go into the cubicle on the right, there are plenty of mirrors inside it."

The voices screamed inside Lisa's head. She wanted to ask for a fitting room without mirrors. The thought of seeing herself from all angles terrified her. The only large mirror in her flat was banished to one wall. It was tucked away in a corner where it required some effort to see it.

She forced a smile and walked towards the cubicle, fearing what she might see. After the fuss Jack had made, she had no choice other than to accept the invitation. Two customers causing problems would be more than the shop could cope with.

Holding her breath, Lisa slipped into the dress. She dared not look up to risk seeing her reflection. Nervously, she fidgeted with its fit. It was shuffled into position with a wriggle of her hips and a couple of small pulls upwards. She waited for the moment when she would discover it was too tight. That never came. The satin slipped around her as if it was tailor-made to her size.

Finally, Lisa allowed her head to rise. She peered towards a mirror and was shocked at what she saw. The dress looked every bit as good as it felt. It was made for her. Her reflection was one to savour.

Edging out of the changing room, she looked around nervously. The voices in her head told her that something was wrong. She was trembling. Her whole body was shaking with the feeling of adrenalin that was rushing through her. All she needed was for someone to tell her that everything was alright.

"Wow!" exclaimed the lady assistant.

Lisa half-smiled. She wondered whether she was just well-trained.

"Is it okay?" she asked nervously.

"You look stunning," added Jack's assistant. He was standing with his arms folded, waiting for Jack to reappear.

Lisa never heard his words. The look on the lady's face had been enough. With excitement, Lisa spun around to search out the nearest mirror. Her movement towards it was unusually swift.

"My goodness," muttered Lisa under her breath. It was as beautiful as the lady had suggested.

"I take it madam is happy with that option."

"I am," enthused Lisa.

"Would you like to try on some other dresses?"

"No, thank you. This is perfect."

"Not quite," said the lady. It offered a moment of concern for Lisa. "You do need some different shoes with that dress."

"That's fine," said Lisa, with relief, "I have plenty of shoes which will go with it."

The conversation was halted by Jack stumbling out of his changing room. He was wrestling with a bow tie that was threatening to strangle him. He had the look of a man who had been dragged through the streets, with barely anything hanging correctly. He glanced up at Lisa and offered a look of surprise before focussing his efforts on trying to resolve the issue with his collar. After limited success, he gave up the struggle.

"Do you want some help with that, sir?"

"No, I'm fine."

"How does it feel?" asked Lisa.

"Not as good as you look," he replied, without realising the magnitude of what he had said.

"Is that a Jack Husker compliment?" she asked. "That really would be a wow moment."

"It is," he grumbled. "Now get me out of this penguin suit."

"Does it fit?"

"It's close enough. Just get me out of it."

Jack marched back into the changing area. Reluctantly, Lisa went back to her cubicle to take the dress off. Part of her wished that she could wear it for the rest of the afternoon. In the cubicle next to her, she could hear Jack grunting as he fought to be rid of the suit. She stifled her laughter and focused on making sure the dress remained undamaged.

When she re-emerged, Jack was already there. His outfit had been thrown onto the counter. He looked irritated as if the whole day had been ruined. With the evening event to come, it was not about to get any better.

"I'll pay for both if you want," said Jack.

"That's great, thanks," replied Lisa.

"And how does sir wish to pay for this?"

"Credit card."

"Thank you, sir. That will be one hundred and forty-nine pounds ninety."

"I want to wear it for one evening, not buy the bloody thing four times over."

"That's fine," interrupted Lisa. "Can you make sure we have a receipt?"

"Yes, stitched in gold," muttered Jack as Lisa stood there. For so many reasons, she was barely able to wipe the smile off her face.

Chapter 9

Marcus and Laura Tummel were sitting in the car in silence. Marcus was driving, his eyes flitting between the road and his wife. There had been words exchanged before they had got into his Land Rover Discovery. They had been harsh. Claws had been sunk in both directions. Since then, neither had felt the need to break the ice. It allowed the frostiness to linger between them.

The traffic had come to a halt. It was typical for the late summer, with the holidaymakers pouring into that part of Yorkshire. Marcus muttered under his breath and glanced across to see if Laura would react. All she did was tighten her arms across her chest. Her knees were angled towards the door to maximise the distance between them.

"Are you going to keep this up until we get to Harrogate?" he snarled.

Laura said nothing. Her eyes did not flicker. She would release her fury when the appropriate time came. Until then, the pressure would continue to build.

As the cars ahead started to move, Marcus's eyes returned to the road. Just outside York, they came to a standstill once more.

A motorhome had broken down and the traffic was stacking up behind it. Thankfully, it was on the opposite side. A middle-aged couple were standing next to it. Their helpless looks were an attempt to gain some assistance. No one slowed, other than to squeeze past. The occasional horn sounded the displeasure that everyone felt.

"They should be taxed double for having one of those things on the road," said Marcus.

Again, Laura offered nothing. Briefly, her lips moved before her words were dragged back in. The unusual sound she made in stifling it caught her husband's attention. He wanted her to speak, just so he could aim another barb in her direction. Her dominance in the previous argument had left him with daggers that were yet to be thrown.

"What is wrong with you?" he demanded.

"What do you mean?" scowled Laura.

"You've been a misery since we left Malton."

"Do you really want me to answer that?"

"Yes, I do!" snapped Marcus. The brakes slammed on with the next obstruction in the road. Once stopped, he turned to face his wife. His fierce look was trained directly at her.

"Try not to kill us," she hissed.

"Why? Might that cheer you up?"

"Fuck you."

"Sorry, I don't do requests."

"You don't do much these days....unless it involves one of the stable girls."

"What is that supposed to mean?"

"You know damn well what it means."

"No, I don't. Enlighten me."

"Don't give me that; I heard you. Did you hear me, Marcus? I heard you in there. That poor little cow was too scared to tell you to get off, you sick bastard."

"And what about Kit?"

"Don't start that again. Concentrate on driving. We are already late for our own party."

"I bet he was screaming, just to get away."

"You're a piece of shit, Marcus."

"And you're married to it."

***

Kelly Knox stared into the mirror of her bedroom. She was worried. The reality of going undercover had struck her. When she had been at the briefing, it had seemed so simple and was made to sound more exciting than it now felt. She had listened to the instructions carefully, particularly the pitfalls to avoid. It all felt like a blur as she tried to remember what she was supposed to do if something went wrong.

Thankfully, there had been no suggestion of wires or listening devices for her to conceal under her clothing. Not that she could have. The little black dress that she had chosen to wear was tighter than when she had last put it on. In her nervous state, it felt like it had shrunk three sizes in the past few minutes. A glance in the mirror left her fearing that the fabric might burst at any moment.

Downstairs, her parents were sitting in their front room. Still living at home, her time to move out was long overdue. Assignments like this reminded her of that. There was always the need to explain why she was working late. Kelly would not dare show them what she was wearing. Not now and certainly not when she returned. As far as her parents were concerned, she was doing nothing more than catching up on paperwork at the station.

"Do you want anything to eat before you go out?" called her mother, her voice echoing in the stairwell.

Kelly shouted out her refusal. Her answer was forced by a combination of the restrictive dress and the way she was feeling. She could not stomach any food. She felt sick, just as DCI Louth had told her that she would. The warnings of Jack and Lisa were still ringing in her head. Neither believed she was ready. She had insisted that she was. Now she was less convinced than ever.

"Do you need a lift to the station? Your Dad can take you."

"No, I'm getting picked up," she replied. It was a lie but only a small one. A taxi was booked to pick her up one street away, out of sight of her parents' prying eyes.

Kelly touched up her make-up and took two deep breaths. She moved slowly towards the stairs and lingered at the top. She waited until she was certain that her parents would not intercept her. When the opportunity came, she dashed towards the front door. Her coat was swept from the rack on her way past.

She called out her farewell as she opened the door. She was gone before her father came to see her off. It was hard to walk in her heels and yet she had to move quickly. Kelly dashed around the corner and only stopped when she was sure that she could not be seen.

The taxi was parked exactly where she had instructed it to wait. Kelly checked it was for her and then slipped into the back. She looked forward and saw that the driver was staring at her in the mirror. She said nothing as she strapped the seatbelt across her. Once settled in her seat, she looked forward with a stern gaze towards those prying eyes.

"Where to, love?"

"The casino, please."

"It's a bit early for that. That place is a road to ruin."

"I'm just meeting someone there; that's all."

"Lucky guy," he grumbled.

Kelly did not feel like pointing out that, in the modern world, it could be a woman. Why bother? The man had made up his mind and nothing was going to change it. She sat back in her seat and tried to relax on the short journey to the casino. There was so much self-doubt bouncing around in her head.

It only took five minutes to get there. That time was spent staring into the mirror to watch the driver's wandering eyes. Each time they exchanged looks, he averted his gaze back to the road. He irritated Kelly. She already felt uncomfortable about what she was wearing.

"Do you need a lift back or are you staying over?" asked the driver.

"I've got a lift back sorted, thanks."

"I'll give you my mobile number in case you need it." He reached back to hand over a card.

"Thanks," said Kelly. She placed it into her bag and decided it was time to end the conversation. "I'll put it next to my police badge."

There was silence. The driver turned away and allowed his eyes to stare through the front window. Not another sound was offered until Kelly spoke.

"How much?" she asked.

"It's on the house," he said. "We always do our bit for law and order."

"No, we pay our way. How much is it?"

"Your choice; it's eight pounds sixty."

"Here, keep the change," said Kelly. She handed the driver a crisp ten-pound note from her purse. She left the car and looked back with a smile. No eyes were watching her any more.

As the taxi drove off, Kelly noted the registration. She scribbled it on the reverse of the card next to the driver's number. She pushed it into her bag and looked up to see the casino bearing down from above. Her first thought was to admonish herself for offering up her identity. It was stupid but fun at the same time. The look on the driver's face made it worth the risk.

Kelly walked towards the casino door. She accepted the offer from the doorman to see her in. He accompanied her to the front desk and wished her a pleasant evening.

"Can I help you?" asked the receptionist, her smiling face greeting Kelly.

"Yes, I'm meeting a friend. Am I able to sign in as a guest?"

"Strictly speaking, you can only go in as a guest if you are with a member. I take it you are not a member."

"No, I've never been here before."

"Is your friend a member?"

"I think so."

"Can I ask his or her name?"

"Sarah Lucas."

"Let me have a look. Lucas…Sarah Lucas, there she is. She hasn't been in for a while."

"That's right. She's been out of the country with work. She got back last week. Sarah said this would be a great place to meet."

"I'm not supposed to let you in without her but if you are just going in to have a drink, I'll sign you in as her guest. You are here just for a drink, aren't you?"

"Oh yes, I don't gamble," said Kelly.

"How long do you think Sarah will be?"

"She said half an hour. If you know Sarah, that could mean anything."

The receptionist smiled. She accepted DCI Louth's scripted back-story while Kelly waited for her approval to go in.

"Can I take your name, please?"

"My name?"

"Yes, for the guest card."

"Oh, Kelly."

"Have you got a second name, Kelly?"

"Sorry; it's Kelly Shaw." It was pre-rehearsed and it still did not feel comfortable. Her stumbling words caused the receptionist to frown.

"Okay, Kelly, sign here."

Panic filled her. She had no signature for Kelly Shaw. All she could do was pick up the pen and scribble the name in formal handwriting. It looked juvenile but it achieved what was needed. The card was printed and handed over as soon as the ink was dry. Kelly was quick to thank the lady. She slipped the card into a side pocket of her bag in case it was needed later.

"Is there somewhere I can leave my coat?"

"Just see the cloakroom attendant on your way in and he will give you a ticket for it."

Kelly thanked her again and went inside. She allowed the coat to slip off her shoulders as she moved through the door. She was shocked when she saw how big the casino was. It seemed to expand as far as the eye could see. Roulette tables and various card games went across the expanse of the room.

It was busier than she was expecting. Her eyes worked their way around the room. The majority of the tables had somebody on them. Even at an early hour, there seemed to be plenty of people ready to gamble. Kelly could not believe the excitement and tension that was permeating through the open space.

Kelly handed in her coat and moved towards the bar. She ordered a tonic water while wishing she could add some gin to calm her nerves. Some ice and a slice of lemon made the drink look convincing. She settled on a stool which offered a view across to where the majority of the games were being played. The whole place felt so alien to her. It was like a scene from a movie that had been produced in a language she was yet to learn.

Within minutes, Kelly saw a man approaching from her side. She recognised him as Jordan Bilby from the photos she had been shown. She smiled out of politeness and then looked down at her drink. Only when he started speaking to her did she feel the need to swivel towards him.

"What is a pretty young lady like you doing drinking alone?" he asked.

His smile lit up his face. Kelly was shocked by how good-looking he was. The warning bells of Louth were dancing around in her head. He had told her about his suave patter and his reputation with the opposite sex.

"I'm waiting for a friend."

"I take it you didn't fancy a flutter while you were waiting."

"I don't gamble."

"Is that don't or won't?"

"A bit of both, I suppose. My mother always said it was a disease."

"Not if it is done for fun," he smiled. He offered out a hand. "I'm Jordan; I own the place."

Kelly accepted his hand and gave it a light shake. She noted the way he looked deep into her eyes when he did it.

"Sorry, I wasn't trying to be rude. I'm sure it is fun for some people. I'm Kelly."

"Come on, Kelly. I'll show you what you are missing."

"No, really, I can't. I've got to wait for my friend."

"Then I will make sure I deliver you straight back here for when your friend arrives."

He took her hand and eased her down from the stool with a small tug. Kelly slipped off her seat without ever intending to. She jolted when she landed and grabbed for the hem of her dress. Her first task was to make sure its shortness did not embarrass her.

As soon as she was upright, she felt another pull on her arm. Jordan was already setting off across the floor of the casino. His hand was tight on hers to make sure that she followed.

"Slow down; I can't walk that fast in these heels."

Jordan laughed and then apologised. He turned and swept her towards one of the roulette tables. Immediately, she felt her body being pressed up against it. In front of her was a grid of numbers. They made no more sense than when they had been explained to her in the station.

"Let's have a bit of fun."

"I told you; I don't gamble."

"No, but I do."

"What, in your own casino?"

"Of course. It guarantees that I'm a winner," he laughed.

Jordan waved his hand at the croupier. It resulted in a pile of chips being pushed towards him. Kelly had no idea of their worth, nor what he was doing. Each chip went down on the table with impressive speed and dexterity. Some were placed in squares; others were on lines. The remainder were pushed onto a corner. It felt like a science that Kelly did not understand.

"There, we've covered two lines, a block of four and two individual numbers. If we win, it is your turn."

Kelly's eyes looked sceptically at the table. Jordan watched her closely, gauging her interest in the event. He smiled when her line of sight never moved from the silver ball that was running around the wheel. Her fixation with it gave him the information he needed.

He prayed that one of his numbers would come up. And yet something about Kelly told him that he might get a second chance. He didn't need it. When the ball settled, his grin widened across his face. Eight was the number he would have hand-picked if he had chosen the result himself.

"That's one of ours!" shrieked Kelly as a mountain of chips was pushed over in her direction.

"It certainly is," said Jordan. "Now it's your turn."

Nervously, Kelly picked up one of the chips. She examined it, unsure what the value was in cash. She looked at Jordan who nodded in the direction of the table. Her uncertainty was met with a smile. A reassuring hand was placed on the back of hers.

"That's it, just relax. You need to wait for the number to come into your head." His voice was far softer than before.

"How much am I betting?"

"As much as you want. You are in complete control."

His grip closed around her hand and guided it onto the table. Kelly went back to the eight that had rewarded them on the previous spin. She covered the number as well as the corners around it. At Jordan's nod, she bet on two further lines.

Kelly enjoyed the feeling that was pulsing through her. The rattle of the wheel threatened to overwhelm her with nerves. Jordan's hand remained fixed to hers. He gripped it tighter when the wheel spun to make sure she noticed he was there. He only released his hold when one of her numbers came up. Kelly turned and hugged him tightly. In his arms, she watched a stack of chips being moved towards her.

"What happens now?" she asked excitedly.

"You cash it out and enjoy your winnings."

"They are *our* winnings. We won them together."

"No, Kelly, they are *your* winnings. Make sure you enjoy them. I am afraid I have to go because I have another commitment this evening. I do hope to see you in here again," he added. He kissed the back of her hand before slipping away with a smile.

Kelly stared down at the chips that were piled up in front of her. She had no idea what she was supposed to do next. The value of them was a mystery. The dealer waited quietly for her instruction. When nothing was forthcoming, she offered Kelly a prompt.

"Would madam care to have another bet?"

"No, I think I'll cash out as Jordan said," replied Kelly.

"Certainly, madam. The cashier is the window over in the corner. Enjoy the rest of your evening."

"Thank you," said Kelly. She scooped up her chips and walked in the direction she had been shown.

Kelly deposited the chips at the cashier's window. Her eyes opened wide when the cash was counted out in front of her. It was hundreds of pounds that were being placed down. The twenty-pound notes were continually pressed onto the pile for what felt like an endless passage of time. It left her shaking with excitement. The stack of money was more than she had seen in a long while.

Over eight hundred pounds was handed over to Kelly. She froze as she stared down towards it. She had no comprehension of what had just happened. In a matter of minutes, that cash had materialised from nowhere.

"Would madam like a bag for that?"

"No," she forced out in response. "It's fine."

Fumbling awkwardly, she crumpled the money into her purse and moved back to the bar. Jordan was gone and her mythical friend was not going to appear. She needed something a lot stronger than tonic water with lemon and ice. It would be downed in one just to stop her body from shaking.

***

Jack sat in the back of the taxi and fiddled with his collar. His hands slipped inside it to loosen the restriction around his neck. Every movement made it feel worse, the adjustments doing nothing to put him at ease. All it brought was an admonishment from Lisa. She reached over to move his bow tie back to where it had been.

"Leave your collar alone. It's fine."

"It's not fine," spluttered Jack. "It's bloody uncomfortable; that's what it is."

"That's because you keep fiddling with it. If you leave it alone, you'll get used to it."

"I don't want to get used to it. I don't want to get used to any of this ridiculous clobber."

Lisa tried her best not to react. Never had someone looked more out of place in a dinner suit. Jack had the innate ability to look scruffy, no matter what he wore. It hardly helped that he had chosen the first one he had tried on. He had not even attempted to select anything which fitted.

"Girls have to suffer as well. My feet will be on fire in these heels by the end of the night."

"Then put some more comfortable shoes on."

"Why don't I go in trainers instead?"

"I wouldn't mind," shrugged Jack.

"I don't think our hosts would be overly impressed."

"So what?"

"It's called respecting others. Do you think there is any chance that we can treat this night as a date?"

"I thought we were here on official police business."

"We are. That doesn't mean we can't have a good time. The two are not mutually exclusive."

"I think you have been reading too many books about modern policing."

"At least I have tried reading a book."

"So have I...once...I think. I guess I must have read something at school."

"You make me laugh," smiled Lisa. She leaned over to put Jack's bow tie back in place before kissing him once on the cheek.

"What was that for?"

"For being Jack Husker; that's all."

Lisa allowed herself a moment to relax on the journey to Harrogate. Her mind was intoxicated with how good she looked. The mirror had not lied even when she checked it for a second time. The dress felt perfect on her frame. She was already weighing up the cost of buying it, just so she could wear it again.

"How long before we are there?" asked Jack. It interrupted Lisa's thoughts even though the question was aimed at the driver.

"About five minutes, mate," the driver replied.

Jack huffed and slumped back in his seat. He stared blankly out of the window, wishing he was anywhere else in the world. Lisa offered an affectionate hand towards him. Jack did not see it. He was oblivious to anything going on in the car. She pulled it back towards her and glanced at her phone. The silence of the journey was only broken when the driver pulled up at the hotel.

"I take it this is on an account?" queried the driver.

"It is," said Jack.

"You know they don't include a tip in that, don't you?"

"Don't they? I blame the Tories for that."

"They leave it up to the passengers."

Jack shrugged and got out of the car. He was not going to take the bait being dangled in front of him. It left Lisa flushing bright red with embarrassment. Her antidote was to push a five-pound note towards the front of the car. There were times that she would do anything to take away the shame that Jack left behind him.

"Bless you, madam, and good luck."

"Good luck? What for?"

The driver looked over to where Jack was standing and then smiled at Lisa.

"Do you need me to answer that?"

"No, I don't," she sighed. She climbed out of the car and smoothed down her dress with a shake of her head.

Jack waited for Lisa to catch up. He gazed up at the grandeur of the hotel. The country manor exuded wealth as did the cars that were pulling up alongside it. Their expense confirmed that the guests were all affluent invitees. Compared to those vehicles, the taxi looked so out of place. Some disparaging looks were offered by others around them. Jack smiled and fiddled with his collar. Lisa approached him and slapped the back of his hand.

"What was that for?"

"For not leaving it alone and for abandoning me in the taxi."

"That was just a show of equal rights. I don't want to be seen as a masculine oaf who doesn't allow a lady to do anything."

"Let me offer you some advice. Next time, play the part of a sexist pig and pay the tip. This lady doesn't go in for all that equality tripe."

"Duly noted. Shall we have a look around?"

"No, we are going inside to enjoy ourselves. We are not investigating a crime scene."

"Not yet," smiled Jack. "When we see the prices at the bar, we might have a case of moral indecency to consider."

Lisa linked her arm through Jack's to bring the two of them closer together. Jack never fought it even though he felt conspicuous on the hotel's steps. To his surprise, nobody seemed to be looking at them. All eyes were turned towards the other arrivals.

Each car was being vetted to assess whether the occupants were of the appropriate class.

They moved inside and were welcomed by a man in a full top hat and tails. The staff were immaculate and made Jack feel underdressed even in his suit. Coats were being taken and invitations checked. It left Jack wishing that he had left theirs behind.

Once accepted into the event, they were passed on to professional greeters. The introductions were so pre-rehearsed they felt like they were being read from a script. At the end of the formalities, their full names were announced. Jack shook his head in bewilderment as they were finally confronted by their hosts.

"Ah, Jack and Lisa, so delighted that you could make it," beamed Marcus Tummel. His eyes moved up and down Lisa's dress.

"Lisa, you look fabulous," said Laura Tummel in a dress that was even more impressive than Lisa's.

"I am so glad we could come," said Lisa. She was keen to get the words out before Jack had the opportunity to be rude.

"Likewise," Jack nodded. They were quickly shunted on to allow the next guests to receive the same welcome.

"Try to pretend that you mean it," whispered Lisa under her breath.

"Now that we are past the Gestapo, can we get a drink?" asked Jack.

"That was a bit full on," admitted Lisa. "Why don't you play the part of the honourable gentleman and buy this lady a drink?"

"Is that in my role of a sexist pig?" he laughed.

"Of course."

"In that case, what do you fancy?"

"Is this where I say, you, Jack?"

"Only if you don't want a drink."

"I'll have a dry white wine, please."

"Large?"

"I think you know the answer to that. This dress doesn't have much room for food but it has all the space you could need for drinking."

Jack took Lisa's order and moved over to the bar. It was a circular effort placed on one side of the room. Ill-designed for the surroundings, it took up far too much space even with the absence of bar stools. Not wishing to stand alone, Lisa followed closely. She left behind Marcus and Laura who were still offering the same choreographed greeting to every arrival.

"What beers do you have?" asked Jack.

Jack listened as the impeccably dressed barman reeled off a list of bottled lagers.

"No, I asked, what beers do you have?"

"Those are the beers, sir. I recommend the Peroni."

"I bet you do. You don't have to drink it. Have you got anything a little heavier?"

"We don't have much call for bitters at these events."

"Okay, I'll just have a scotch. I take it you have malts."

"We certainly do, sir. Any preference or shall I surprise you?"

"You have already surprised me with your lack of beers. Just give me a middle-of-the-road one. And stick one block of ice in it, will you?"

"And for the lady?"

Jack looked up. He had forgotten about Lisa. Thankfully, she had not noticed. "A large glass of dry white wine, please."

"No problem, sir."

While they waited, Jack surveyed the room. Lisa did likewise. Neither was able to switch off even for a few seconds. Eyes lingered on anyone they recognised, with a few semi-public figures catching their attention. Lisa noted one local news presenter who had a young man glued to his arm. Who would have thought that but then why would you? His normal personality was fixed by the lens staring directly at him. Jack's eyes had long since moved passed him. He was finding interest in the way the Tummels presented themselves in public.

"Interesting couple, aren't they?" he noted.

"Yes, I never had him down as gay," said Lisa.

"Gay? I don't think so."

"I would say he is. That lad stuck to his arm is not an ornament."

"What lad? Where are you looking? I'm talking about the Tummels."

"Right, sorry. I was with our local television host."

"You mean that guy over there. I've never seen him before in my life."

"Do you watch television?"

"No."

"You do own one, don't you?"

"I think so."

"How can you not be sure whether you own a television or not?"

"I used to have one. I've had so many people walk out on me, one of them might have taken it with them."

"And you don't know?"

"Why should I? It was in a corner of the living room when I last saw it. I don't do a regular stock take to check that it is still there."

Lisa rolled her eyes. She was wasting her time by continuing the line of questioning.

"Go on, tell me about the Tummels."

"What do you notice about them?" asked Jack.

"You mean other than him practically undressing me with his eyes? If you had been watching, you would have dived in to protect my honour."

"Would I? Oh, yes, I would have done exactly that. Anything else?"

"Like what?"

"How about Laura?"

"She looks stunning in that dress and please do not pretend that you didn't notice."

"I noticed. Everyone in this room noticed, with one exception."

"You mean…"

"That's right. Look around at the eyes in the room. Most of the men are glancing furtively in her direction. The only person who is not interested is her husband. I mentioned it to Louth at the races and he just laughed at me."

"What are you trying to say?"

"I am just saying that the relationship and this function are all for show."

Jack turned back towards Lisa who was nodding. It was timed perfectly to coincide with the drinks arriving. Two glasses were pushed across the bar. First Lisa's wine and then Jack's whisky, with its single block of ice standing like an island in the middle.

"That just needs a polar bear on it," laughed Lisa.

"You're right," said Jack. He turned to the barman with mischief. "I don't suppose you have a polar bear, do you?"

"Is that a cocktail?"

"That's right. Three parts ice, three parts vodka, four cherries and two umbrellas, plus you need to jump three times. How about I just pay for the drinks?"

"Certainly, sir, that will be…"

"Stop!" interrupted Jack. "Just take it from this; I can't bear to hear the bad news." He handed over a twenty-pound note and said goodbye to the money.

When the change came, it was as disappointing as Jack expected. A small collection of coins was returned. Jack swept them into his pocket and ushered Lisa over to a table. On the way, she sipped her drink. Jack was already halfway through his and had allowed his eyes to return to the Tummels. The frostiness was obvious. Even when they stood together, there was a clear sense of separation between the couple.

"We better make the most of the wine at the table or it will be an expensive night," offered Lisa. "It'll be worth it, though."

"Why do you say that?"

"When else do I get to see you dressed up?"

"I dress up every day."

"Yes, as a middle-aged detective."

"That's better than a middle-aged tramp, which is what you meant."

"Enjoy your drink," laughed Lisa. "It cost you enough."

"Not as much as the next one will. I'm having a double if it saves me from the table wine. Same again?"

"I've barely had a sip."

"In that case, I'll get you a small one."

"We both know that's a false economy. Just line them up and I'll drink faster," said Lisa. She drained most of her glass with one large swig. It had Jack nodding his head in admiration.

Chapter 10

Lisa rolled over in bed and wished that she hadn't. Her stomach was churning even with the slightest movement. Her head was pounding and her eyes were so heavy. They felt like they would fall from their sockets if she leant forward. She groaned, took hold of the pillow and buried her face into it to block out the light. It made no difference. That hung-over feeling was still there.

Just as concerning was the noise that was coming from her living room. Someone was moving around outside her bedroom. Not just in the building but inside her flat. Fighting the urge to ignore it, she dragged herself up a few inches. After a deep breath, she readied herself to make the monumental effort of getting out of bed.

She never needed to move. Her blurry eyes recognised the sight of the door moving. She squinted to focus and was unable to persuade her eyes to behave. Through the haze, a head popped into view. It was the smiling face of Jack that was peering around the door. He was dressed and looked fresh. For that, she hated him with all the venom her throbbing head could muster.

"Morning, sleepy head."

"Is it?"

"Yes, and it has been for the past few hours."

"What time is it?"

"Eleven o'clock. Don't worry; Louth knows that we are not coming in this morning. I told him that we had some other things to do. Do you want a coffee?"

"I'm not sure I could face it. What time did we get back?"

"About three o'clock in the morning."

Lisa pulled herself up in bed. For the first time, her awareness returned. Her senses offered some realism to the vulnerable state she was in.

"Oh, shit, I'm naked," she groaned loudly, the volume causing her to wince in anguish.

She grabbed for the covers and dragged them upwards with enough force for her feet to appear at the bottom of the bed. Jack laughed at her discomfort. It was hard not to derive some pleasure from her suffering.

"Did we, you know?" asked Lisa.

"Did we what?" smiled Jack.

"You know damn well what I'm asking."

"Do I?"

"Just tell me what happened when we got back." As she barked the question, the pain rifled through her. She put her hand to the side of her head and tried to blink it away by pressing against the torment.

"Was it that memorable?" he laughed.

"I'm not going to get angry. I just want to know."

"I'll tell you later," offered Jack. "Why don't I make some coffee?"

"Jack, tell me now! I don't want a bloody coffee!"

"I do. It will also give you a chance to put some socks on. Those feet of yours look like they are in danger of catching a cold."

By the time Lisa had tried to object, he was gone. She thumped the duvet in frustration. She regretted the outburst when the vibration went through her body. She cursed how she was feeling. Her lack of discipline had caused it. Not Jack's. For once, it was her fault and that made it so much worse.

Across the room, her dress was hanging limply on the chair. Beside it, she could see her discarded underwear on the floor. Her heels had been kicked off in the middle of the room. She wished that she could wind back the clock to a time when her head did not hurt.

Jack returned five minutes later carrying two cups of black coffee. Lisa had slipped on a pair of tracksuit bottoms and thrown an old t-shirt over the top. Her clothes from the night before had been picked up. Any embarrassment had been hidden away in the wash basket. Only the dress and her shoes offered any evidence of their night out. Desperately, she tried to remember what had taken place. It just brought more pain to her head.

"I'm not sure I will be able to drink this."

"Try a sip."

"And then you are going to fill in the blanks from last night, aren't you?"

"Where would you like me to start?"

"Let's start with what happened when we got back to the flat."

"Not the event?"

"I want to know what happened between us. We can discuss the rest after that."

"Do you want the censored version or the one with all the juicy details?"

A deflated feeling saw Lisa's head lower. She hated the thought that she had shown herself up in front of a man she had grown close to. She could live with the intimacy of what they had done but not the humiliation of being out of control. She wondered what she had revealed about herself and how embarrassing she had been.

"Just give it to me gently," she sighed.

"That sounds like the opposite of what you said last night," laughed Jack. When Lisa's face flushed with anger, he offered an immediate apology. "Stop worrying. Nothing happened."

"So why do I ache so badly this morning?"

"I don't know. It has got nothing to do with me and nor has your sore head. You're the one who insisted on large glasses of wine."

"Did we sleep together?"

"No."

"That's a relief."

"Thanks for that."

"Sorry, I didn't mean it like that. I just don't want to be the type of girl who only does things when she is drunk. That doesn't sound any better, does it? You know what I mean, Jack."

"I'm not sure I do but let's stop worrying about it. When we got back, you were in a bit of a state. You fetched a glass of water, dropped most of it down me and then went to bed. I gave you one kiss on the cheek and undid the zip on your dress, which you asked me to do."

"Didn't you undress me?"

"No."

"Why not?"

"Because you were not in any fit state. I said goodnight and you went into the bedroom. You banged and crashed around for a few minutes and then it all went quiet. When I popped my head in to check on you, it was dark and you were fast asleep under the covers."

"So you didn't come in?"

"No, I slept on your sofa and then left this morning to go and get some fresh clothes from home."

"Jack, I'm so sorry."

"What for?"

"For not...well, you know. It should have been a date."

"It was."

"Except I don't remember it."

"Then you missed the best part."

"Which was?"

"While you were busy with Marcus Tummel..."

"Oh no. Tell me, I didn't."

"You did a great job of keeping him occupied," smiled Jack. "While you were doing that, the real action unfolded."

"Which was?"

"A certain Jordan Bilby turned up and let's just say that he made an immediate move towards Laura Tummel. Mind you, he had to fight his way through plenty of admirers to get to her."

"Do you think something might be going on?"

"Who knows? I think we might have a new line for our enquiry. Are you up for a car ride?"

"I'm not sure I can make it, why?"

"Louth called a few minutes ago. They've got another body for us to look at. Same location and it looks like the same MO."

"I'm not sure I can go. I feel sick."

"In that case, can your car go? Either way; you're in no fit state to drive."

"The keys are in the kitchen. Be careful with her. She's very precious to me."

"I'll be as gentle with her as I was with you last night."

"Is that a good thing?" groaned Lisa.

"You tell me. After all, you're the one with a head full of regrets."

***

Jack drove quickly to the crime scene. The thought of Lisa bounced around in his head. He felt good about last night. Not just at the way he had got her home safely when she had wanted to continue drinking. It was what had happened back at the flat. When she had demanded he take her to bed, he had managed to sidestep the problem. He had no intention of telling her how drunk she had been or the crude advance she had made on him. Some things were best left as a secret, particularly in a new relationship. Maybe once they were more comfortable together, they would find time to laugh about it.

He was thankful the table wine had limited his drinking. He had only had three whiskies all night while Lisa had allowed her glass to be filled repeatedly. He would have made the same mistake if he had liked the wine. Faced with its unpleasantness, Jack had stuck to water and then persuaded a barman to get him a coffee. That meant no sore head and a morning without regret.

At the crime scene, the white tent was already up. It always sent a shudder through him when he saw it. It confirmed that somebody's family member was underneath. It could be a child's father that would not be coming home. It never felt any easier even as Jack's years advanced. It remained an unpleasant part of the job. That first sight or the smell of a scene was one which always seemed to linger.

As he approached, the whole thing felt familiar. The scene was the same as the pictures he had seen of Josie Raynor. The position of the body felt close enough to suggest that the tent could have used the same anchors or maybe even been left up for the purpose. How did they miss the second body on that search? More likely, the body had been dumped since. So many thoughts were circling in his head. For once, they did not involve Lisa or how she had looked when she had tried to drag him into her bedroom.

Jack parked the car on the verge. He took more care than usual to get it off the road. It was Lisa's car, not some overused wreck from the station. He would never forgive himself if he returned it with any damage. He had seen the pride in her when she had first shown it to him. The last thing he wanted was to add to her woes. Her sore head was enough penance for her night of indulgence.

Ben Hughes was working when Jack walked up to him. The sole other person at the scene was a uniform stationed at the entrance. Ben smiled at Jack and beckoned him over with an informality which Jack liked. Jack was getting to know him as an efficient crime scene officer. He was also someone who was not afraid to offer an opinion. Jack didn't always agree with it but at least it gave him something to work with.

"Got the short straw this time," smiled Ben.

"I just fancied a ride out."

"In Lisa's new car, I see."

"Nothing escapes you, does it?"

"It is my job to notice things."

"I suppose. She wasn't using it and I needed a car, so here I am."

"Don't worry; I won't cross-examine you on your story. How is she?"

"Good, thanks. How's the stiff? I take it you have a body under there."

"Yes, we've got a middle-aged man. Like the other one, it looks like he has been shot in the head. That comes with all the usual caveats, which I won't bore you with."

"Same gun?"

"Ruddy hell, Jack. How good do you think I am? I've had the body less than an hour and it is not in the best condition, I might add."

"How long do you think he has been in the water?"

"A while. I can't be too sure but we are talking days rather than hours."

"Do you think he could have been in there when the last body was found?"

"It's possible."

"Then you know I have to ask the question."

"You're right to ask. We didn't rummage around overly hard last time as this area is believed to have a few unexploded bombs from the war. I know some of your colleagues might want us to run the risk but we are always very careful about things like that. We had a quick scour of the area. We certainly didn't go trawling around in the mud. This one was weighed down with a couple of blocks. There wasn't going to be much chance of finding him without a bit of excavation."

"How did you find him?"

"By accident. A fisherman came down in the night and hooked into the body. He dragged the line in and a leg popped up to the surface. It gave him a proper fright by all accounts, not that he hung around to be questioned. He shouldn't have been fishing here. To be fair to him, he called it in."

"Do we know who it was?"

"No. He rang from the phone box in Coneysthorpe in the middle of the night. By the time a car got down here, he was long gone. I don't think he is likely to come back."

"Do you think he has something to hide?"

"Who knows? We can do the usual traces but we are probably better off concentrating on the body. It's just a shame that it rained last night. We are going to be pretty light on evidence close to the scene."

"Which brings us back to the body," said Jack. "Any clues?"

"It's a pretty distinctive corpse. There are a few tattoos and plenty of dental work. He's had a wedding ring taken off his finger. A watch has also been removed. Other than that, whoever dumped him hasn't done much to disguise his identity. I am confident we will ID this one within a couple of days.

"Mid-forties, did you say?"

"I said middle-aged. That could be mid-forties. Do you have somebody in mind?"

"I might," said Jack. "Let's just say that I have a missing person who might be a pretty good shout. I'll jot the details down to pass on to the pathologist. How confident are you that it links to the last one?"

"You tell me, Jack. We are talking about two bodies in the same location and they have both got bullet holes in their foreheads. I'm not a fully-blown detective but that's a fairly good link by most standards."

Jack laughed. Even he had to admit that it was hard not to make the obvious connection.

***

Kelly spent the morning staring at the pile of bank notes on her dressing table. It was her day off and yet she felt unable to do anything while the money was sitting there. Guilt had filled her from the moment she had arrived home in the taxi. Those winnings were part of the investigation and would need to be handed in. The first thing she had done was to take the money out of her purse. The second was to promise herself that she would take it to the station early the following morning.

Except, she hadn't. She had got up, eaten her breakfast and then sat down on her bed with a coffee. She had stared at the money until it induced a trance-like state. She never drank the coffee; nor did she move. The conundrum that money offered rendered her breathless. It was not hers and yet something told her that she should keep it.

Her mind was filled with thoughts of how easily it had been won. Two spins of the wheel had given her over eight hundred pounds. In barely a couple of minutes of undercover work, the wealth was in her hands. It was more than her bank balance had seen in an age.

By early afternoon, Kelly had not moved from her bedroom. Thoughts turned back to her night and her interaction with Jordan. He had been so charming with her. Everything he had done had made her feel comfortable in his presence. And yet when the opportunity came to get closer, he had left her alone.

That intrigued her. He had not made his move like every other man she had ever met.

Maybe he had a girl tucked away in the back or maybe he was different to the other men in her life. Without a second thought, Kelly phoned for a taxi. Within twenty minutes, she found herself in the back of a car.

"Where to, love?" asked the driver.

"The casino, please."

"That place is a road to ruin," said the taxi driver. Kelly wondered whether they all worked off the same script.

"I'm not going there to gamble," said Kelly before realising it was the same conversation she had shared the night before.

"Of course you aren't, love. Nobody ever does. It's a waste of a pretty young girl if you ask me."

Kelly ignored the driver and stared out of the window. Her mind was filled with thoughts of Jordan Bilby and what his motivations might be. Was she attractive to him or was she just another pretty young girl in his casino for the real punters to stare at? It was part of his job to get girls like her in through the door.

The afternoon traffic allowed the taxi to pick its way through the streets with ease. It felt strange to be visiting a casino in the daylight, particularly on her day off. Kelly had dressed more soberly; her outfit more suitable for an office than a night out. It did not stop the driver from staring at her when she left the car and walked into the building.

As she entered, she signed in at the desk. Her name came up as 'membership pending'. Her last act before she had left had been to put in her application. It was enough to see her granted entry.

A brief conversation advised her that her card would be through in a couple of days. Kelly did not care. She just needed to be able to do her job and get in when she pleased.

Inside, the atmosphere felt different. It was quiet. The buzz of an evening session was not there. Large parts of the casino floor were closed down, with the action concentrated on a handful of tables. The demographic had also changed. It was now heavily weighted towards females. Their smaller frames were hunched over the tables, with the occasional high-pitched shriek echoing around the cavernous space.

Kelly made her way over to the bar. She ordered a tonic water and placed herself down on the same seat as the night before. She looked around in the hope that Jordan Bilby would appear. He was the reason that she had chosen to come to the casino on her day off. Without him, there was little to interest her.

Jordan Bilby did not show his face. Her only interaction was with a barman who went about his work. He was polite and offered an acceptable level of conversation though it was clear that he didn't want to talk. After a period of silence, Kelly smiled and took her drink over to one of the tables. She chose the busiest one where four ladies were gathered around a roulette wheel. They were staring at it intensely.

None of the players noticed her. Their minds were focused on the game taking place. Less than twenty-four hours before, that had been Kelly. The fortune that had spent the night on her dressing table had been generated by two spins of a wheel.

She tried to understand the strategy that each of the ladies was following. Bets were going on quarters and lines, together with a smattering of individual numbers. They all had their own method of betting. None showed any interest in what the others were doing. It was all about them and what their next bet would be.

After the bets had been placed, there was a lull. It was a period of reflection before the small metal ball was released into the wheel. Everyone held their breath. Kelly watched in silence until one lady cried out with the thrill of a win. Three disappointed faces stood back to allow the table to be cleared. Once empty, more chips were piled on. They filled the same squares as the previous spin. Kelly concluded that the lady covering the full lines knew most about what she was doing.

"Are you betting?" asked the croupier. His eyes looked over in Kelly's direction.

"Not at the moment," she replied. She felt the tingle of the previous evening's excitement pulse through her.

"When you do, you can take my place," said one of the ladies bluntly. Her attractive face caught Kelly by surprise.

Her recognition of her was instant. Her father's passion for horse racing had soaked in. Every trainer and every jockey were names and faces never to be forgotten. She smiled and nodded her thanks to Laura Tummel before allowing her to resume at the table.

The next whoop of delight came from Laura when the metal ball settled into the number thirty-four. It was the largest stack on the table and it resulted in a mountain of chips being pushed in front of her. Without knowing the value of each chip, Kelly had no idea what she had won. All she knew was that it made her haul from the previous night seem like pocket change in comparison.

"I knew that beauty would come up," beamed Laura. She scooped the chips onto a tray and eased away from the table. A single chip went in the direction of the croupier. As she left, she offered a smile in Kelly's direction. "Always bet on your vital statistics and age," she grinned.

"In your dreams," muttered Kelly under her breath. Her eyes fixed on Laura as she walked across the casino floor. "Now where are you going?" she wondered.

The answer was a door to the right. She slipped through it into what appeared to be the back offices. It was the same door that Jordan Bilby had disappeared into the previous night. Kelly took out her phone and sent a quick text to Lisa. It was to update her on what she had seen. She was eager to make her first undercover assignment a success.

As soon as she had sent the text, she regretted it. It was too late to recall it, meaning questions would be asked. What was she doing in the casino when it was supposed to be her day off? She had not told anyone that she was going. That had broken the first rule of her assignment.

Thoughts turned back to the money that was sitting on her dressing table. What was she supposed to say if anyone found out about it? That money had been won doing something she was not supposed to. Louth had been clear that she was there to observe. Under no circumstances was she to participate.

In her distracted state, she did not notice the drunken man stumble across the floor. He fell sideways and crashed into Kelly, sending her spiralling downwards. He landed on her and then rolled off to the side. Kelly looked shocked at the sudden moment of violence. She used a stool to drag herself up to her feet.

The man got up beside her. His eyes were wild and uncontrolled. He could barely focus and did not seem to notice that he had fallen to the ground. She watched the security team descend upon him. Two men came from nowhere and grabbed hold of his arms.

"Right, Spencer, you have had enough. Time to go home."

"One more bet; that's all I want. One more lousy bet."

"You are going," was the reply.

Kelly watched the drunk being manhandled away from the tables. The lad was barely thirty. He was held up by the two guards who were marching him through the front of the casino. As Kelly brushed herself down, a kindly voice was heard in front of her. She turned to see a concerned face.

"Are you alright?" asked the croupier.

"Yes, I think so. I might have a few bruises tomorrow but I'm okay."

"Sorry about that. I am afraid Spencer doesn't know when to call it a day."

***

Jack walked back to the car. In his head was the description of Darren Brand. He was trying to decide whether the corpse was him. The similarities were there even if it was hardly a match.

But why would there be a match? The body had been left to deteriorate. It would look like any other man of a similar build.

He took a moment to gaze across the lake. He noted the splendour of the house in the distance. It was a glamorous place to meet such a grisly end. The location was the last place he would attempt to hide a body.

He opened the door and was greeted by the distinctive smell of a new car. It was a welcome invasion to his nostrils and not something he had ever enjoyed personally. It took away the stench of death which hung in the air. Jack checked his feet for mud as his thoughts turned back to Lisa. She would be starting to recover from her night of excess.

Jack took out his phone and called her. If he knew how to operate either her car or his phone, he would have tried to do it hands-free. Unable to decode such mysteries, Jack sat in the car and allowed his feet to remain outside. The call rang three times before Lisa's quiet voice answered tentatively.

"Hi, Jack."

"How are you feeling?"

"In a word...crap."

"Are you still in bed or did you manage to get up?"

"I've got some clothes on if that's what you meant."

"It wasn't, but thanks for the update. Have you been out?"

"No chance. I've just collapsed on the sofa. I think I'm going to write the day off. How's the corpse?"

"Dead."

"They normally are. Any clues?"

"Yes, he's in a better condition than you are today."

"Thanks. How about anything which might help us solve the case?"

"He's a middle-aged man with a bullet hole in the centre of his forehead."

"As with Josie Raynor?"

"Exactly the same."

"Do you have any idea who it is?"

"There are plenty of distinctive marks, so he should be easy to identify. At this stage, I am taking a punt on it being Darren Brand. Even with the state the body is in, it has an uncanny resemblance."

"I thought you were going to say that."

"I never like to disappoint."

"You never do that, Jack. Would you like to hear something else that is interesting?"

"Go on."

"Kelly has been back to the casino."

"I thought it was her day off."

"It is. Don't worry, I've made a note to keep an eye on her. She says that she is just keen."

"Yeah, right. And I'm tee-total."

"Guess who she saw in there."

"Jordan Bilby would be my wild guess."

"Better than that."

"That isn't a high bar to clear."

"Try again."

"How about DCI Louth with a show-girl on each arm?"

"Now you are just being silly. She saw a certain Laura Tummel."

"Is she sure?"

"She is one hundred percent sure. She reckons her father is a horse-racing fanatic."

"Casinos on her day off and a background in horses," mused Jack. "I think we might have to watch that girl closely."

"Any excuse, you dirty old man."

Jack laughed out loud. Lisa's accusation could not have been further from the truth. Kelly was attractive, that was for sure. She would never be of interest to Jack.

"I resent dirty. I had a bath last month."

"You don't argue with 'old' then?"

"I might need to take a plea bargain on that one."

"Would it be that easy to find you guilty?"

"How about I pop over with a takeaway tonight and you can question me yourself?"

"Seriously, Jack, I can't. I'm not going to be able to stomach anything for a while."

"Then get yourself off to bed. I have a sneaky feeling that we might be going out for a drive tomorrow."

"To the Tummels?"

"Possibly."

"In my car, I presume?"

"Someone has got to use it and that someone needs to be sober."

"That's a low blow."

"It is thoroughly deserved," laughed Jack.

"I think I might be the one who needs a plea bargain this time," offered Lisa.

"Sorry, you're guilty as charged. The prosecution will not be backing down on that one."

"I guess not," admitted Lisa. "Now, are you going to tell me what really happened when we got back last night?"

"I told you earlier."

"And now I want the truth."

"What makes you think it wasn't the truth?"

"Let's just say that I've had a couple of flashbacks. In neither of them did I get undressed in the bedroom."

Jack paused for a moment and tried to hide his discomfort. It was no time to change his story from the one that he had offered earlier.

"It was exactly as I told you," he insisted.

"Jack, are you going to tell me?" Lisa's voice took on a sterner tone.

"Get some rest and I'll see you tomorrow."

"Okay, and thanks."

"For what?"

"For being a gentleman when you could have taken advantage."

"I don't know what you are talking about," he replied as he ended the call with a grin.

Chapter 11

Jack got up early. He was feeling good. His early night had paid him back with interest. He had enjoyed one pint in his local and had then walked home. With Lisa's car parked outside his house, he was tucked up in bed by ten o'clock.

He had contemplated texting Lisa to offer his good night wishes. He decided not to, knowing she was likely to be asleep. If he woke her, she might start asking awkward questions. He was in no mood for further interrogation, not when it could only embarrass her. In time, he would have to tell her about the advance she had made on him. Not now. He would allow her to retain her dignity for a little longer.

He wandered out of the house and took a left turn down the street. It was a short walk to a cafe he often passed by. It was not his usual choice but good enough, particularly when he had so little in the house.

"Just a coffee and two slices of toast to take away, please."

"Coming right up," said the man behind the counter. Offering an efficient manner and a smile, the whole transaction was completed in the time it took for the toast to brown.

Jack slipped the bag into his pocket and walked back to his house. He smiled when he saw Lisa's car in front of it. It gleamed at him in the morning sun. It lit up his day almost as much as its owner.

He settled onto a chair in his kitchen and forced down the first slice of toast. He was not particularly hungry though knew it was not a day to skip breakfast. A visit to a mortuary should not be done on an empty stomach. He would need something to line it and it was not one of his usual fry-ups. That would be a mistake when the smell of the place would assault his nostrils the moment he entered the building.

Jack checked his phone. There was nothing from Lisa; not even a text to ask him what time they were heading over to see the Tummels. He pondered sending her a quick message before changing his mind. He had no idea how long the mortuary visit might take. If the body was not the first in, he would be left in a queue. No amount of pestering was going to see him given priority over anyone else. Not with the procedures they worked to. He would be made to wait his turn.

Jack finished his coffee while staring out of his front window. The more he looked at it, the more the car seemed to look back at him. Maybe he needed to invest in one or better still, he could move in with a lady who had. That was a thought for the future.

He tipped the final swig of his coffee down the sink and slipped on his jacket. Jack got into the car and drove the short distance to the mortuary. When he turned into the car park, he was the only car outside the building. Jack checked the time and sighed. He knew that he might have a long wait ahead of him.

After twenty minutes, a familiar face pulled up alongside him. It was Cathy Duggan who glanced across and offered her smile. Jack readied himself to meet a lady he knew from his past. A shiver went through him when he thought about the complications that might bring.

"DI Jack Husker; it's been a while," she announced. Her tone forced him to blush.

"Hi, Cathy. It's good to see you. I didn't know you were back in York."

"Of course, you didn't. That's the only reason you haven't been in touch, isn't it?"

Jack felt tongue-tied. His lips were moving but there was no sound coming out. Twice, he tried to offer a response. He was pleased when Cathy saved him from his moment of difficulty.

"Seriously, Jack, it's good to see you. I met that special lady of yours the other day."

"You mean, Lisa?"

"I take it the car belongs to her. It must be serious. I can't imagine you spending that sort of cash on anything."

"Yes, it's hers. What brings you back to York?"

"A man. Sorry, Jack. You missed your chance."

"Anyone I know?"

"No, he is one of the few around here without a criminal record."

"You hope," laughed Jack.

"I bloody well do. I can't face the thought of you locking up my boyfriend. We have just bought a house together in Fulford. I am hoping he is the one."

"They must be paying you too much if you can afford to live in Fulford."

"It's the amount of overtime. Your lot don't catch enough murderers, so I'm kept very busy. Are we going to carry on with the small talk or are you coming inside?"

"Let's go inside but be gentle with me. I've only just had my breakfast."

"And those are words I never thought I would hear Jack Husker say."

Once again, Jack blushed. This time, it was as red as the colour of Cathy Duggan's nail varnish.

***

The visit was short. The body had been brought in late during the previous afternoon. Cathy had set to work on it immediately. The identification had been swift, with the match to Darren Brand made quickly. All that was waiting was a positive ID from his wife. Once she had confirmed that it was him, Cathy Duggan's work was done.

The cause of death was a single shot to the head. A ballistics examination was expected to confirm that the bullet was fired from the same gun that had killed Josie Raynor. It was all too easy though it put them no nearer to finding the perpetrator. Two people had died in identical ways and had been left in the same location.

Jack and Cathy walked out of the building after going over the details. Jack was pleased to get out. He needed to enjoy the fresh air outside. Being in that confined space was bad enough. To be in there with Cathy Duggan made it harder. There were things from their past that he had no wish to rake up now that they had both moved on.

"How long do you think he was in the lake?"

"Certainly a few days."

"Long enough to have been there when Josie Raynor was found?"

"There is a fair chance that he was. I can't be sure. I would love to give you an exact time and date but that just isn't possible."

"That's fine. You've given me as much as I could have hoped for. I'll let you get on."

"You take it steady, Jack. It is good to see you and I mean that."

"You too," said Jack. He leaned over and gave Cathy a peck on the cheek.

"You should save that for Lisa. I've had my fair share from you over the years."

Jack turned and walked away before the colour of his face gave away his level of discomfort.

***

Jack left the mortuary and drove straight to Lisa's flat. On the journey, his mind drifted back to his time with Cathy Duggan. They were two headstrong people who were never likely to be a compatible couple. There had been good times but it had been tempestuous, with neither able to back down for a second. That had led to arguments and an inevitable split.

The act of separation was the most surprising part of their relationship. It was amicable and left them both wondering why it had ever gone wrong. Cathy was moving away from York which made it easier than if she was staying. Jack smiled. It was one relationship in his life that he could look back on without regret.

Lisa was waiting for Jack outside her flat. He waved at her as he pulled the car into the car park. He fought the urge to compare Cathy to Lisa. One thing that Cathy had got right was that he had found somebody special. Lisa was someone who deserved better than the Jack Husker of old. Quite how long he could remain on his best behaviour was another question.

"Jump in," he instructed.

"Do I get to drive? It is my car," said Lisa.

"Maybe on the way back. I've adjusted the seat now."

"You're priceless."

"Yes, just like a museum artefact. Anyway, what are you doing at home when you should be at work?"

"Catching up on paperwork."

"Yeah, right," he frowned. "Two bunk-offs in two days. You'll end up with a reputation."

"That's rich coming from you. What's the plan?"

"I think a trip to see Marcus and Laura Tummel might be the order of the day. Let's find out what her relationship is with

Jordan Bilby. We should make sure that we ask her in front of Marcus."

"You don't think he knows about her casino visits, do you?"

"I would be pretty confident about that."

"And what about Jordan?" asked Lisa. "Do we need to pay him another visit?"

"For now, leave Kelly to do her work. If we are right about the Laura connection, he'll know we are asking questions pretty quickly."

"Are you as worried as I am about Kelly going to the casino on her day off?"

"A little," admitted Jack. "We should definitely keep an eye on her."

Jack drove carefully, aware that Lisa was watching his every move. It felt like he was undertaking his driving test all over again. Any late change of gear or over-revving of the engine was met with a frown. Jack did not like it. He felt tense with Lisa watching him so closely. He feared how she would react if he made a mistake. Her fierce manner when crossed offered an uncanny resemblance to Cathy Duggan.

"What are we expecting to find when we get there?" asked Lisa.

"Who knows?" shrugged Jack. "Let's just call it an old-fashioned fishing trip."

Jack was pleased to pull off the A64. It put them to the west of Malton on a series of weaving country lanes. He drove slowly past acres of fields. A turn-off down a private road saw them pass a sign for the stables.

They were met by a grand entrance and a long straight road between two fields of crops. Jack could see the stables in the distance. As he approached, he was surprised by the size of the yard. There was a series of large buildings and houses which hinted at staff accommodation. It looked big enough to accommodate an entire workforce. Jack had no idea how many people were needed to run a racing business. He turned towards Lisa. For the first time, she was looking out of the car instead of studying his driving.

"This is some place," noted Jack. "I reckon they might have a few quid."

"And I thought Laura was with Marcus for his sparkling personality."

Jack slowed the car to allow them extra time to look out. There was no obvious place to park in the spacious yard. Vehicles seemed to be dotted around at random. He pulled up alongside an old farm vehicle. It hid the car behind it and put them out of sight of anyone who was passing. Like Jack, the farm vehicle had seen better days, giving him a sense that he belonged.

"I'm driving back," said Lisa.

"We'll see," replied Jack.

He exited the car before Lisa asked for her keys. He walked a few paces and surveyed everything around him. Lisa got out and moved around the car to stand with him. She looked across the yard and then directly towards Jack.

"I'm serious, Jack. I'm driving back."

"That's fine. Where would you like to start? I suggest we stick together on this one."

"Do you think there will be trouble?"

"I am just trying to avoid getting lost. I also have a feeling that when we find the happy couple, neither of us is going to want to miss the show."

Jack followed Lisa into the barn in front of them. Built with concrete blocks up to halfway, it was clad in timber to the roof. The roof was quite new, with transparent areas added to bring in daylight. Despite that attempt for illumination, it still needed electric lights to see clearly.

They circled around, searching for any signs of life. The barn was empty except for machinery and sacks of feed. Slipping through the shadows, Jack came out shaking his head. He and Lisa stood near the door having seen nothing of interest.

As they emerged back into the yard, they heard footsteps. Their heads turned to see a girl running from one of the buildings. She was young, with her hair tied back in a scruffy blond ponytail. She looked dressed to work with the horses.

Lisa hurried away from Jack and went after her. It forced the girl to quicken her pace. Lisa called out, which made the girl stop. She half-turned and then began to edge away towards one of the houses.

"Are you okay?" asked Lisa.

"I'm fine," sobbed the girl before she ran into the building and slammed the door behind her.

Lisa returned to Jack and offered a puzzled expression. Something felt wrong about the encounter. They looked around and shook their heads. There was nothing to cause her distress. The yard appeared deserted.

"Shall I go after her?" asked Lisa.

"I would," replied Jack. Before Lisa could move, he placed his hand on her arm. "Hang on; someone else is coming."

"Is that where the young lass came from?" asked Lisa.

"I think so. Look who it is."

They watched Marcus Tummel come into view. Jack smiled and offered his greeting by saluting him in an exaggerated manner. The stable owner looked annoyed at the sudden intrusion into his day. Jack was not welcome in his yard and he was not afraid to show it.

"Excuse me; have you got a warrant to be here?"

"Have you done something to make us need one?" asked Jack.

"Of course not. Now get out before I..."

"Call the police?" asked Lisa, with a straight face.

"Yes, very good. They teach you well. Do they also teach you to leave when you are not invited?"

"Perhaps after a chat, they do," smiled Jack.

"What if I don't want a chat?"

"Then you don't have to have one," confirmed Jack. "I'll just go away and fill in the blanks myself."

"What is that supposed to mean?"

"It means that we have to guess the links between you, your wife, a certain casino owner and two dead bodies. It's amazing how quickly these stories grow legs when the press get hold of them."

"Is that a threat?"

"No, Mr Tummel, it is an offer for us to sit down and have a pleasant chat."

A big sigh displayed Marcus Tummel's exasperation. He was fuming. His eyes were bearing down spitefully on the detectives. His options were limited and he knew it. If he kicked them off his property, the impact could come back to haunt him. After some prolonged thought, he beckoned them towards a picnic bench at the side of the barn.

"We could go inside," said Jack.

"No, we couldn't," corrected Marcus. "You asked for a chat, not a guided tour."

"The bench is fine," confirmed Lisa.

"It had better be," growled Marcus.

"May I ask one question before we do have that chat?" asked Lisa.

"If you must," shrugged Marcus.

"Why was that girl upset?"

"What girl?"

"The one who came out of the barn before you."

"Sorry, you've lost me. I didn't see a girl."

"Then how about I go and see her while you have a chat with DI Husker?"

"How about you don't? The offer is for a chat with me and nothing else. Take it or leave it."

Jack and Lisa nodded their acceptance, knowing it was the best offer they were going to get.

***

Marcus Tummel sat on the picnic bench looking bored. His arrogant swagger did little to make the detectives warm to him. Something had riled him. He was a very different man from the one they had met in Harrogate.

"Is Laura here?" asked Jack.

"No."

"When is she likely to be back?"

"I don't know."

"Where is she?"

"You would need to ask her. We are not one of those couples who keep watch over each other. She lives her life; I live mine. In case you hadn't noticed, we are both very busy people."

Marcus smiled, first at Jack and then at Lisa. It was a forced expression that took on a sneering form.

"How long have you owned these stables?" asked Lisa.

"That is an irrelevant question. Are we done?"

"How many staff work here?" tried Jack.

"Enough to run it. Some days that could be a couple. On other days, there could be a dozen or more. Like most businesses, we match workers to work."

"How many are on site today?" asked Jack.

"I don't know."

"I thought you managed the stables. Surely, you would know."

"Where is this heading? If there is something you wish to know, just ask me directly and stop playing games."

"Okay," said Lisa. "Do you know Jordan Bilby?"

"Good question," he smiled. "Yes, I do."

"What is your relationship to him?" she continued.

"He runs a casino in York and we run a stable yard. We cross paths at various charity functions, as you know. We share a common interest in raising funds for good causes."

"Out of interest, what charities do you support?"

"The injured jockeys' fund is our main one. It is a very good cause if you would care to make a donation."

"What has Mr Bilby got to do with jockeys?" interrupted Lisa.

"Nothing, as far as I am aware. The world of gambling and horses has a little bit of an overlap, so we tend to move in the same circles."

"Have you been to his casino?" continued Lisa. Jack was impressed with the way she was increasing the pressure on him.

"I did go there in the early days but not recently. Watching a ball-bearing spin in a mechanical wheel has never done much for me. These days, I simply don't have the time."

"Does Laura go to the casino?"

"I don't think so," he shrugged.

"I guess I would have to ask her," said Lisa, choosing to interrupt him once more.

"You would."

"And when can I do that?"

"You can ask her as soon as she gets back. I will ask her to contact you. I'm guessing you can still be reached on nine...nine...err, is it nine?"

"Try my mobile number instead," said Lisa. She pushed a card across the table.

"I'm not sure I should be taking a phone number from a police lady."

"Trust me, you should. It means that we can get to know each other a little better," she replied.

"You mean better than we did at our charity event," he grinned. It sent a sickening feeling through Lisa's stomach.

"Yes, I'm far more receptive when I have my handcuffs with me," she scowled.

Jack struggled to contain his smile. Lisa was visibly growing in her seat. As Marcus eased back, she sat further forward. His swagger was disappearing by the second. There was no doubt who was on top in the exchange. In desperation, Marcus glanced over to Jack.

"Are you a racing man?"

"Not really, why?"

"It's just that you were at the races and the charity event. Now you have turned up here. I just wondered whether you had a personal interest."

"It is just part of the job. I would be keen for a tour of the stables though."

"Sorry, we've got too much work to be getting on with."

"I don't think you heard me properly. We *would* be keen for a tour of the stables. I could, of course, ask that young girl we saw to show us around if you prefer. That is when she has finished sobbing."

Marcus Tummel scowled. He narrowed his eyes to stare Jack down. The hatred was written across his face. Jack had touched a nerve. The detective intended to ensure it was twisted hard.

"Stay here and I'll find someone to give you a quick tour."

"That's very kind of you," smiled Jack. He nodded at Marcus as he got up and walked away from where they were sitting.

"What was all that about?" asked Lisa.

"What do you mean?"

"Why didn't he just show us around for ten minutes and then see us off the premises?"

"I don't know. Maybe it was an affront to his ego. Something is going on."

"Who do you think he'll send out? It can't be that girl."

"I think she will be doing a disappearing act."

"Not permanently?" queried Lisa, her eyes opening wide with worry.

"I meant until after we have gone. I don't get the impression that Marcus is the sort of man who would want to lose a pretty girl too easily."

"Do you mean what I think you mean?"

"Hopefully not. Mind you, she didn't run out of that stable block without a good reason."

Lisa screwed up her nose to indicate the unpleasant thoughts in her head. The look surprised Jack who had not seen her grimace in such a way. That was one to file away for the future. If he saw her do it again, the alarm bells would be sounding in his head.

Before he could offer anything else, their attention was drawn to someone approaching. He was a small wiry man in his thirties who could only be a jockey.

"DI Jack Husker and DS Lisa Ramsey," said Jack, offering up his warrant card.

"Kit Grady; head jockey. Marcus said you wanted a tour of the facilities."

"That's right."

"Is there anything in particular you want to see?"

"We are just after a quick look around," said Lisa. Her smile was designed to get his attention. "We are just being nosy. Call it a perk of the job."

"No problem; follow me."

Kit set off at a pace that screamed efficiency. He seemed happy to oblige even if he looked bemused at what the detectives wanted. He went straight to the main stable block. It was the one the girl had run out of. He offered no commentary as he walked, suggesting that part of the role had not been explained to him.

"How many jockeys do you have here?" asked Lisa in a desperate attempt to engage him in conversation.

"I'm the only one on a retainer. The others are just booked for rides."

"What about stable lads and lasses?" added Jack.

"There are plenty of them. Some are full-time; others are casual. You don't know who you will be seeing from one day to the next."

"We saw one of them on the way in," said Lisa. "Young lassie; blonde hair."

"That's probably Pippa. She lives in the house over there," he said, pointing to the building the girl had run into.

"Do many live on site?"

"I think there are three of them at the moment. I might be wrong. We call it Marcus's harem. You had better make that off the record." He smiled. It was the first moment of emotion that Kit had shown.

"Don't worry; we're not here to investigate any relationships, illicit or otherwise."

"That's a relief," laughed Kit in a manner that was more exaggerated than it should have been.

"I take it there are a few," smiled Lisa.

"It's a stable yard. There are plenty."

"What about you, Kit? Do you stay in Marcus's harem?"

"No, I have a cottage down the road."

"But you visit."

"Not the harem, I don't," he laughed.

"Come on, Kit," offered Jack. "You must be tempted."

"They are all a bit young for me. I prefer a slightly more mature lady." He smiled at Lisa when he said it.

"Like Laura Tummel?" queried Lisa.

"That's Marcus's wife. I don't think so."

"Come on; you wouldn't be the first to be tempted," she insisted.

"As I said, she is Marcus's wife."

"That doesn't mean she cannot be your lover," said Lisa boldly.

Kit blushed. The colour of his face gave him away.

"Can we move on?"

"Only if you answer one more question."

"Go on," he said cautiously.

"Where is Laura today?"

There was silence. The jockey angled his face away as if resisting the urge to answer. Kit made it obvious that the question felt uncomfortable.

"Kit, where is she?" demanded Lisa, raising the tone of her voice.

"I don't know. It's none of my business, wherever she is."

"I think you do know," said Lisa.

"You'll get me sacked," protested Kit. "Just promise me this is on the…you-know-what."

"It is," said Lisa, with a reassuring nod.

"Let's just say that she has a few other admirers as well as myself. That one does like a lot of attention."

"Is one of them Jordan Bilby?" asked Jack.

"I don't know. She does spend a fair bit of time with him."

"Thank you," said Lisa. "You have been more than helpful."

Kit looked crestfallen. He appeared deep in thought when they finished. Leaving him behind, Jack and Lisa set off towards the car. Their pace seemed to quicken the further they walked.

"Come on," said Jack. "Bagsy me driving."

"But it's my car?"

"Yes, and I bagsied it first."

Jack marched across the yard. It left Lisa to shake her head behind him. They walked quickly until they were close to the car. Without warning, Jack deviated away and stared past one of the buildings. His eyes were directed to a girl who had her back turned. She was working with the horses in the neighbouring field. As Lisa caught up, she looked first at the girl and then at Jack.

"Do you want to make it any more obvious that you are staring at her?"

"I know her."

"That's even more worrying from that view."

"Not like that," he laughed. "I think that is the councillor's daughter."

"Which councillor?"

Before he could answer, the girl turned around and looked across towards Jack and Lisa. Her recognition was instant. She patted her horse twice and then jogged over to the detectives. Jack raised his hand to acknowledge her. It was a face that he remembered from the past.

"It's been a while," she smiled softly.

"It certainly has, Elizabeth. Do you remember DS Lisa Ramsey? Lisa, you must remember Elizabeth Moss; David Moss's daughter."

The recollection came flooding back. Their paths had crossed in the most grizzly of circumstances. It was a while ago and yet there would still be unhealed wounds. Elizabeth was unlikely to ever lose the memories.

"I take it you work here," said Jack.

"Work here; live here; I never leave the place. After Steven, I needed a change of scene."

"I can understand that. How's your father these days?"

"You mean after you hit him."

"Did I?" blushed Jack. "Oh yes, I did. He was being an utter prat. Sorry, no offence intended."

"None taken. We're only vaguely in touch these days. We fell out after the loss of Steven. We text occasionally but that is about it. Hey, if you see him, don't tell him where I am living. I could do without him turning up here and having a row with Marcus."

"And would he?"

"Of course, he would. You know what he is like."

"I certainly do."

"So what brings you here?" asked Elizabeth. "We're not in trouble, are we?"

"No, it's just background stuff. We have a case in York. The Tummels know some of the characters involved. We are just trying to fill in a few of the missing details. You know, family, friends, who they mix with, etcetera."

"Unfortunately, I know the process only too well."

"More importantly, how are you getting on?"

"Great; I love it here. I've always been into horses."

"How are the Tummels?"

Elizabeth went silent. It was not a question that she wanted to answer.

"Well?"

"Okay, I guess," she offered reluctantly.

"Just okay? That's the sort of thing people say when everything is not okay. Tell us about Marcus."

"He runs the place."

"With a rod of iron?" asked Lisa.

"That's not my place to say."

"How about you tell us about the other stable girls who live here?" continued Jack.

"What is there to tell? There are three of us. Pippa, Becky and me. Mind you, Becky is away at the moment. She's at a family birthday or something like that."

"What about Pippa? We saw her earlier. Why would Pippa be running from a stable block in tears, with Marcus emerging a few paces behind her?"

"He must have told her off."

"Just told her off?"

"I'm sorry, I don't know. You will have to ask Pippa or Marcus."

"I think you do know, Elizabeth. When you are ready to tell us, you have my number."

"There isn't anything to tell."

"What about Laura? What's she like?"

"We see less of her. She is away from the yard a lot of the time."

"Where does she go?"

"I don't know."

"Is she with Kit?"

Elizabeth blushed bright red. She looked around to check who was listening before moving a pace closer towards the detectives.

"Look, she has a bit of a thing with Kit, but they are discrete. I caught them once in a less-than-flattering position in a barn. That's about as much as I know."

"Does Marcus know?"

"I don't think so and you didn't hear it from me if he finds out. I need to get on."

"That's fine, but keep in touch. I have a feeling we might be talking quite a lot over the next few days."

***

Jack and Lisa allowed Elizabeth to go back to work. Jack knew that she was holding plenty back. Eventually, she would tell them everything they wanted to know. The girl was a 'slow burner' when it came to offering up information.

His work on the Steven Reeves case would hold Jack in good standing. Whether that was enough for her to open up rather than just provide gossip about the Tummels was less clear. Sordid behaviour and affairs provided useful background information. Without evidence or a complaint from an innocent party, there was nothing that would allow them to move forward.

Without a word being exchanged between Jack and Lisa, they got into the car. Jack drove while Lisa thought nothing about taking the passenger seat. Both were reflecting on what they had heard and were processing the information in their heads. It was Lisa who cracked first. Her mind was still fixed on Pippa running from the barn with Marcus not too far behind her.

"Do you think Marcus is having an affair with Pippa?" she asked.

"Possibly."

"Or do you think he was just trying it on with her?"

"That's possible too. The other option is he could have been rejecting her advances and that was why she was upset," countered Jack.

"That's typical of you to take the man's view," said Lisa.

"My point is that we just don't know. It could have been him rejecting her or her rejecting him. It could even be mutual and both were upset. Or he could have been trying to force himself on her."

"That would be the most likely," insisted Lisa.

"That's typical of you to take the female's view," laughed Jack. "It is just as likely that it was an ordinary work matter and he was giving her a dressing down for something. Have you also thought that in a building of that size, they might have been in there separately?"

"Where is the fun in thinking that?" laughed Lisa.

"Either way, I don't think it gets us any closer to what we are after," said Jack.

"I'm not sure I agree with that. We now know that Laura Tummel is having at least one affair. We believe Marcus has an eye for the stable girls and we know that Kit is happy to go behind one of his employer's backs to sleep with the other one. Quite why, I'm not sure, but he does."

"Some people go for older partners," quipped Jack.

"Yes, I've never understood that," responded Lisa. She rolled her eyes in his direction. "It seems like a lot of hassle to me."

"Maybe that's what makes it interesting."

"You're probably right but that doesn't answer the main question of the day," said Lisa.

"Which is the connection to Jordan Bilby," guessed Jack.

"No. The more pertinent question is why are you driving my car again?"

"It's an age thing," laughed Jack. "Seniority always takes precedence."

"Yes, in post office queues and at the bus stop. Now, can we go home, Grandad?"

"Only if you've packed the tartan rug and the boiled sweets for the journey," laughed Jack.

Chapter 12

Kelly had spent the afternoon thinking about the money from the casino. Those eight hundred pounds weighed heavily on her mind. So little effort had been required to make it hers. Its value was nothing to Jordan Bilby and yet it meant the world to her. It was the difference between a normal life and struggling to keep her head above the water.

The lure of that financial respite made it hard to think rationally. The more she thought about it, the more that money was hers. There was no way that it could be classed as police funds when it had nothing to do with the case. It was pure luck that it had been given to her. She had been left with no choice but to accept it if she was going to keep up the pretence of being a customer.

Once Kelly had made her decision, there was no going back. She left the station early and returned home with the money on her mind. She collected three hundred pounds of it and put it into her purse. Her destination was her favourite boutique dress shop on Stonegate. It had been a while since she had been in there and even longer since she had been able to treat herself.

The excitement of the trip was difficult to contain. She intended to buy an outfit which she could wear for the job. It would also be one that would catch Jordan Bilby's eye. If she was going to watch him, she had to look good to do so. A girl wearing the same dress on multiple nights offered no allure to anyone.

It did not take long for her to find something she liked. Kelly's slender figure slipped into the first two dresses that she took to the fitting room. Both hugged her tightly and clung to her shape. She emerged from behind the curtain to use the full-length mirror in the shop. A twirl caught her eye as well as the drifting gaze of a boyfriend who was waiting for his girl to emerge. Kelly smiled when she saw the desire written across his face. She could only hope that his girlfriend would receive the same reaction.

The way his face lit up chose the dress for her. The dark blue mini-dress was the one they both preferred. Kelly returned to the changing area. While inside, she noticed the girl he had been waiting for. She was standing in front of the smaller mirror, looking unsure. She was making her adjustments ahead of going out to model for her boyfriend.

Kelly smiled politely towards her. She was not going to say anything to upset her. The girl looked awful, with her oversized frame having been shoe-horned into a dress that was far too small. It created bulges in all the wrong places and looked worse when she walked. As she went to parade in front of him, Kelly glanced out at the spectacle. She saw the lad nodding. It was cringing to watch his deceit.

"Unlucky," muttered Kelly. She admonished herself for being such a bitch.

She changed quickly and tucked the dress over her arm. A last look at it brought a smile before she walked back into the shop. She left the rejected dress on the rail and moved over to the counter. The assistant was waiting for her at the till.

"How was that one?"

"I'll take it."

"Perfect; that will be one hundred and sixty pounds."

"Will you take cash?"

"No problem," smiled the assistant.

Kelly counted the cash onto the counter while the assistant bagged up the dress. It felt good to be rewarding herself with something so nice. She had earned it by going undercover. She took the bag eagerly and tucked the receipt inside it.

She slipped past the couple who were still discussing the dress the larger girl was wearing. Kelly smiled and offered a wink to the boyfriend. His head turned to watch her leave. It earned him an angry slap on his arm. For the lad, it was worth every moment of the discomfort.

***

Less than two hours later, Kelly walked back into the casino. She moved confidently in her new dress, with her strappy black heels making her feel four inches taller. She knew the routine. A quick signature against her name confirmed that her membership was pending. It left her wondering whether anyone was a full member or whether the whole thing was an elaborate charade.

She made for her usual haven of the bar. This time, she had plenty of cash with her. The change from her three hundred pounds was still in her purse. There was thirty pounds of her own in there with it. She certainly had enough for a wild night if she wanted one. As she approached, she smiled at the barman and settled onto the stool in front of him. Was she on duty? A quick scan of her options soon answered the question.

"I'll have a gin and tonic, please. Bombay Sapphire."

"Ice and a slice?"

"Yes, please."

She looked across at the gaming tables and noted a few familiar faces from last time. There was no Laura Tummel though some of the others were there. They were all focussing acutely on the action. What struck her was that everyone was in the same position. It felt like the success of their evening was dependent on a lucky seat. Her gaze went across to the table where Jordan had handed her the winnings. It was empty. Her desire to move over there was only dampened by the sound of the barman delivering her drink.

"One gin and tonic, madam."

"Thank you," she replied softly. She took the glass up to her lips and then stopped. It was the moment when her eyes caught sight of the man she had seen thrown out. She thought back to that night and remembered his name as Spencer.

Drunk and slurring, he was throwing chips energetically at the table. His voice was growing in volume by the second. The security team were loitering around him but not moving in. They were allowing him his freedom until it was too late. Kelly watched him lean against the table for support. He was drunk and he erupted when he suffered a big loss.

The explosion was accompanied by him swinging his arms aggressively. He was loud and got worse when the security team grabbed hold of him. He was dragged towards the front door, screaming out his expletives along the way. Kelly watched him as did most of the others in the casino. It felt like the whole thing could have been avoided with some earlier action. Kelly turned to the barman for answers.

"What was all that about?"

"He doesn't like losing," shrugged the barman who was not showing any real interest.

"He was thrown out last night as well."

"Some people never learn."

"Why is he allowed back in?"

"I'm sorry, I can't answer that. I just run the bar. Let me know if you want another one."

"Not yet," smiled Kelly. She took another sip from her drink. She looked around and watched how others were reacting to their losses. Nobody seemed to take it as personally as Spencer did. She wondered how much he had lost. Maybe it was everything he had.

Her attention was taken by a voice behind her. It was familiar and sent a tingle through her body. She tried to remain calm as she slid her legs around to face him. Once turned, she offered up her smile.

"Fancy seeing you again," beamed Jordan Bilby. His hand reached up to signal for a drink. "Meeting a friend again?"

"No, I am just passing."

Jordan's eyes swept down her dress. They lingered on her for a little too long. He studied her and then looked up with a smile. "Just passing, you say. You do look stunning for a lady who is just passing. May I ask where you are heading?"

"A lady never tells," smiled Kelly. She felt pleased with the mystery of her response.

"No, but she can accept company. Can I get you another drink?"

"Why not?" she smiled, ignoring the rejection she had given the barman less than two minutes ago.

"What are you having?"

"A gin and tonic, please."

"Make that two," he offered. He nodded in the barman's direction. "Mind if I take a seat?"

"It's your casino."

"Even in my casino, I don't force my company on anyone."

"I'm glad to hear it. You are welcome to join me."

Jordan slipped onto the stool opposite Kelly. His attraction to her was obvious. His eyes were flitting around to take every opportunity to stare at her. Kelly was the type of girl who intrigued him.

"I think it might be time for you to tell me a bit more about yourself. You know plenty about me, so let's hear something about you." Jordan smiled and looked deep into her eyes.

"It's all pretty dull," sighed Kelly.

"How about we start with what you do for a living? That can't be too dull."

"I'm between jobs. I've just moved to the city."

"Are you looking for work?"

"I suppose I could be."

"That is something I might be able to help a pretty girl with."

"Thanks, but I'm not sure I would want to tell people that I work in a casino."

"You don't have to tell them. Everyone has a dark side with a few secrets."

"Do you?"

"Of course, I do. I wouldn't be much fun if I didn't."

"Tell me one of your secrets."

"Why would I do that? What do I get out of telling you?"

"I might accept that offer of a job."

"I think we can make the stakes a little higher than that," smiled Jordan softly. He leaned over and placed his hand on Kelly's arm. "I want you to take everything in your purse and go and put it on a single spin of that roulette wheel. Then I'll show you one of my darkest secrets."

Kelly was trembling. She could feel the electricity pulsing through her body. It was a strange cocktail; a heady mixture of fear and excitement, all bubbling away in one intoxicating mix. She wanted to do it and yet she couldn't. There was too much to lose. Jordan looked into her eyes and allowed his presence to bear down on her. All Kelly wanted to do was run out of the building.

"I don't know how much I have in my purse."

"That is part of the thrill and you are stalling for time. Take the risk, Kelly. Girls who take risks have so much more fun."

Before she could refuse, her purse was open. She pulled out the notes and grasped them in one hand. She was shaking and fighting the urge to comply. Everything about Jordan made her want to do it.

"Go on, Kelly. You can do it. Not just the notes. It has to be all of it," he whispered. "Every last penny you have on you; I want it tipped out onto the table."

"But that includes my taxi money to get home."

"That is part of the excitement. To enjoy the thrill, you have to take risks."

As if hypnotised by his words, Kelly slid from her stool. She walked over to the empty roulette table and tipped out her money. She dropped the notes and shook out her purse to confirm that there was nothing left inside it. Once it was all on the table, she stared back at Jordan.

The croupier glanced at Jordan. A single nod confirmed that the bet should be taken. Kelly shuffled the money away from her to cover some of the numbers. It took forever. She looked up towards the young girl to seek her approval. Had she done it right? All she got was a smile.

"No more bets," said the croupier, her words like a weight pressing on Kelly's chest.

Kelly watched the wheel being put into motion. She was transfixed and did not notice Jordan approach her or when his hand slipped fully around her. He gripped her waist and pulled her into him. There was no resistance offered. Electricity was pumping through her. Her eyes went to the croupier's hand as the ball was flicked into the wheel. She felt fear, then excitement before utter terror ripped through her body.

"Ride it, Kelly; ride the excitement," said Jordan, his grip around her unrelenting.

Kelly could not move. She blinked her eyes and was unable to clear her blurry vision. They closed as the ball slowed and settled into a number. She couldn't watch. Her mind had long since forgotten what she had bet on. Through the numbness, she prayed that it would be one of her numbers. Beside her, Jordan held her tight to his side and savoured every moment of her suffering.

"Red five," announced the croupier. Her eyes were down to review the bets on the table.

"I think that is one of mine," offered Kelly. "I think I won. I did…I won!" she screamed. She jumped in the air as Jordan continued to hold her.

She turned and threw her arms around him, grabbing as tight as her strength allowed. Jordan did little to fight her as she enveloped him in both arms. He accepted her attention, knowing he would play the long game. Kelly would pay him back so many times for the money he had invested.

The croupier smiled. She pushed a combination of cash and chips in Kelly's direction. It was far more than she had put on, leaving Kelly's head spinning. She could not comprehend how much was there. It was a sizeable sum of money that was being eased towards her.

"I'm sorry, I haven't got cash to give back to you. You can exchange the chips at the cashier's desk."

"That's fine," said Kelly. She was still shaking from the experience.

"Someone is a clever girl," said Jordan. He leaned over and kissed her softly on the cheek. It lingered as did his hand before it slipped from her and linked through her arm. He guided Kelly away from the table. "Now it is my turn to show you a secret."

"What about my winnings?"

"They will be waiting for you when we get back," he said. He waved his hand to instruct the croupier to deal with it. "I think it is time for me to show you where the big boys and girls go to play."

Jordan made sure that he had a firm hold on Kelly's arm. He walked her across the casino floor. Her mind was still scrambled from the bet. Her head swivelled back towards the table. She was anxious to know how much she had won. Kelly had seen the stack of chips being pushed in her direction. All she needed to know was what they were worth.

For a few seconds, it seemed like she had imagined the whole thing. It felt like Jordan was taking her away from her winnings. Did she trust him to give her the money? She didn't but she was ready to buckle up and enjoy the ride.

Jordan took Kelly through a side door and away from the casino floor. It brought them into an unused office and then beyond to a narrow corridor. As the pace quickened, she struggled to keep up in her high heels. It was not an outfit designed for a lady to move quickly. To her side, Jordan's arm had slipped back around her waist. He was not about to let her fall.

"Where are we going?"

"I told you. You are going to see where the big boys and girls go to play."

A sense of fear gripped her as they passed through two more doors. One had a guard standing outside. He was a large shaven-headed man who looked like he could inflict some serious pain. The bouncer stepped aside and nodded to Jordan. Brief pleasantries were exchanged before a left turn took them through another door.

"This is like a rabbit warren," giggled Kelly.

"It is a deceptive building," said Jordan as he eased Kelly inside. "It's been added to many times over the years. There are doors and corridors everywhere."

The room they entered was the size of a large living room. Its only windows were four veluxes sunk into the ceiling. It was devoid of any features, other than two card tables spaced well apart and a drinks trolley to the side. The furthest of the tables had seven people gathered around it. Heads were down and a game was in progress.

"This feels like the inner sanctum," whispered Kelly. Her voice was hushed to avoid disturbing those inside.

"It certainly is. You are very privileged to be allowed in here. It is invite only and is restricted to special guests."

"Why have you brought me in here?"

"I think you might be the sort of girl who likes a game with higher stakes."

Her attention was taken by one of the players. A good-looking man in his late thirties stood up and eased quietly away from the table. He walked across to Jordan. A quick handshake was exchanged between them. Then his focus went onto Kelly and drifted slowly down her body. He smiled as he looked up and stared deep into her eyes.

"Are you coming to play with us? I'm Jason."

"Kelly," she said with a nervous tone. A hand was held out and shaken.

"We always have space for one more."

"I'm just giving Kelly the VIP tour. You might be seeing Kelly again. She is making a bit of a name for herself with her success on the floor."

"Then we need to get her in here, don't we? We always welcome a pretty face."

Kelly blushed. She could not help but think that Jason would also qualify in that category.

"We'll see," she said softly.

"Maybe you and I could go head-to-head," said Jason as he allowed his eyes some freedom to roam. "I would like that a lot."

"I don't think I am quite ready for that yet," admitted Kelly.

"Then you need to test yourself. The only way to do that is with high stakes. The higher the better. If you will excuse me, I need to get myself a drink. Then I am going to eliminate these mugs. I do hope we meet again soon, Kelly," he smiled.

"You will," nodded Jordan. "That I can be sure of."

Kelly watched Jason help himself to a drink from the trolley at the side. He poured a large whisky from a decanter. She noted the way he glanced back to have another look at her. He seemed to be studying everything about her.

"I take it he is a good player," offered Kelly.

"He is probably the best high-stakes poker player in the casino."

"What sort of stakes are we talking about?" she asked.

"Let's just say that he only plays for serious money."

Kelly looked across towards Jordan. His face was beaming down at her. He had that glint of someone with unlimited confidence. Kelly felt uncomfortable in his presence and yet there was a sense of excitement that came with it. With Jordan, every day was different to the monotony life often brought.

"I'm not sure I have the kind of money to play in those sorts of games," she shrugged.

"Then you need to offer a different form of collateral. There are always people willing to stake you if the right guarantees are offered."

Chapter 13

Jack rang Lisa just as she woke. It was early, with the sun barely shining in through her curtains. She felt drowsy. Her eyes were still full of sleep even though her phone had sprung to life on the bedside table.

"Jack, what is it?"

"I need your car."

"Don't I even get a good morning?"

"Good morning. I need to borrow your car."

"You only gave me the keys back last night."

"Yes, and now I need them again."

"When?"

"I'll be there in fifteen minutes."

"Jack, it is seven o'clock in the morning."

"Is it? Oh dear; I'm late."

"For what?"

"There is no time to explain. I just need your car. I'll be there in fifteen minutes."

"Jack...Jack..."

He had hung up. It was dead long before Lisa had started to speak. She pushed herself up and shook the sleep from her head. There was regret that the phone had been left by her bed. Just for one morning, she would have liked to wake up with the alarm. Lisa eased back the covers and forced herself out of bed. Jack would be around within minutes. When he sunk his teeth into something, politeness never stood in his way.

Lisa had a quick shower and got dressed. The buzz of the intercom came as she finished drying her hair. She allowed Jack to come up. The coffee machine was turned on in an attempt to slow him down. She doubted that it would work. He had sounded like a man on a mission.

He barely came into the flat. His reluctance to engage put Lisa on edge. It felt like she had done something wrong. Was it her or was something else troubling him?

"Do you want a coffee?" she asked. Her voice was tentative, with the question tailing off towards the end. There was no point finishing it. Jack was not listening.

"I just need your keys."

"Jack, what is this about? Even car rental companies get a few minutes before they hand over a car."

"It's the Tummels. There has been an incident reported. Some form of assault."

"Right, I'll come with you."

"No, you get to the station and do some more digging. The uniforms are already there. I am only going to get the inside track before they make a mess of it."

"And you want to borrow my car to get there?" Lisa said with a puzzled expression.

"Exactly."

Lisa took the keys from the side table and threw them into his hands. She shook her head towards Jack. "Just call me Avis, why don't you?"

"I reckon you've been called a lot worse than that," laughed Jack. He exited the flat just before a cushion crashed into the door behind him.

***

Jack drove as quickly as he dared. He knew that any speeding offences would go back to Lisa and leave him with some difficult questions to answer. That would be an awkward conversation. He made sure the needle stayed on the right side of eighty. He could get away with a few miles per hour even with the sharp-eyed civilians in their camera vans.

On the approach to the stables, he could see a lot of activity. A large police van and a squad car were already parked up. One set of blue lights was still flashing though more through the absent-mindedness of the officer rather than the need to warn others. Jack parked Lisa's car and got out. He flashed his warrant card in the direction of the officer. It was a girl he had not seen before.

"DI Jack Husker," he offered.

"PC Jenny Blake," she smiled while shifting from foot to foot.

"Are you new?"

"First day," she beamed. She had a mixture of nervous energy and uncertainty rolled into one.

"Well, Jenny, it doesn't get any more exciting than this. I take it this is a domestic."

"I'm not sure. Sergeant Fenwick is in the far building. He's in charge."

"Thanks," said Jack, mindful that the young PC did not need any more stress in her life. Her first day would be hard enough without him giving her a grilling.

Jack followed her directions into the stables. There were raised voices, with three uniforms trying to resolve the situation. They were gathered in one corner of the building. A saddle and a bucket were strewn on the floor, possibly sent tumbling in the incident. As Jack approached, their heads turned. That was the moment that he saw Marcus Tummel and Kit Grady being separated by the officers. Jack nodded his head as a greeting before turning towards a man he knew only too well.

"Hi, George; it's been a while," said Jack. He smiled at Sergeant Fenwick.

"I knew it wouldn't be long before you turned up. Am I muscling in on your patch?"

"Not really. I normally stick to the city. Can I ask what the story is?"

"Yes," interrupted Marcus. "You are all trespassing on my land."

"What Mr Tummel means is that we were called to a disturbance at his property," corrected Sergeant George Fenwick.

"Not by me, you weren't," insisted Marcus.

"A concerned citizen called us."

"Who? I'm a mile from the nearest neighbour."

"I cannot answer that, Mr Tummel. All I know is that we received a call. As officers of the law, we have to investigate."

"What a load of claptrap. Jack, can you sort this out?"

"I might be able to if I understood what was going on. I am sure you have made every effort to explain the situation."

"Nothing is going on as I keep telling these idiots."

Jack looked at Marcus Tummel and then at Kit Grady. He noted that Kit's shirt was ripped. The top two buttons were gone. A bruise appeared to be forming on his cheek, suggesting that something blunt had struck it hard. Jack had no doubt that the same mark would be found on Marcus's fist if he was kind enough to show him.

"I think we will need some statements," said Jack.

"For crying out loud; nothing happened!" bellowed Marcus, his voice echoing around the stables. "Did it, Kit?"

"Err...no, Mr Tummel. Nothing happened."

"See."

"Very good," said Jack. "George, can I leave you to take the statements?"

"It would be my pleasure."

Jack walked out of the building. It was the ideal opportunity to have a look around without Marcus Tummel circling over him. He had a reason to be on the property. That would allow him into the other buildings. He wondered whether Pippa might be willing to talk or whether she preferred to forget about the incident. With Marcus Tummel about to be drowned in George Fenwick's questions, he had plenty of time to find out.

***

Jack was pleased to leave Marcus to someone else. He had enjoyed the display of annoyance the man did nothing to hide. There were so many things he did not like about him. That alone was reason enough to make his life difficult. George Fenwick would do exactly that. He was one of the best at irritating his suspects. A stickler for doing things by the rules, he would drive Marcus mad with his pedanticness.

At the house, Jack knocked lightly on the door. He made sure that it was barely loud enough to be heard. It was far better to go in and apologise than give fair warning that he was approaching. So many times, he had caught people in the act of a crime or understood subtleties which would otherwise have remained hidden. After allowing a moment of silence, he pushed the door open. All he saw was an empty kitchen.

"Hello, is anyone home?" said Jack quietly.

His approach was halted by the sound of feet on the stairs. Aware of his imminent discovery, Jack called out. This time, it was loud enough to wake the dead. He stood waiting for the footsteps to reveal themselves and then watched the distinctive form of Laura Tummel come into view. Still radiating her glamour, Jack smiled and awaited her frosty tones.

"I'm sorry to disturb you, Mrs Tummel. The door had been left open."

"For heaven's sake, it's one thing after another. What is going on out there?"

"I don't know. I have only just arrived. The officers appear to be taking statements from both your husband and Mr Grady. Are you aware of what has gone on between them?"

"I think they have had a bit of a disagreement about something," she replied dismissively. Her indifference to the incident was not fooling Jack for one moment.

"Do you know what that disagreement was about?"

Laura Tummel went silent. Her face flushed with a deep shade of red. She looked uncomfortable once the focus had turned to her. "I don't know."

"I think you do. Why don't you tell me about it over a cup of coffee?"

"There is nothing to tell."

"Okay, let's try that again. How about you tell me over a coffee in the comfort of your kitchen rather than down at the station?"

"You wouldn't."

"Try me," replied Jack.

"A coffee, you say?"

"A coffee and a little chat; just between the two of us."

Laura Tummel sighed loudly. She resigned herself to the request. Jack was a persistent maverick who would insist on getting his way. Making coffee bought her some time. It also offered a faint ray of hope that something else would take his attention while she did it.

"How do you take it?" she asked.

"Just with a drop of milk if you have some."

"I think we can manage some milk. This isn't the third world, you know. Do you think they will charge Marcus?"

The question came like a bolt of lightning. It caught Jack by surprise. When he did not answer, she turned to face him with the coffee pot held firmly in her hand.

For once, Jack found himself struggling for words. He was left to mouth a simple, "Don't know." It earned him a small amount of respite while his host finished at the worktop. That blunt question left him wondering whether she would be interrogating him instead of the other way around.

Laura brought over two cups of coffee. They were placed down in the centre of the table. She took the chair opposite Jack. Once seated, her eyes seemed to stare straight through him.

For Jack, it was a reminder of how attractive she was. Her large eyes were her dominant feature. It was not difficult to see why Marcus was with her and yet she was more than a piece of eye-candy for his arm. She was a proper businesswoman, with many commenting that she was the main driving force behind their success. They were rumours Jack did not find hard to believe.

"You were going to tell me what is going on between Marcus and Kit," said Jack.

"I think you know the answer to that," growled Laura.

"Humour me, please. I would rather hear it from you."

"I hope you aren't going to use the term 'horse's mouth' to refer to me."

"Certainly not," lied Jack. He was thankful that he had not said what was in his head.

"Marcus thinks Kit and I are having an affair."

"And are you?"

"I don't think that is a police matter, do you?"

"It is if your husband attacks your alleged lover."

"Are you going to arrest anyone?"

"I don't know. It will depend on the statements and whether anyone intends to make a complaint."

"Nobody will make a complaint."

"They might not but what happens after we leave?"

"I don't know," sighed Laura, the life visibly draining from her body.

"Will you be alright?"

"What do you mean?"

"Well, if your husband is prone to violence, are you going to be safe?"

"Of course I will be safe. Marcus would never do anything to hurt me. He loves me."

"And do you love him?"

An uncomfortable silence told Jack everything. Laura looked troubled as if her world was dependent on an answer she could not give. The longer she remained quiet, the more it confirmed how difficult the relationship was. Laura chewed her lip and then uttered some words that she soon regretted.

"Let's just say that we were once close. Marcus now finds the stable girls more to his liking. Sorry, I shouldn't have said that."

"Yes, you should. Does that extend to Pippa?"

Laura looked confused. She was wary of asking the question. Her eyes had regained a steely edge and were targeted at Jack. "Why are you asking about Pippa specifically? We have several stable girls."

"We saw her leaving the stables in tears when we came yesterday."

"You were here yesterday?" she queried.

"Yes, we spoke to Marcus."

"He never said anything."

"We spoke to Kit as well."

"Did you?" asked Laura innocently. She bit her bottom lip between her teeth.

"Can you think of any reason why Pippa would be coming out of the stables in tears?"

"I dread to think," sighed Laura. Her head shook slowly when she said it.

"So do I," mused Jack. "How about I ask her? Is she here?"

"Probably not. I think I had better go and see my husband, don't you?"

"You are not going anywhere, Laura. Not until you have told the stable girls that I would like to speak to them."

"What, all of them?"

"Yes, I would like you to ask them to come over one at a time. We might be a while so I am sure a fresh pot of coffee would not go amiss."

***

Pippa Jones was the first girl to be summoned to the kitchen. Fear was written across her face. Her manner was not helped by Laura Tummel hovering over the detective. Pippa's eyes barely looked in Jack's direction. The venom coming from her employer told Jack everything. There would be repercussions if she told the truth.

"Pippa, please take a seat. I'm DI Jack Husker. I think we met briefly the other day. Would you like a coffee?"

"No, I'm fine."

"Are you sure? I'm having one."

"I'm fine."

"Laura, could you leave us to it, please?"

"I would prefer to stay and offer my assistance."

"I am afraid that is not possible. Why don't you go and see how your husband is getting on? I will be keen to talk to him when he is finished with the uniformed officers."

"What about?"

"Don't worry, I'm not about to drop anyone in it. That is provided I see some cooperation."

As he spoke, Jack stared at Pippa. She looked terrified as if her interrogation was about to begin. He felt for her and the other stable girls who were all in a difficult position. If there was a way to get to the facts without speaking to them, he would have left them out of the investigation.

Laura nodded reluctantly and left the room. She closed the door with enough force to ensure that it got everyone's attention. Pippa jolted violently at the sudden sound. She knew the act was a warning from Laura.

"I don't know what I can help you with," Pippa spluttered. She was a little too keen to get the words from her mouth.

Jack allowed a moment of calm to return once they were alone. Pippa looked so young. Her troubled expression highlighted every worry on her otherwise unblemished face. Her discomfort was obvious and would only get worse when the detective sought to unpick her life. Jack allowed himself a wry grin. The move was designed to unnerve her. It was a trick he had often used on the naive. The longer he waited, the more likely she was to talk.

"Tell me about yourself, Pippa."

"What do you mean?"

"Who are you? Where are you from? How long have you worked here? Just give me a feel for who Pippa Jones is?"

"Am I in trouble?" she asked, her voice wavering with each word.

"Not if you tell the truth, you aren't. I'm sure you don't need me to highlight what happens if you don't."

"Is Marcus Tummel going to get arrested?"

"I don't know," shrugged Jack. "What has he done?"

Pippa blushed and stared at the floor. That tell-tale sign made it obvious that she was avoiding the question. Jack leaned forward over the table and brought his hands together. When she was ready to speak, he would listen. As he waited, a knock on the door caused him to spin around. Whoever it was had broken his flow at a crucial time.

The door eased open. Lisa occupied the space in the doorway and offered a stern look. A frown went across Jack's face when their eyes met. She was not someone he was expecting to see.

"What are you doing here?" asked Jack.

"DCI Louth sent me. I'll spare you the details. It revolves around him not trusting you to come alone."

"But you haven't got a car?" frowned Jack.

"Yes, I know. I had to pay for a taxi, which we will discuss later."

"Coffee is on, if you want some," said Jack, eager to change the subject.

"Thanks. Don't tell me, you would like one too while I am on my feet."

"See, we are in tune with each other. That's telepathy."

"Don't push it."

Jack turned back to Pippa who was looking no better than before. Her worried face was giving away her fear of having to speak. Inwardly, she was wondering how little she could say. After the informal exchange with Lisa, Jack went back to offering a fierce stare. That made Pippa shrink in her chair. She was trembling, not just at the thought of speaking to the police, but also at what the Tummels would do afterwards.

"Pippa, this is DS Lisa Ramsey. I think you were just about to tell me everything you know about Marcus Tummel, weren't you?"

"I can't," she offered softly, her eyes staring downwards for protection.

"Shall we make this easier? Why don't we go back to the bit where you were going to tell me about yourself?" As he asked the question, Lisa moved in behind Jack to watch over his shoulder.

"There isn't much to tell," she said in a whisper. "I have worked at the stables for a year. I left college and came here."

"Where did you go to college?"

"Bishop Burton. It's an agricultural college."

"Where's home for you?"

"Beverley."

"Why did you move here?"

"It was a bit too far to travel with the early mornings. Marcus likes the girls to start early. I couldn't have got here by that time. I don't drive, so when Marcus offered me a room, it was hard to turn down."

"How did you find the job?"

"It was advertised in the college. A few of us went for it. I was lucky enough to get it."

"Dare I ask whether you were the prettiest girl to go for it?"

"I guess I was. Do you think that made a difference?"

"I don't know. Maybe not," said Jack, deciding it might be noble to lie. "Tell me what Marcus is like to work for."

"Fine, I guess."

"How is he with the stable girls?"

"Yeah, great."

"Any difficulties?"

"No."

"What, never?"

"Not that I can remember."

"How about yesterday morning?"

"Yesterday morning?"

"You were in tears when you ran out of the stables. Marcus was in there with you."

"Who told you that?"

"Pippa, we saw you with our own eyes."

"Oh...err...yes...I...err...I had just got some bad news."

"Which was?"

"I can't remember."

"That must have been terrible news. What happened in there, Pippa?"

"Nothing."

"Pippa, we need to know."

"I said, nothing. Please, you have to believe me."

"Did he try it on with you? If he did, we can help you."

"Nothing happened. I was just upset. Can I go?"

"You can go whenever you want. Remember, there might come a day when we are the type of friends you need. Just think about that."

Pippa said nothing. She was dwelling on what Jack had said. It was still in her mind when she slipped from the room and allowed herself a deep sigh. It was obvious that she had so much to tell even if she did not want to say it. Jack decided that it was best to leave her to stew. There were two other girls he needed to see. Whether they would offer anything was questionable. Only one of them had to say something and the secrets of the yard would soon begin to unravel.

***

Becky Rose was next to go into the hot seat. Aged twenty-two, she had been with the Tummels for four years. She was a local girl, born and brought up in Malton, with a slight accent from the local area. She spoke with confidence and offered a sense of assurance that Pippa did not have. It felt so different to what had gone before. The girl appeared untroubled by a police presence. She was calm when she came in and paused to get a drink before easing into the seat that Pippa had vacated.

Throughout the introductions, she was friendly and made small talk with the detectives. Once the questions started, she batted away everything she was asked. Not once was there a suggestion that she had anything to offer them. Within minutes, Jack knew he was wasting his time. She would tell them nothing, no matter how hard they pushed her.

"What about Marcus and Laura?" interrupted Lisa. "You have been here for four years, so you must have a pretty good idea about how their relationship works."

"Not really. I'm paid to look after the horses, so that's what I spend my time doing."

"You have time off. You must see things."

"I'm rarely here if I am not working."

"I thought you lived here?" queried Lisa.

"Yes, but my parents are still in Malton. I'm over with them a fair amount."

"Why do you live at the yard if your parents are so close by?"

"Have you tried living with your parents once you are an adult?" asked Becky. "Let's just say that I get a bit more freedom living away from home even if it is only a couple of miles away. In any case, Marcus does me a cheap deal on the rent."

Suddenly, Jack's ears pricked up. The words were what he was waiting to hear. In front of him was a very attractive young lady with an appearance that would command her boss's attention. Jack sensed it was her first moment of weakness. He readied himself to be more incisive with his questions.

"Why does he do that?"

"Can you keep a secret?" she asked softly. Her body moved forward until she was leaning towards the detectives.

"We can," smiled Jack. He eased over the table towards her.

Becky looked around. She checked that nobody was watching or was in earshot of the conversation. It created a tense atmosphere. The feeling of expectation seemed to prolong the hushed silence around them.

"It means that I can check on the horses at any time. Day or night."

Jack looked puzzled. The frown that formed on his face confirmed that he did not understand what she was saying.

"Why is that a secret?"

"Because it means that he doesn't have to pay one of the other girls to do it. He just bungs me a few quid now and again. To be honest, I would do it for nothing. I love horses and when I am here, there is nothing much else to do anyway. Don't tell him that," she grinned.

"And it is just money that he offers?" asked Jack.

"Yes, but that's a secret. I don't want the other girls or the tax man to find out."

"I can promise you that we are not here to represent the tax man. We are here to find out more about the Tummels. Can I ask you, has Marcus ever tried it on with you?"

"Of course he has," laughed Becky. "This is a stable yard. Everyone tries it on with everyone else. If you're investigating affairs in this industry, you are going to be very busy."

"Have you had an affair while you have been here?"

"Not with Marcus, I haven't, if that is what you are implying. Others, yes, but I know when to avoid shitting in my own bed if you know what I mean?"

"I think the expression is that you don't want to bite the hand which feeds you," said Lisa. "Your words got the same message across."

"Good. Then I guess we are done," said Becky. She got up and left Jack and Lisa sitting at the table.

"At least we have confirmed that Marcus has a thing for the girls," said Lisa as soon as Becky had left the room.

"Did we need anyone to confirm that?" asked Jack. "Marcus has a thing for stable girls and Laura is getting ridden by the head jockey. It all feels a bit cosy or it was until Marcus confronted Kit. Do you reckon it has calmed down out there?"

"I would guess so. Let's see what Elizabeth Moss has to offer."

"She won't tell us anything," said Jack.

"You know that and I know that. That doesn't mean that she does. How about I put the frighteners on her and see what happens?" asked Lisa.

"You mean without me?"

"Why not? Let's see if a bit of female aggression goes a long way. You can find out what is happening outside." As she said it, Jack vacated his chair and allowed Lisa to slip into his place.

Jack liked Lisa's idea. He paced up and down, waiting for Elizabeth to appear. As soon as she knocked on the door, he held it open. Jack moved through it on his way out of the room.

"Where are you going?" Elizabeth asked, her face painted with worry.

"I've been called to attend outside. Take a seat. Lisa will speak to you."

"I'm not sure about this," offered Elizabeth.

Jack had already departed through the door. In a panic, Elizabeth's eyes flitted around. She was not quite sure what to make of Lisa. Her stern look was that of someone who did not suffer fools readily. Lisa did nothing to put the young girl at ease.

"He said, take a seat," confirmed Lisa, her voice raised and authoritative in tone.

"Yes, but…"

"Take a seat!" she demanded.

Elizabeth Moss sat down immediately. Her eyes opened wide and her face flushed red. She stared at Lisa, fearful of what the detective might say next.

"I'm not sure I can help you."

"Then let me make it easy for you, Elizabeth. This is what we know so far. You are hiding from your father by living with the Tummels. They are probably keeping you off any official records or paying you cash in hand. Either way, some laws are being broken. Then there is Marcus. We know he has a penchant for stable girls, which may or may not include you."

"But..."

"I haven't finished!" barked Lisa. "Marcus is married to Laura, who we know is sleeping with Kit Grady plus several others that we are yet to confirm. One of those she is close to has an uncanny link to people who keep turning up dead in lakes with bullet holes in their heads."

"Please..."

"Currently, we don't know who is neck-deep in what but I would say the web is closing in around the whole murky set-up pretty damn quickly. In the middle of this mess lies a girl who is keeping her mouth shut and hoping that the whole thing will go away. Well, I'll let you into a secret, princess. It is not going anywhere. People are getting killed; others are getting put inside and a lucky few will get away by the skin of their teeth. Which one of those groups do you fancy being in, Elizabeth?"

Elizabeth Moss broke down in tears. Her head slumped into her arms as the sound of her crying filled the room. Jack listened carefully, hoping to hear if the words were effective. For now, there was just upset and trauma, with the silence punctuated by the young girl's wailing. Only when the sobbing subsided would they find out whether Lisa had just scared a girl with nothing much to say.

"I don't know anything," she insisted after taking a moment to compose herself.

"I think you do, Elizabeth."

"I don't."

"We both know that isn't true."

"It is!" she snapped. Elizabeth Moss stood up and marched from the room.

Jack entered the room once Elizabeth had gone. He was met by a sheepish expression from Lisa. She looked guilty as if she had gone in too hard and scared away a potential witness. Jack said nothing and allowed her a moment to contemplate her thoughts. He could see her discomfort. She was playing back everything she had said. Jack had heard every word and knew that Lisa had done exactly what was needed.

"That went well," he smiled.

"I'm sorry. I made a right mess of that," she blushed.

"No, you didn't. It was perfect. She will be back in touch when she has had a chance to reflect on your conversation. I will give it a maximum of two days."

"I hope you are right, Jack."

"Trust me. On this rare occasion, I am."

Chapter 14

Spencer Pugh stumbled back from the table. He reached out to steady himself. His vision was blurred and his eyes were finding it hard to focus. It had only been one small error. His trembling hand had placed his chips on the ten instead of the eleven alongside it. Those precious few inches were the difference between riches and the rags he now found himself with.

He felt the anger building inside him. The game was rigged and had been for the past few weeks. His results were all the evidence that was needed. He had told them about it. That was when they had thrown him out. The truth never made for comfortable hearing. Somebody had discovered their little secret. One day, they would listen to him or the whole world would hear what he had to say.

Spencer reached into his pocket. He fumbled around inside it for what he had left. There was little other than an old set of keys. His cash had long since gone on that corrupt table. The more he thought about it, the more the fire raged inside him. There were so many people being conned and yet he was the only one prepared to do something about it. That was what separated him from the rest of the mugs in the place. He had a system and the balls to stand up to them. Nobody was going to take him for a fool; not now; not ever. He was Spencer Pugh and he did not accept second place.

"Give me a line of credit!" he barked. It was loud enough to turn heads on the neighbouring tables.

His demand was met by silence. Eyes were shying away, not wanting to engage a drunkard in conversation. He looked around, trying to catch somebody's attention. Every one of those cowards was ignoring him.

"I said, give me a line of credit! Is anyone listening to me?"

They were. With the noise he was making, there was barely anybody in the casino not listening. His voice boomed across the room with enough volume to wake the dead. He nodded with satisfaction at their inquisitive faces. Finally, he had got the audience he deserved. And yet all it took was for a croupier to press a button under his table for Spencer to get more attention than he could ever have wanted.

The security team was upon him in seconds. Three men, all dressed in black trousers and polo shirts, appeared from nowhere. They were equipped with earpieces to enable them to communicate. Two were young and looked like they had been hired for muscle. An older grey-haired man in his late forties appeared to be in charge. He was the one who spoke.

"Is there a problem, sir?" he asked. He recognised Spencer as someone who had been removed on many occasions.

"Is there a problem? I can tell you there is a problem. There is a big fucking problem."

"Sir, please can I ask you to moderate your language? Then we can discuss the matter."

"There is nothing to discuss. You lot are crooks; the whole fucking lot of you."

"I think it is time for you to leave."

"Fuck off! Try and make me."

"It's Spencer, isn't it?"

"What of it?" he slurred, stumbling back with his words.

"Look, Spencer, you are drunk. We are not going to discuss this matter while you are in that state. If you want to come back tomorrow, Mr Bilby, the owner, will happily see you."

"I want to see him now."

"That is not possible. You will need to come back tomorrow."

"Why? Is he scared of being told he is a crook?"

"He is not here. Go home, sober up, and come back tomorrow."

"I'm not going anywhere."

"Spencer, this is your last chance to leave voluntarily."

"I told you; I am not going."

"Yes, you are."

The two lads picked Spencer up and marched him out into the street. The removal was swift. The strength of the men was obvious from the outset. Spencer was lifted from the floor. Their arms hooked under his and carried him out before he could put a foot down in defiance.

Spencer struggled without offering any real resistance. The skirmish would have been one-sided even without the effects of the drink he had consumed. Once outside, he was pushed into a taxi and told to go home. The driver was overpaid for the fare with three twenty-pound notes. It left Spencer slumped in the back of the car with nothing but empty pockets and a sore head to look forward to.

Chapter 15

DCI Louth had called everyone together for an eight o'clock briefing. It had brought a few complaints and the usual comments about why it could not wait for nine. Then came the retort that every hour mattered. With two dead bodies, nobody could offer a suitable response. It was hard to have a reasonable argument when so little was known about the deaths.

For Jack, it had meant leaving the pub a little earlier. For Lisa, it meant not being led astray. She had learned her lesson about trying to match Jack's drinking. Then there were the flashbacks to her night of shame. She wished that Jack would tease her about it just to get it over with. His role as a gentleman was only making it harder to forget.

When PC Anderson walked in nearly five minutes late, everyone was grateful they were already in situ. Louth went for him, like a comedian picking on someone exiting the room for a comfort break. It was sharp and cruel, with the poor officer ripped to shreds. His one crime was to have answered the phone. It delayed him for those precious few minutes.

Everyone in the room knew better than to defend him. To speak out would see the individual take his place. It was better to enjoy their time away from the spotlight, aware that their turn might come next.

"Now that PC Anderson has graced us with his presence, let's go through what we know. Jack, can you summarise the deceased?"

Jack was jolted to his feet. He had not expected to be brought into the action so soon. All heads turned towards him, the look of relief on PC Anderson's face palpable. He now had the chance to slip into the background. Jack knew that it was no time for frivolity or jokes. He offered a summary that was longer than anyone expected.

"As you know, we have two bodies. Both appear to have been killed in the same manner, with a single shot to the head. We believe it is the same gun though ballistics have yet to confirm that. At this stage, we should work on the basis that it probably is.

"The bodies were discovered within metres of each other in the corner of Castle Howard Lake. Both had been in the lake for some time though not necessarily at the same time. The second one may or may not have been dumped after the first was found.

"The first body is that of Josie Raynor. She was thirty-one and lived on her own in a rented flat in the city. We know that she had money troubles and, up to recently, worked as a croupier in the city's casino. She went missing three weeks ago."

"And the second body?" asked Louth.

"I'm getting to it, sir. Darren Brand was a forty-four-year-old family man from Strensall. He had his own business, which he set up himself, though was struggling a little with the financials. We know that he was a gambler and he also had links to the casino. When we spoke to his wife, she reckoned he gambled on a lot more than that."

"That gives us a possible link but no motive," confirmed Louth.

"That's fair," said Jack.

"Kelly, you have been into the casino. What can you tell us about it? Do you want to give everybody the update you gave me yesterday?"

Kelly blushed. Nobody had told her that she might have to speak in the meeting.

"Err, well, it is quite busy, with a few problem gamblers. I have only been in a few times but you tend to see the same faces. You know, regulars and the like. It all seems fairly welcoming though I am not sure how good their record keeping is."

"What do you mean?" asked Louth.

"You seem to be able to get in whether you are a member or not."

"You must be a pretty face," laughed PC Anderson, regaining his confidence by the second.

"Then Jack would get in," said PC Brian Wilkes. He nodded his head at Jack to add one more point to the score chart.

"What about Jordan Bilby?" asked Louth, ignoring the growing disorder in the room.

"I have spoken to him and he is pleasant enough. I also saw Laura Tummel in there," insisted Kelly.

"Did you?" asked Louth, showing his surprise. "Did anyone else know about this?"

"Yes, I did," said Lisa, much to Kelly's relief.

"What is her link?"

"We don't know," replied Lisa. "There is a possible connection between Jordan and Laura. Whether it is more than just friends, we are yet to confirm. Our guess is it might be. We are confident that Laura is having an affair with a jockey while her husband appears to have a thing for stable girls."

"Don't we all?" laughed Brian Wilkes. His eyes stared at Lisa to see if she would blush.

"Is that relevant to the case?" asked Louth. "Remember, we are looking for a murderer, not a philanderer. I would ease off on that line of enquiry unless we are confident it is going to lead somewhere. I don't want us to go down rabbit holes chasing domestic problems."

"If it's alright with you, sir, we will keep it warm but not chase. We may have somebody on the inside on that one if things go the way we think they might. For the sake of waiting for them to come back to us, we might be able to close that one off fully with very little effort."

"I'll leave that to your judgement. Just keep me informed of everything and I mean everything. Let's get out there and get this solved. I want the pace quickened."

Heads nodded with as much enthusiasm as they could muster. Louth was the first to march out of the room. When everyone followed, Jack made a point of catching up to Lisa and took her off to one side. He waited until everyone else was out of earshot. Then he pointed towards the door and made his predictable offer.

"Fancy a coffee; my treat."

"Didn't you hear Louth? He said we had to quicken the pace."

"I know. We might need to jog to the coffee shop."

***

Laura Tummel had watched her horse romp home. Its chestnut colour had streaked through the line four lengths clear of the field. The buzz it gave her never diminished in any way. This time, it was even better. It was a horse they had bought and trained themselves. That was the best feeling; to see the blue and gold streak home, with their jockey onboard. It was hardly life-changing prize money but what did that matter? For that moment of seeing her horse cross the line, she would have gladly given it all away.

Laura waited for Kit to bring the horse back into the paddock. Their second and final runner of the day had certainly made up for the first. Their fancied mare had been well off the pace and had trailed in fourth. Questions had been asked by the stewards as to why it had put up such a poor showing. She wouldn't mind but there was nothing sinister going on. Not this time. Sometimes, a well-prepared horse simply doesn't turn up.

Kit smiled when he saw her waiting. He wanted some time with her. The journey across from Malton had not afforded that luxury. Not with Becky in there with them. Her position in the centre seat had stifled the conversation. All Kit could think about as he drove the truck was whether Laura and he would be in bed together before the day was out. It was what he wanted and he knew that Laura wanted it too. And yet life just seemed to have an uncanny knack of getting in the way of a good old-fashioned bunk-up.

Easing into the enclosure, Kit doffed his cap at Laura. She waved her hand and offered him one of her smiles. She noted the sweat on his forehead, paying testament to the exertion of the race. He was a fit man and yet he barely looked tired. His sinewy physique was made for work. Laura knew that only too well. Her heart was fluttering at the thought of the things he could do to her.

"You made that look easy," she beamed. A series of pats were placed on the horse with each person they passed. Laura added hers and made sure Kit's leg got its fair share of her touch. He grinned and traced the tip of his whip across her to get her attention. Laura frowned, not at the act, but that it had been done in public.

"Not here," she whispered. "Get weighed in and then we can go for a drink while Becky sorts her out."

Kit nodded and eased into the winner's enclosure. He dismounted and unbuckled the girth before slipping the saddle from the horse. In a flash, he was gone. The weighing room was his priority. There were formalities to go through before Laura was able to pick up her prize. It was a routine he knew only too well and one that was not to be messed around with.

Laura turned to Becky and smiled. Her best stable girl was already at work and making sure the horse was well looked after. Her efficiency in the industry was second to none. She was the one stable girl they would not want to lose. That was why Marcus went easy on her and gave her the least attention. Laura knew it. Becky knew it. And so did everyone else who worked at the yard.

"Are you okay loading her up when you have finished the cool down?"

"Yes, that's fine. I'll see you at the box when you are ready."

"I won't be too long."

"Take your time. It's not like we've got far to travel."

Laura nodded and left Becky to do her work. Her thoughts had already turned to the man she needed to see.

Kit was weighed in, showered and changed in less than ten minutes. It was an ability he had perfected over many years. In his younger days, it meant more drinking time. More recently, it meant being able to get more rides, with the occasional liaison with Laura thrown in for good measure.

Despite his haste, she was still waiting for him before he was ready. She was leaning up against the building when he emerged. So sultry and so damn sexy, he could have devoured her right there. A quiet corner would be enough for him to enjoy his final ride of the day.

"Drink?" he asked.

"Or we could find somewhere for just the two of us."

"How long have we got?"

"We should be good for an hour. Becky will sort everything out."

"Let's grab a quick drink and then find somewhere comfortable," he grinned. "I got a right thump against the rail on the back straight. I might need you to rub it better."

Laura laughed. She led the way into the bar and took a table by the door. She ordered two beers and drained a third of hers on the first pass. Over the top of the bottle, she never took her eyes away from Kit.

"Thirsty? I'm the one who has done the work," said Kit.

"Maybe I'm just eager," she offered as she took the level down below halfway.

Kit was barely beyond the first sip. His mouth was savouring the coolness of the beer. The stress of the race still needed to be eased along with the tension that a winner always brought.

"Well, Miss Eager, answer me this. When are you going to leave him?"

"Soon," she assured him.

"When is soon?"

"I told you; let me get the finances sorted out first," she replied. Laura finished her bottle with one long satisfying gulp. "More importantly, what does a woman have to do to get laid around here?"

"Allow me to finish my beer," laughed Kit. He quickened his drinking pace under her ever-watchful stare.

Chapter 16

Dan Millings was finishing off for the day when Jack walked in. He sighed, perhaps louder than he intended to, before flushing red with embarrassment. An apology followed quickly, his words not quite able to cover his tracks. Jack was not going to let him off easily when there was some sport to be enjoyed at Dan's expense.

"Good to feel welcome, eh?"

"Sorry, Jack, it's been a long day. I didn't mean it."

"You don't have to apologise. We older folk know we are a burden on you youngsters."

"Jack, seriously, it's not like that," continued Dan. He glanced up to see Jack laughing. Just the look on his face was enough to force a shake of Dan's head. "One of these days, I'm going to get one over on you."

"Maybe. Until then, stick the coffee on and power up your computer. I've got a little bit of homework to do."

"Won't you get into trouble if you copy mine?"

"Only if you get the answers wrong. Rule number one is always copy off a smart kid."

Dan walked over to the coffee machine. Jack watched enviously. That machine was the best one in the station. Jack had tried to order one for his department and it had been rejected. That meant Dan would be getting a regular visitor.

"Still no luck getting one of these," said Dan.

"Nothing doing. I keep getting told there are cutbacks. One of these days, I'll come and take yours."

"Then you would lose your sanctuary."

"Fair point. In that case, you had better make it a large cup, just to keep me going."

"You mean until you reach the pub."

"Absolutely. A man can die of dehydration otherwise."

"Somehow, I don't think that is likely."

Jack waited while Dan worked his magic. The office was empty, the others in his team having left on time. Jack doubted whether they ever felt the need to do any extra hours. Dan was hardly the toughest taskmaster even if he had a competitive streak for results.

It was good to see the lad happy. They had been partners when Dan was shot. That guilt would never leave Jack. Could he have coped with the death of his partner at that time? Jack knew the answer and it only allowed the demons back into his mind.

"Milk?" asked Dan.

"Just a drop, thanks."

Dan offered the cup to Jack. The aroma was already a pleasant invasion of his nostrils. Dan took a cup of his own and toasted his colleague. Something told him that Jack was about to make his life difficult.

"Okay, what do you need me to do?" asked Dan.

"I'm just here for the coffee," smiled Jack.

"Not at this time of the day, you aren't. It has gone opening time and you said there was homework to do."

"Shucks, you rumbled me. I wanted to have another look at Josie Raynor."

"The morgue's that way," said Dan, with a wave of his arm. "Sorry, that was a bit of a sick joke."

"I just want to understand a bit more about her background."

"Anything in particular?"

"Yes, but I don't know what. I just want something if you know what I mean."

"I take it you're close to a breakthrough?"

"Yes and no. I think I am. I just don't know what it is."

Dan moved over to his computer. He pulled up a second chair for Jack to sit on. His first act was to drag up her record, which offered more entries than Jack was expecting. As it was loading, Dan went to a metal filing cupboard. He thumbed through it until he found a red folder. Dan lifted it out and placed it in front of Jack. His encouraging hand beckoned him to open its contents.

"What's this?"

"The old records. We haven't got it all computerised yet. It's a bit of a pain but we have to juggle between the two at the moment. I've only just found that one in the old system. I was going to pop up and see you in the morning."

"What are you telling me?" frowned Jack.

"I am telling you that the paper records cover the first time she went missing."

"Josie Raynor has been missing before?"

"Exactly. About ten years ago, she disappeared for a few weeks. Nobody ever discovered where she went and, to be honest, I am not sure you would be that interested."

Jack sat back. The lack of enthusiasm in Dan's statement disappointed him. He thought he had something and yet Dan was now telling him that the disappearance meant nothing.

"I don't understand," offered Jack.

"The bit you will be interested in is what happened immediately before she went missing."

"Go on."

"She was fired from her employment with a certain Marcus Tummel. According to her file, she put in a complaint about him. Within a couple of weeks, she was dismissed. She then went missing, only to turn up a few weeks later."

"Now I am interested. What job did she do?"

"It's listed as general duties at the stables."

"In other words, she was a stable girl."

"I would say so."

"And Marcus made a move on her."

"I never said that."

"And she objected, so he fired her."

"I definitely did not say that either."

"You did, Dan, but not in so many words."

Jack rubbed his chin and nodded. A man he initially disliked was now someone he was beginning to despise. He had no time for anyone who used their position to their advantage. It made him sick to think about what was going on at the stables.

"I think a drink might be in order," said Jack.

"Are we celebrating or drowning our sorrows?" laughed Dan.

"Neither. We are just being sociable. Are you coming?"

"Sorry, I've got a date tonight."

"With the nurse?"

"You got it."

"Who's putting on their uniform this time?"

"Don't judge everyone by your standards, Jack."

"I wasn't. I was judging them by yours."

Dan smiled and shook his head. He missed being Jack Husker's partner.

***

Kelly arrived at the casino at eight o'clock. It had been on her mind throughout the day. Her heart was fluttering each time she thought about Jordan Bilby. How did he do that to her? The man she was supposed to be watching left her with a dizzy feeling. It was that strange mix of sophistication and bad boy mixed into one.

She had come close to revealing her attraction to him when DCI Louth had challenged her about her work. The way Lisa had looked at her suggested that she knew. She could see through her denial. Thankfully, Lisa was distracted by Jack and his complexities. Faced with that bouncing through her mind, all Kelly had to do was play for time.

As she signed in, she noticed that her membership had changed. No longer pending, she was now a full member. Her name flashed up as having VIP status. It was obvious who had arranged that. The knowing smile of the middle-aged lady behind the desk made her feel dirty. At the same time, it sent a tingle of excitement through her.

"You tart," she whispered to herself as she took her card. She smiled at the security guard and entered the casino. Kelly felt good. She was wearing another new dress paid for out of her winnings. There was plenty of money in her bag to have a good night. Not police wages; it was cash that she had won. That made it worth so much more.

The casino was quiet. Kelly's eyes scanned the room for the problem gamblers. Most of them were congregated on one side. The shaker was in; the lady who trembled with adrenalin every time the roulette wheel was put into motion. No doubt attractive in her younger days, it looked like the effects of gambling and drinking had taken their toll. Her ragged hair and ill-fitting dress were symptoms of a lifestyle that had come back to haunt her. Kelly had little sympathy, not when it was so easy to walk away.

At the bar, she noted the absence of familiar faces. A new barman took her order. He smiled politely as he did to every customer. In expectation, she gazed around, hoping that Jordan would appear from his office. For once, he was absent. It left Kelly with a feeling which tended towards loneliness. Without him, there was little to interest her. Another glance across the room confirmed that nobody else had noticed her. That felt so much worse than when unwanted attention buzzed around her.

She finished her drink within minutes. She ordered another and followed it up with a third. She checked her phone repeatedly, hoping that something would come up. Thankfully, Jordan had not given her his number. If he had, she would have texted him. Her discipline was not strong enough to resist.

Her mother had always told her to play it cool with men. She couldn't. When someone took her eye, Kelly was hopeless. She would dive in with both feet and worry about the consequences later. Often, she would emerge with a head full of regrets.

A smile from a croupier caught her attention. She eased from her stool and walked over to buy some chips. Fifty pounds from her purse was replaced by what felt like a very small stack. She laid out the betting tokens in front of her. It was her table and she only had the croupier for company.

All of a sudden, it felt harder to place the bets. There was no voice on her shoulder to guide her through it. She stared vacantly at the table while the croupier waited for Kelly to make her move.

"Would you like some help?"

"Yes, please," she replied. The relief in her voice was obvious.

"It's easy really. You can either bet on colours or odds versus evens. After that, you have rows, columns, blocks or individual numbers." With each bet option offered, he laid his chip shovel onto the table to point at an example of where the bet would go. Kelly smiled in appreciation even if it all felt difficult. "There are minimum bets for some of the categories which I can talk you through as well. The most important thing is not to bet more than you can afford to lose."

"Thank you," whispered Kelly softly. "Can I ask what most people bet on?"

"Birthdays are the most common. What day were you born?"

"Tuesday."

"Sorry, what date?"

"The eleventh of May."

"A lot of people would bet on eleven and its four corners to cover the numbers around it. That makes sure that you don't lose out if you were born a day or two away from where fate determined."

"Does betting on your birthday make it more likely that you will win?"

"Not at all, but you have to start somewhere," he grinned.

Kelly looked down at her stack of chips. She had been given one-pound and five-pound chips, the value marked by number and colour. She placed a pound cautiously on the eleven and then on the four corners as suggested. A smile to the croupier was met with a reassuring nod.

As he turned the wheel and flicked the ball around the rim, Kelly's heart started to race. She felt faint. Her eyes were barely able to focus, despite her attempts to watch the numbers on which she had bet. If she was allowed to, she would have taken the bet back. That was stupid. Only five pounds of her previous winnings were at stake and yet it felt like so much more. Without Jordan there, she was flying solo for the first time.

The ball went around the bowl for an age and then settled into the number twelve. Kelly sighed and bemoaned her lack of fortune. She felt her stomach turning over at the loss. Such feelings were quickly dispersed by the croupier who looked at her with a smile.

"We have a winner," he said.

"I thought I had lost?" queried Kelly. "I bet on eleven."

"And the corners, which gives you nine chips to your one on that winner."

"But I lose the other chips, don't I?"

"That's right. Overall, you are a few pounds ahead," he confirmed. He pushed the chips towards her.

Kelly eyed the small pile in front of her. She knew what she needed to do even if it sent a tingle of uncertainty through her.

"I think I might need a larger bet to get back anything worthwhile."

"I can't advise you either way on that. Just remember, you should only bet what you can afford to lose."

"Yes, but I'm ahead," said Kelly. "That means I can bet whatever I like."

The croupier said nothing. He watched Kelly push her five-pound chips onto the table. Again, the number eleven was covered, as was twelve, with some of the corners added in for good measure. He waited while she finished making late adjustments. Once she smiled towards him, he set the wheel in motion. With most of Kelly's stack down on the table, a thirty-five left her beat.

"For fuck's sake!" she exclaimed, her voice loud enough for others to hear.

"That's the game, I am afraid. Never mind."

"Just a setback," she said. She laid the rest of the chips down and watched the same number come up.

Kelly exchanged another one hundred pounds into chips. Her purse was full of her previous winnings, the money staring back at her with reassurance. It meant that she could recoup her losses. She covered the same numbers, plus thirty-five for insurance. Again, nothing came up. The ball dropped in twenty-six, leaving Kelly stony-faced at the table.

"It might be time for a break," advised the croupier.

"One more go," Kelly declared.

She increased her bet and got lucky. The number seven was one of her corners and it put Kelly back into credit. Excitedly, she jumped up and let out a cry of delight. Heads turned to offer up their looks of disapproval. Kelly did not care. She called for a drink and stared at the table, mesmerised by the game in front of her.

From far enough away to remain unseen, Jordan Bilby was watching her. He was biding his time and licking his lips at what he was witnessing. For such a novice, Kelly displayed such intensity with her betting. He had never seen someone so engrossed with their first few bets. She was a girl that he had to find out more about. First, he needed to discover her limits.

He caught the croupier's eyes. A nod instructed him to keep her at the table. If he needed to, he would send over a second punter to offer a distraction alongside her. For now, Kelly seemed happy to bet alone. That solitary win had ignited something inside her.

Jordan studied Kelly's approach. He was surprised at the speed with which she bet. After that initial hesitancy, she was now piling her chips onto the table freely. She never looked up, other than to confirm with the croupier that her actions were valid.

Every few minutes, she seemed to take more cash from her bag and exchange it for chips.

The leakage of funds was significant for anyone, let alone a newcomer. It would not take long for Kelly to return her previous winnings. A couple of good wins made Jordan feel better. Those occasional successes would only increase the grip the game had on her.

After a string of losses, Jordan could see Kelly's behaviour becoming erratic. That was the moment when he felt the need to go over. It was time to guard his asset. If she lost all her money, he would not see her again. The girl had to be closely managed if she was to fulfil her potential.

"Kelly, it's good to see you," he offered. He picked up her hand and kissed it softly on the back. As she turned, he noted the stressed look on her face. It screamed of someone who had spent too long at the table. "Let me get you a drink."

"I could probably do with a break," she sighed.

Jordan guided her away from the table. His arm slipped around her when she stood up. She was unsteady and unsure of her footing. The combination of gambling and drinking was obvious.

"Gin and tonic?"

"Yes, please," said Kelly eagerly.

He waited until they were both sitting down before he started a conversation. All the time, Jordan's eyes were on her. He was assessing her level of intoxication while he chose his words carefully. It was not a time to make a mistake.

Away from the roulette table, Kelly sounded more coherent. Risking some unthreatening conversation, Jordan complimented her on her dress. Kelly smiled and pulled at the hem nervously. As she started to relax, her mind drifted onto the losses she had suffered.

"How has your night been?" asked Jordan.

"Rubbish; I lost."

"I am sure you are still well ahead overall."

"I guess so," blushed Kelly. She could not remember how much she had spent on the dresses.

"Are you going to have another go?"

"I would like to but I'm pretty much out of chips."

"Then get some more," he shrugged.

"I don't think it is quite that easy. I'm out of funds."

Jordan reached into his pocket with purpose. He grinned and winked once with a glinting smile. He threw some chips down in front of her. Kelly looked at them and then back towards him. Jordan shrugged. He was only showing compassion.

"Try these."

"What are they?" she asked.

Unlike the chips she had purchased, they had no value marking. They were gold, with the letters VIP etched across them. The edging of the discs was marked in black. To Kelly, it made no sense.

"They are VIP chips. You have got to be pretty special to get your hands on them."

"What happens if I lose them?"

"Don't worry, we won't come after you. We're not that sort of casino."

Kelly picked up one of the chips and noted the additional weight. They were so much heavier than those she had been given before. Her heart pounded when she played with them in her hands. Her head told her to put them back down. She couldn't. They felt too good. She was special if he was entrusting her to have them.

"Are you going to help me put the bet on?"

"No, Kelly, that's up to you. I need to get some work done."

"All work and no play," she said.

"Makes Jordan a very rich boy," he replied with a grin.

***

Jack walked into The Cellars with a series of thoughts dancing through his brain. His meeting with Dan was still fresh in his mind. The links he was making were causing his head to spin. The revelation had been that Josie Raynor had a connection to the Tummels. That created the possibility that Josie was one of Marcus's girls. It did not need a detective to know what he would have done to her. That didn't answer the question of where Jordan Bilby fitted in. Perhaps he was just a distraction for Laura to allow Marcus the freedom he craved.

"Evening, Jack," said Alf. He did not bother to ask him what he wanted. One of his hands was already on a glass while the other was pulling a porcelain handle towards him. A creamy pint was beginning to flow downwards. For a while, Jack had stayed off the booze. Now, he was back to being Alf's most regular customer. "No Lisa tonight?"

"What is it with this fascination with Lisa? We're not Siamese twins." It was blunt enough to cause Alf to stand back in shock.

"I was only making polite conversation," insisted Alf.

Jack looked up with regret. He had taken out his frustration on the wrong person.

"Sorry, Alf, that was unnecessary. Let me buy you a drink."

"You're fine, Jack, though you could pay me for this one. You are a bit behind."

"Does this cover it?"

Jack slipped three twenty-pound notes across the bar. He took the pint from Alf and savoured the first taste.

"It will leave you about fifteen quid to the good. I'll pop it in your pot."

"Cheers, Alf, and sorry."

"Forget it. It's all part of being a landlord. When you're ready, someone over there wants a word with you."

"Anyone I want to talk to?"

"Definitely not, but it's too late to hide. He's seen you, so you don't have many options unless you want to abandon your pint and make a run for it."

"Unless it is my former mother-in-law, I am not running away from my beer for anyone."

Jack's eyes looked across the bar. They made contact with Andy Hutton. There was barely anybody in the world he despised more than that man. Most journalists got short shrift. Andy Hutton got a very special reaction.

"What does he want?" sighed Jack.

"There is only one way to find out," said Alf. He eased away to make sure he did not get mixed up in the conversation.

Jack took his pint and walked over towards Hutton. The journalist nodded and smiled inanely. The look on his face was somewhere between that of a man breaking wind and sitting on a cactus. A stool was kicked out as an offer. Jack shook his head in response. He was not planning on staying long in his presence.

"Are you going to fill this up for me?" asked Hutton. He thrust his empty glass in Jack's direction.

"Only if you want me to take it into the gents," snarled Jack.

"And there was I thinking your legendary bad manners were exaggerated."

"I can assure you they weren't. I take it you want a word with me."

"Do I?"

"I am not going to play your games. Either you do or I will go and enjoy my pint in peace."

"Okay, I would like a word. Take a seat."

"I prefer to stand. It means I can get away quicker if anyone sees me near you."

"Fair enough. I won't give you the full spiel about us being peas from a pod and all that crap. I know you'll only throw it back at me. I was just wondering whether you have thought about our conversation from the other night."

"What conversation?"

"The one where we said that we could help each other."

"Oh yes, I remember. You want me to help you out because you find it too difficult to make up stories on your own."

Hutton shook his head. "Jack, we could work together."

"Okay, here's the deal," smiled Jack. "How about you let me know when you are on fire and I will contemplate putting you out?"

"Just contemplate?" Hutton laughed.

"I don't make promises I may not keep. I might have something better to do, like cutting my toenails."

"You've made your point. What's your problem?"

"You."

"I tell you what. How about you give me something to work on and I'll go away?"

"Why would I do that?"

"I'm sure there might be something I could do for you in return."

"Like what?"

"I don't know. Is there anyone you want smoking out?"

"The only rat I know is out of his hole and in full view."

"What about those bodies in the lake?"

"There is no point smoking them out. They're dead."

"Someone must have put them in there."

"Bloody hell; you're right. That's the case solved. I should have come to you sooner. We could have ruled out the corpses going for a midnight swim by themselves."

"Come on, Jack, you know the game. Throw me a titbit."

"I haven't got any."

"We both know that is a lie. Give me an inside tip."

"An inside tip?"

"Something between old friends or adversaries, whichever you prefer."

Jack rubbed his chin and then leaned in a little closer. His face went uncomfortably close to Andy Hutton's. He could smell him from a mile away, his sweaty stench masked by an over-application of cologne.

"This is the only tip I am giving you," insisted Jack.

Andy Hutton nodded and moved a little closer.

"Don't eat the free peanuts at the bar."

"Yeah, yeah, I know. They have traces of you-know-what on them from people's hands."

"No, you're wrong. It's because if I know you are going to eat them, I'll have pissed in the bowl."

Jack downed his pint in one and moved away. He placed the glass on the bar and bid goodnight to Alf. He walked straight back out onto the cold streets of the city. A sober night was better than one spent talking to vermin like Andy Hutton.

Chapter 17

Jack woke to the vibration of his phone. It was a missed call from a number he did not recognise. Not that it narrowed things down. His contacts had grown in recent times and yet there were still less than ten numbers in there. Most of his calls came up without any form of identification and were happily ignored. If someone needed to speak to him, they would try again or leave a message.

Hauling himself out of bed, he glanced at the screen. He had a feeling that this call was different. There was no logic to the thought. It was just a hunch. Jack stared at the phone and wandered towards the bedroom window. That was when he realised how early it was. There was barely anyone on the street. He put the phone to his ear and pressed his messages. He was met by a soft female voice.

"It's Elizabeth Moss. Can we meet? Don't call me. Just text me when you are free to talk and I'll call you."

All Jack did was text the letters 'OK' and the phone sprang to life in his hand.

"I didn't think you would be up yet. I hope I didn't wake you," she said in a whispered tone.

"I have been up for a while," lied Jack. He did not want to put a barrier between them. "Is everything alright?"

"Let's talk. Not now, because I have only got a moment. Somewhere away from here."

"How about a cafe in town?" asked Jack.

"No, we'll be seen. Do you mind meeting in a lay-by?"

"Of course not," he replied.

"Do you know the Malton to Pickering road?"

"I know where it is."

"There is a lay-by almost opposite a farm shop about a mile from the A64. I'll see you there."

"When?"

"Eight o'clock. I've got to go."

"I'll be there."

Jack was there by seven thirty-five. Once again, he used Lisa's car. She had rolled her eyes when he told her that he needed it. Jack could sense the irritation in her. Despite her annoyance, not once did she consider refusing. She handed the keys over and left Jack to look after her baby.

The guilt hit him when he was halfway to Malton. Barely two hundred miles were on the clock. He had done far more of them than she had. Maybe next time, he would take a taxi or ask Lisa to drive.

Elizabeth Moss turned up five minutes late. Jack expected her to. She had to get away from the stables. Living on-site, Marcus would be aware of every movement she made. With his eyes on all the girls, he would want to know where she was going. Jack was ready to wait all day if he needed to. The girl was a key source of information and would not be hurried.

She approached slowly and tucked her car in beside his. Jack did not move. He waited for Elizabeth to walk over. From the road, her distinctive red Volvo would be out of sight. The car was a legacy of a pampered upbringing and was far too expensive for a stable girl of her age. It would be a burden for her but not one she was about to get rid of.

Elizabeth Moss slipped into the seat next to Jack. He glanced across at her. There was no wonder Marcus was watching her. She was dressed in tight blue jeans, with a cream hoodie thrown over her top. Her blonde hair was tied back in a ponytail. Her appearance was stunning despite having the look of someone who had changed in a hurry.

"It's good to see you, Elizabeth," smiled Jack. He tried to soften the tone of his voice when he spoke.

"I haven't got long," she replied, dispensing with the need for a greeting. "Sorry, I'm in a bit of a state. I didn't have time to get changed properly."

"You're fine," he assured her. "Tough day?"

"Every day is a tough day at that place."

"I guess that is why you want to talk to me."

"I just know that you'll listen. When I saw you at the stables the other day, it brought back memories. Not good ones, mind you. I can see myself ending up in a mess again. It was tough losing Steven but it told me that I needed to get away from my father. I guess all that has happened is Marcus has stepped into that role. Then again, he sees himself as something very different to how I see him."

"Do you think he has a potential relationship in mind?" asked Jack, choosing his words carefully.

"I'm not sure I do. It's all a bit weird if you know what I mean."

"I might need you to explain that," replied Jack.

"We all know that he has a thing for some of the girls. That's where it feels odd. It's not all of them; just those he selects when he feels like it. At the moment, that's Pippa."

"Do you think they are having an affair?"

"I don't know. Pippa has never said anything. There is definitely something going on."

"Have you talked to her about it?"

"I've tried. She says nothing. It's almost like she has taken a vow of silence. She's scared."

"How long has it been like that?"

"Probably three months; perhaps more. Before that, there was another girl."

"What happened to her?"

"I don't know. One day she was there; the next she was gone. She didn't even pack her things. Marcus slung everything of hers into a bin bag and that was it."

"What was her name?"

"We only knew her as Flick. I guess it was short for Felicity or something like that. None of us knew her that well. When she wasn't with Marcus, she kept to herself."

"What did she look like?"

"She was very pretty. I think you could have guessed that."

"Was she blonde?"

"No, she had light brown hair. In many ways, she looked like a younger version of Laura."

"That's interesting," nodded Jack. "Are you sure you don't have a name for her?"

Elizabeth shook her head. "I hardly spoke to her. Once I realised that Marcus was interested in her, I did not make any effort to get closer. The other girls would say the same thing. You can ask them."

Elizabeth smiled nervously. It was an uncomfortable look that told Jack she had more to say. He allowed her a moment and then, when nothing was forthcoming, he asked the question that was on his mind. Whether she would answer it, he was not sure. Something told him that Elizabeth was not quite ready to tell him everything about life at the yard.

"So why are you now worried?" asked Jack.

There was another period of silence before Elizabeth finally spoke.

"Things with Pippa have changed recently. They are not as close as they used to be. I sense my turn is coming."

"What do you think he will want from you?"

"I don't know," sighed Elizabeth. "It makes me sick to think about it."

"Are you scared?"

"I'm terrified, Jack."

"What makes you think that he is going to turn his attention to you?"

"It's small things. You know, the odd comment here and there; the occasional touch or an arm going around me. There's nothing you could pick him up on in isolation without it looking like you were making a fuss. It's as if he is pushing the boundaries to see how I'll react. Each time, there is a bit more contact. I know my time is coming."

Jack watched her shudder visibly when she said it. Her pretty face had changed from worry to fear. Her body was on edge. She looked across at Jack with piercing eyes.

"You will help, won't you?" she asked.

"You know I will."

"Thank you."

"But I will need information."

"Like what?"

"Did you ever see Josie Raynor at the stables?"

"I don't know the name. Should I?"

"Probably not," admitted Jack. "She was well before your time. Are there any other girls he has tried it on with? What about Becky Rose?"

"There is no way he would touch her. She has his measure and is not afraid to stand up to him. I think she had a fling with a jockey at one point. I can't be sure."

"Is that with Kit Grady?"

"No way; he is Laura's. Becky is too smart to fall into that trap."

"In what way?"

"Let's just say that Laura is not the type to let someone stand in her way. A night with Kit would be a one-way ticket out of the yard. That lady does not accept playing second fiddle to anyone."

"Where does all this leave you, Elizabeth?"

"I think it might be time for me to leave. I've been thinking about going home for a while. I can't run from my father forever. I've made my point to him."

"What will you do?"

"I'll go home, sob a little and then get pampered. In a year or so, I'll be allowed back out into the world. I might even do a bit of travelling after that."

"Would you consider delaying those plans?"

"Why?"

"I could do with somebody on the inside. Not for long; just until we find out what is going on."

"Do you think the Tummels are involved in something?"

Jack sighed loudly. "We just don't know. We might be looking in the wrong place. Then again, we might not be. There is too much smoke for them not to be up to something."

"What about my safety?"

"You have my number. If anything happens, call me. Any time; night or day. We will get you out of there and that is a promise."

"I know it is," she smiled. She leaned over and gave Jack a hug that he was neither expecting nor wanted.

***

Lisa muttered under her breath when she got into the taxi. It had irritated her to call one. That sense of annoyance had now turned to anger. The monthly car payment had been taken from her bank that morning. That made it worse. For all that expense, all she could do was stare at an empty parking space. Once again, Jack had caught her out. The sleepiness in her eyes had made her vulnerable. He had breached her stubbornness and she had handed over her keys without a thought.

Once woken by Jack, Lisa had forced herself to get up. She had showered and dressed before going through her plans for the day. Over breakfast, she had made up her mind that Kit Grady deserved another visit. He had been booked for two rides at Beverley as a rare foray to ride for a different trainer. No doubt the money would be good and he would go there with Laura Tummel's full blessing. Maybe Laura would find a way to go with him, which gave Lisa all the more reason to go.

In the back of the taxi, Lisa mulled over her approach. Was she going to play the detective and keep to a simple script? Or was she a racing fan ready to fawn over him like a groupie with her eyes on the star performer? It would be difficult to convince him that she was there for any other reason than work. All she could hope was that Kit might have an ego and would succumb to her flirting. Lisa smiled and settled back into her seat. She would play whatever role she needed to get some information.

On the way to the track, she sent a curt text to Jack. It was a simple enquiry to find out when she might see her car. When he didn't respond, her thoughts turned back to the racing and the horses that Kit was due to ride.

A quick scroll through a couple of articles confirmed that he was not going there to make up the numbers. In both races, his horse was expected to romp home. It was nice work if you could get it. Kit seemed to have a way of making sure he always backed the right horse.

The lack of chat from the driver was welcome and allowed Lisa to get lost in her thoughts. Once she had finished researching her target, she watched the countryside fly by. Her mind drifted back to her car. No matter what she did, she could not get the sense of irritation out of her head. Jack was taking advantage of her and it needed to stop.

That feeling of annoyance was not helped when the driver stopped the car on the outskirts of the track. He shrugged off Lisa's request to go closer. It forced her to get out and walk the final three hundred yards. She flashed her warrant card at the gate to secure her passage inside. She had no intention of paying. Nor would she be staying to the end.

Lisa had arrived later than planned though it was still early enough to see Kit. She made her way towards the jockeys' room where he would prepare himself for his two rides. She gazed around and wondered whether he had already gone inside.

Lisa took up a position where she could watch the flow of jockeys coming out for the second race. The first race was finished, with the riders already weighed in after a race with only five runners. It had been a romp home for the favourite, which seemed to generate some excitement. The odds would be poor though an early winner always provided a good feeling.

For the first time, Lisa caught sight of Kit. His wiry frame was leaning up against a wall. He was chatting to another of the jockeys, a near clone in appearance. They all seemed to fit the same description. All slight of frame, they looked like they needed a good dinner.

Kit saw her out of the corner of his eye. He frowned briefly and cocked his head to one side to suggest that he was thinking. A few more words to his colleague saw him break from his conversation. He walked over to Lisa, offering a sense that something was on his mind.

"Fancy seeing you here."

"I could say the same about you. I didn't know the Tummels had any horses here."

"They don't. I'm guesting for Ray Thomas."

"If I had known you were here, I could have got some free tickets from you," smiled Lisa.

"Isn't that bribery and corruption?" he laughed.

"Only if it is work-related."

"Don't tell me; you are here purely for pleasure."

"I am. I love a day out at the races, particularly the smaller tracks."

"So who did you back in the first?"

"What do you mean?" stumbled Lisa.

"Which horse did you back? I just want to know whether you would make a decent tipster."

"I backed the winner, which makes me a better tipster than most jockeys."

"True enough," laughed Kit.

"How many rides have you got today?" asked Lisa. She was determined to play dumb when she needed to.

"Two; the three o'clock and the three-forty."

"Fancy them?"

"Both should romp home."

"Should I be backing you?"

"Only if you can get decent odds. I think they have both been backed down to something stupid. Once my name gets put with them, people tend to pile in. I have a reputation as being able to get the best out of an old nag."

"Are we still talking about horses or have we moved on to Laura Tummel?"

"Very good," laughed Kit. "No comment."

"I thought we had got past all that silence rubbish."

"Maybe; maybe not. Let's see what mood I'm in after my two rides. If I win, I might be prepared to open up a little. You would need to press the right buttons, of course."

Lisa scowled to send a message that she was not a toy to be played with.

Kit smiled and bid Lisa farewell. It left her to look around while Kit made his way into the jockeys' room. The track felt small compared to her recent visit to York. She had been with a friend on a hen do where she had been dragged around in a haze. Even on a day out, she didn't care much for the spectacle and even less for the drunkenness it seemed to be an excuse for.

Smartly dressed gentlemen were found to be anything but and the term 'ladies' could only be applied loosely.

Thankfully, Beverley seemed calmer. The characters stood out while the drinking was more moderated. It was still early though the carnage of York felt a long way from what she was seeing. In the distance, there were police vans though the uniformed officers were nowhere to be seen. That allowed her to relax and took away her fear of being called upon.

As she walked around the course, she wondered what was going through Kit's mind. Away from Laura Tummel, did he feel that he had the freedom to have some fun? In the small world the racing industry operated in, any shenanigans would soon get spoken about. If they did, the meal ticket he enjoyed would be over. She had to know more. Somehow, she had to find a way to pin Kit down before he thought he could do the same to her.

Chapter 18

At twenty-past two in the afternoon, Spencer Pugh walked nervously towards the building. His heart was beating a little too hard for his chest. The conversation he had shared had been brief. It was the chance he had been waiting for. By taking a risk, he could clear his debts and gain the respect he deserved.

That risk needed to be taken. There was too much hanging over him. Wherever he went, he could feel the axe looming above his head. Sharks, the lot of them, they were all out to feast on his blood. He would not be able to run for much longer. His past was catching up on him and that deadly blade was about to come down on his neck.

He squeezed the handle and eased the door open. Spencer was hit by the darkness. He squinted to take in his surroundings. There was a small room to his side and a corridor stretching out before him. The eerie light barely offered enough illumination to see where he was walking. A strange smell filled the void and hinted at something sinister. It was not quite the stench of death but it was close to how he would imagine it.

Spencer contemplated whether it was right to proceed. Did he have a choice? The answer forced him to slip inside and close the door behind him. He remembered the instructions he had been given just a few minutes ago. Go through the unmarked door and follow the corridor to the end.

Tiptoeing forward, he strained his eyes to focus. In front of him, the shape of a door could be seen. He knew what was waiting inside and yet he had been told nothing. One shot at redemption was what it had been described as. After that, all his troubles would be gone. He could turn his life around. That was the promise they had made. It was also the promise he had made to himself.

He had to do it for himself because his parents had disowned him. His family and friends were all now distant acquaintances. Even the cards at birthdays and Christmas had stopped arriving. He would be lucky to get any of them to attend his funeral. If he got himself back on track, it would be years before he had to worry about that.

He walked forward and reached for the second door handle. Dark and damp, the smell had grown stronger and filled his nostrils with unpleasantness. Spencer could feel his gut tightening, the urge to be sick filling his mind. He had nothing to offer. His last meal was two days ago. If they found him dead, they would have nothing to follow up on. All his stomach would contain was the cocktail of alcohol which had been consumed to calm his shredded nerves.

Spencer took a deep breath and immediately regretted his decision. His hand shot to his mouth to fight his involuntary retching. He turned the handle and pushed through into the room. He looked across and set eyes on an individual seated at the table.

"It's you!" exclaimed Spencer. His eyes opened up to the widest stare. He was unable to comprehend what he was seeing and yet it all made sense.

"Good afternoon, Mr Pugh. Shall we put an end to your problems?"

"I guess," he sighed, the life visibly draining from his body. Suddenly, his confusion returned. It left him staring blankly at his opponent. "I don't understand."

"There is nothing to understand. You are here to play cards; that's all. Shall we play?"

Spencer's eyes scanned the room and noted the lack of furniture. There was just a table and two chairs, with chips stacked to each side. Alongside the chips, there was some money in a series of neat piles. The gun on the opposite side made his heart skip a beat. Just seeing it confirmed the stakes they were playing for.

"Where is the rest of the money?" he demanded.

"In the case if you want to count it. The combination is six-six-six."

"I do. Call me picky but I reckon I will only get one shot to check it."

"You will only get one shot whatever the outcome is, Mr Pugh. Be my guest if you want to do a quick count. Just don't take too long about it."

He ignored the words and went over to the case. The combination was already set to allow the latches to open. He laid the case flat while making sure he kept an eye on his opponent. A satisfying click allowed him to reveal the riches inside.

"Wow!" he exclaimed as he let out a deep exhale of breath. The case was full, with every inch taken by banknotes. "One million, you say?"

"Minus the bit on the table, which doesn't quite fit in. I should buy a slightly bigger case. I don't think you'll mind putting that bit in your pockets, will you? It can be some spending money for the way home."

"Can I take it out?"

"Take it out, count it, smell it. You do whatever you need to do. Just make sure you put it all back."

Spencer reached in and took out a stack of bundles. They felt heavy. The weight of the money rested comfortably in his hands. He fanned it with his thumb, his eyes scanning for anomalies. All he saw was the continual movement of twenty-pound notes across his eyes.

"It's all there. This isn't like the movies where they slip paper in between the notes to rip people off."

"I've never seen so much money," he replied. He took out another bundle and riffled it against his face.

"It's all yours if you win."

"What's in it for you?"

"For me, Mr Pugh, it is all about the game. Shall I shuffle?"

Spencer took one final breath and nodded. He slipped the money back into the case and turned to face his opponent.

***

At twenty-past-three, Lisa walked into the jockeys' room. She was stopped at the door by another wiry clone. A flash of her warrant card and a whispered threat granted her unrestricted passage. It brought her into a small changing room where the space was filled with the stench of masculine bodies. The sound of a shower running in the background confirmed that she was in an area that no lady would normally be allowed inside.

She had waited until most of the jockeys had left. The few that remained were those who were waiting for their next ride. Two were sitting on a bench offering their view of the previous race. One was Kit Grady, the other a near identical twin who looked just as malnourished as his colleague.

"What are you doing in here?" barked the twin, the angry scowl on his face conveying his feelings. "This place is for jockeys only."

"I'm here to see Kit. Unless you want to see a grown man cry, I suggest you give us five minutes."

"I'll stay if it is all the same, love."

"No, you won't," said Lisa. She flashed her ID. "You will disappear for five minutes or you won't be making your next ride."

"Just be quick; I need to get ready."

"That will depend on Kit and how quick he can be with a lady," she smiled.

The twin cursed and slipped out of the room, leaving Kit and Lisa alone. The shower was still going and sending a wisp of steam into the room. In minutes, there would be others who needed to be in there. Lisa checked to make sure that nobody could overhear them. Then she turned to Kit who had not moved since she had entered.

"Nice ride in the last," she offered. He had ridden home by fifteen lengths, with the horse barely breaking a sweat.

"Seriously, you need to get out. The stewards will go mad if they see you in here."

"Then I suggest you start talking."

"What about? I thought you were here to enjoy a day at the races."

"I am. However, the day just got better. I think the expression is two birds and one stone."

"What do you want?"

"How about you tell me what is going on at the stables?"

"We've been through this. You are barking up the wrong tree; no offence intended."

Lisa folded her arms and offered an unimpressed look. She could sense that Kit was playing her in the hope that she would crawl back under a stone. This time was different. Her intrusion onto his patch made him vulnerable. It was her best opportunity to put the squeeze on a man who would otherwise be unwilling to talk.

"Let's start with Marcus Tummel. Tell me about him."

"I've told you all there is to know."

"No, Kit, you have hinted at it. I want to know exactly what is going on between him and the stable girls. Don't leave anything out. Otherwise, we are going to give him every lurid detail of your affair with Laura."

"What affair?"

"The one that everyone except Marcus knows you are having. Actually, I think Marcus has a pretty good idea. He didn't hit you for the sake of it."

"Look, Laura and I just have a bit of fun now and again. It's nothing serious."

"But it is behind Marcus's back."

"Of course it is."

"Are you Laura's only extra-marital affair?"

"I think 'affair' is a bit of an exaggeration."

"What would you call it?"

"I told you; a bit of fun."

"For you or her?"

Lisa paused when she saw a jockey appear from the shower. He was naked from the waist up, with a blue towel wrapped around his bottom half. Kit shook his head in the younger lad's direction. The signal sent him away without stopping to question what was going on.

"For both of us. Come on, we need to get ready for the next race."

"Then you had better talk quickly. Keep going."

"I've told you. It's nothing serious for either of us. It's a bit of fun and it is pretty much coming to an end."

"Bored of you, is she?"

"You would have to ask her that."

"I am asking you. Maybe she has got somebody else. What about Jordan Bilby? Is he another bit of fun for her?"

"I don't know," shrugged Kit.

"What's your suspicion? You jockeys are great ones for form and hunches, so what do you reckon?"

"If I was a betting man, I would say the odds were pretty low."

"Odds-on?"

"Maybe not that low, but close. He's a good-looking lad and let's just say that she has a voracious appetite. If it is not him, it will be somebody else. Who knows, maybe your colleague fits the bill. What was he called? Was it Jack?"

"I'm pretty sure that he doesn't fit anyone's bill. Now, we never finished talking about Marcus. Tell me about him and the stable girls."

"I think that might get me in trouble."

"You're already in trouble, so start talking."

Kit looked around to make sure that nobody was in earshot. He moved closer to Lisa. It put him into a position where he could whisper. She noted his expression change. His eyes had gone cold as hatred spread across his face. Lisa felt a chilling shudder go down her spine as she waited for the news to break.

"He forces himself on them."

"As in rape?"

"As good as. He would argue that they are willing. Anyone else would say that he doesn't leave them much choice. It's that or get out."

"You mean he fires them."

"I don't know. One or two have disappeared suddenly. I've always had my suspicions about something sinister."

"Are you saying that he has killed them?" asked Lisa as she recoiled back a few inches.

"I don't know. I try to stay as far away from him and the girls as possible."

"So why do you ride for him?"

"In this game, you have to go where the good horses are. It's all about winners and contacts. If I left on bad terms, I would never get another contract. Marcus would make sure of it. That would leave me to freelance, which is a tough world to be in."

"So you turn a blind eye to any shenanigans," confirmed Lisa.

"I'm sorry if that makes you think bad of me but that's the way it is. The girls are adults. They have to look after themselves."

"And do you enjoy taking advantage of the girls as well?"

"Absolutely not. I had a couple of relationships in the early days. Since then, nothing."

"With the stable girls?"

"Yes, but not the type you see now. When I first came to the stables, there were a couple of older girls. Marcus soon cleared them out."

"Were they not his type?"

"He prefers them younger. You will have seen that. They all conform to a template. He recruits them personally."

"Which ones has he had affairs with?"

"That is not for me to say."

"Kit, I want some names."

The jockey let out a deep sigh. He shook his head and then glanced up at the clock. He was on borrowed time if he was to avoid the wrath of the stewards.

"Just be clear, you haven't heard any of this from me. Okay?" Kit's eyes offered a tone of insistence.

"That's fine."

"Pippa, for certain. I walked into a stable last week. He had her pinned down."

"Did you stop him?"

"I didn't get involved. You can call me whatever you like. In my world, I call it discretion."

"I call it something else."

"Fine, but I'm telling you what I saw."

"Who else?"

"That Elizabeth girl. He has certainly got eyes on her. Then there's Becky. They were close for a while but that didn't seem to go on for long."

"Any others?"

"Plenty. Most of them have gone. They tend to disappear quickly. Come on, that's all I know," he urged as the door opened and two jockeys entered from outside.

Lisa smiled at them before turning back to Kit with a steely glare. She stared deep into his eyes and never allowed herself to blink.

"We will finish this conversation another time. I'll leave you boys to finish playing horsies."

With her words lingering in the air, Lisa walked out. She dialled Jack's number on her way back to the car park. He did not answer. Her message relayed a summary of the information that Kit had given her. As the call finished, she turned to the rows of parked cars and cursed. Once again, she would need to order a taxi.

***

Despite the cool temperature, the sweat was building on Spencer Pugh's forehead. He was trembling and struggling to hold his hands steady. His eyes glanced up at the clock to note the time. It was four o'clock. They were over an hour into the game and he had already lost over half of his chips. Inside, his stomach was churning. His remaining life was represented by what he had left on the table. Those initial stacks were now down to two and a half columns. Like his health, his chips were ebbing away before him.

"I need a break," he huffed loudly.

"No breaks," was the reply. "We break when it is over."

"Please, just five minutes."

"I said, no breaks."

The voice was full of authority and made Spencer shudder. His body trembled. The intoxicating mix of alcohol, adrenalin and a lack of food had left him fighting to maintain his senses. Opposite him, his opponent was showing no such signs of weariness.

"You know the rules. The game ends when it ends."

He looked directly at his opponent, hoping for a reaction. There was nothing; no emotion or even an acknowledgement of his presence. All he saw was the cold calculating face of someone who had no time for anything but the game. Spencer stared in desperation, almost pleading over the table. It was hopeless. The cards had been dealt and his two were face down in front of him.

Edging the corners up, his mind thought back to the life he had lost. The son of a vicar, his mother was a talented hairdresser. They were both loving though strict and far too busy to show much affection. His father, who had time for everybody who walked into his church, had little time for his own kids. Not just him, but also his poor sister. Angela had taken an overdose at the age of nineteen.

Unable to find her place in life, she had sought what she believed was the easy way out. Except it was far from easy. Her strong body had hung on for three long days. The doctors had covered her in tubes and wires just to keep her going. Her death had defined his teenage years.

After Angela's demise, his parents had only become stricter. Finally, he had pushed them away, unable to cope with the suffocation any longer. In his dark days, gambling had provided his one escape. It was a necessary demon that he knew he could control. The drink followed and then so did the losses before the walls began to close in around him.

"Are you going to make a play?"

Through hazy eyes, he stared at his cards. A ten and an eight of hearts stared back at him. It was no hand to make a move on though he had long since detached himself from the reality of the game. He was flying around the room, with his parents demanding that he come down. All he could see was the school that he had spent his early years in. He saw an innocent young boy whose happiness was a distant memory.

Then came the surge of anger as the bullying kicked in. It had started when his sister had died and offered up the hurt that he needed to feel. There were no relationships or friendships that other adolescents enjoyed. All Spencer could see were the devils and demons circulating through the people he recognised. The flames licked up at him and forced him to cower from the heat. He had to get out if he was going to rid his body of the fire.

"I can't do this any more!" he screamed.

The chair was sent flying back when he made his move. He ran to the door and fought to prise it open. Battling the lock, he dragged it towards him. When it was unsuccessful, he smashed his fists against it.

"Sit down, Mr Pugh. You cannot get out until the game has finished."

"I can't do it! Let me out!"

"Mr Pugh, will you please sit down?"

"Let me out! I need to get out! I'm suffocating!"

"Mr Pugh, for the final time, will you please sit down? If you don't, you will forfeit the game."

"No!" screamed Spencer at the top of his voice.

It was the last thing he said before a single gunshot from behind brought the game to an end. His opponent snarled with anger. It had been a wasted couple of hours. Now, someone else was going to suffer and would offer the satisfaction that Spencer had failed to provide.

CHAPTER 19

JACK DID NOT PICK up the message from Lisa for over an hour. When he did, he called her straight back. She told him everything. With each word, she sensed Jack's fury growing. Any warnings she offered went unheard. Jack's only thoughts were about Marcus Tummel.

He rushed to the car as soon as the call had ended. There had been no conversation about whose car it was, just the lurid facts that Kit had told Lisa. No details had been spared. It made Jack boil with rage. His hatred for Marcus Tummel could not have been greater. He despised the man for using his position to take advantage of those who were unable to fight back.

It explained why the girls were not prepared to speak out. They all knew the consequences if they did. The threats would come with unwanted attention until they submitted in silence. Jack thought of Pippa running from the stables in tears and the hassled nature of Marcus when he followed.

As he thought through the possibilities, Jack's foot pressed harder on the accelerator. The car sped along the A64 until the dial approached three figures. Thankfully, he was close to the turn-off for the stables. The fire in his eyes was ready to be unleashed. Lisa had warned him not to go in too hard. What else was he supposed to do? Any other approach would see Marcus dismiss his words as malicious gossip.

The hard part was getting the girls to talk. It was unlikely that any of them would be willing to offer a statement. Would they face him in court if it went to a trial? Jack knew that getting a conviction would be impossible.

He contemplated phoning Elizabeth Moss to tell her to leave. And yet he needed her to remain on the inside. She was the one possible witness he could call upon. Would she talk when he needed her to or would she clam up under pressure? It was hard to know. First, he had to confront Marcus and threaten to expose him for what he was.

Driving in through the gateway, Jack noted how quiet the yard was. Marcus's car was parked up, with few signs of life elsewhere. Jack headed over to the house and knocked on the front door out of politeness. When nobody answered, he tried the handle. He peered in through the window when he found it locked. He repeated the act at the staff house and was offered little reward.

Jack eased back from the building. He stared up at the first-floor windows in the hope that he would see movement. So many people pretended they were not in and then made the mistake of looking out. There had to be somebody looking after the yard. That thought was confirmed with a scream.

Reacting to the high-pitched sound of a female in trouble, Jack ran to the small stable block behind the main building. The distressed cry had been piercing. After the cry came silence. Jack was close to the building when the air was filled by the bellowing voice of Marcus Tummel.

Jack crashed through the door without warning anyone that he was going in. He stared across at two figures in the far corner of the building. A young girl had been thrown over a dirty wooden bench. Behind her, Marcus stood with a riding whip high above his head.

"Leave her alone, you bastard!" Jack cried out. It forced Marcus to turn around and lower the whip.

"Get out of here!" snapped Marcus. "This is an internal matter."

"No, it's about a bully getting his kicks."

"You have no right to be here. Get out!"

"You'd love that, wouldn't you? If I go, you'll flay the skin off the poor girl. If you lay another finger on her, it won't be the law you have to answer to; it will be me."

"Who do you think you are; Judge Dredd? Unless you have got a warrant, you can fuck off!"

To prove his point, Marcus took the whip back above him. He sneered at Jack and locked his eyes on him. His muscles tensed to suggest that his next step was to strike down at the girl. Jack's reaction was instant. He lunged for the whip and allowed his hand to intercept its path when Marcus Tummel aimed it at him.

Jack fought the anguish burning through his palm. The two men wrestled for the whip until Jack snatched it away from Marcus's grasp. As the two men faced off like rutting stags, Jack cracked the leather hard across Marcus's face. It split his cheek open and forced a drop of blood to run down from the wound.

Marcus reached up to confirm that he had been cut. His eyes opened wide as the young girl turned around in fear. It was Pippa Jones who was staring up from a prone position. She was trembling in front of the two men.

"I'm going to have you for assault," snarled Marcus. "You're finished."

"Try it; I dare you. Pippa, you can go. He's done with you...for good."

Pippa ran from the stables as quickly as she could. Jack waited for her to be clear of the building before turning his attention to his foe. Only then did he realise how much damage he had done to Marcus's cheek. The blood was dripping from a wound that Jack had found satisfaction in inflicting. There was no remorse to be offered for a bully who had got what he deserved.

"You are going to regret this," growled Marcus.

"We'll see when I've finished asking you a few questions," grinned Jack. "Then I will decide whether to arrest you. Are you ready for the first one?"

"Funnily enough, no."

"Let me ask it anyway. How many girls have you done that to?"

"No comment."

"Is it just Pippa or do all the girls get a turn?"

"No comment."

"What about Laura? Does she like it?"

"No comment."

"Or is she too tough for you?"

"No comment."

"Do you get your kicks with those who can't fight back?"

"No comment."

"What about Josie Raynor? Did she get a turn?"

"No comment."

"We are going to be here for a long while at this rate. I will try that again. What can you tell me about Josie Raynor? As a clue, she was another one from your harem."

"I don't remember her. Girls come and go in my world. Have we finished or can I go and get this cleaned up?" Marcus dabbed at his cheek in fury.

"I can give you one on the other side as well if you want."

"You have not heard the last of this. There will be hell to pay."

"I don't doubt it," Jack laughed. "I wouldn't want to have to explain to Laura what you did to earn that. That one is a feisty lady. Tell me, is she off shagging again?"

Marcus launched himself forward at Jack who raised the whip. He held it out between them as if it were a sword that would strike down. Marcus restrained himself and stared intently at Jack. He dared not bridge the gap between them when he knew that he would come off second best. Jack held his position until Marcus backed down.

"Get out of here!" he snarled.

"I'm on my way. Just one word of advice. If I hear that you have touched any of the girls again and I mean any of them, you and I are going to have more than words."

"Is that a threat?"

"It is and you would do well to listen to it."

As he left, Jack threw the whip directly at Marcus. It bounced off his chest and landed on the floor at his feet. Marcus's furious stare never left Jack for a second.

***

Jack was still raging when he turned back onto the road outside the Tummels' gate. He had nothing but contempt for a man who had misused his authority for pleasure. His thoughts were for Pippa and the ordeal that she had faced. He had bought her some time. Jack knew that she would not be safe for long.

He wondered whether he had made things worse for Elizabeth Moss. Someone was going to incur Marcus's wrath for what he had done. Would Marcus turn his attention from Pippa to her? He would contact her once the dust had settled on his visit. To do it too soon would make her stand out as an informer.

As he drove, Jack dialled Lisa's number. It was too complicated to get her hands-free system working, so he slowed down and spoke to her on speaker. He needed to tell her what he had seen. Lisa had provided the information, which meant she should hear about it first. Louth would be briefed later and would get a far more economical version of the truth.

"How did it go?" asked Lisa. "Did you do anything stupid?"

"That depends on your definition of stupid."

"Jack, what have you done?"

"Nothing that I regret."

Lisa's eyes rolled with each detail he told her. It started with a disapproving response and then she seemed to defrost. Once Jack offered the full story, any disappointment was gone. She had no sympathy for Marcus but feared the repercussions that would come.

"Do you think he will press charges?"

"I doubt it. I think he will be cleverer than that. I don't think he will fancy offering a full confessional to Laura, let alone a court."

"You still shouldn't have done it."

"Yes, I should. You didn't see the fear in that girl's eyes. She was terrified of him."

"Do you think we should arrest him?"

"I did think about that."

"Was that before or after you hit him?"

"Both. I decided there was no point. None of the girls will offer a statement. They are too scared to speak out."

"So what happens now? Do we sit here and hope that he says nothing?"

"Don't be silly. We do what you should always do when you come across a hornet's nest."

"Which is?"

"You poke it with a bloody great stick until something comes out."

"Have you got a big stick?"

"I think I might have exactly the right type of stick for the job," smiled Jack.

Lisa ended the conversation after she had offered another warning. She knew that it was pointless though still felt the need to say it. When Jack was riled, he would strike out. There was nothing she could do to stop him.

Jack did not hesitate before he made his next call. He could barely contain the grin on his face as he linked together two people that he detested. It was a perfect match; two rats ready to gnaw at each other until they had devoured whatever flesh remained. The last one standing would probably have gorged itself to death.

"Andy Hutton speaking," came the reply.

"Andy; Jack Husker. How are you?" Jack's tone was unusually friendly.

"Somewhat surprised. I never thought I would hear from you. How are you, Jack?"

"All the better for hearing your voice."

"Okay, let's cut the bullshit. What do you want?"

"I might have a little titbit for you."

"Really?" The tone of shock in Andy Hutton's voice was obvious.

"To be fair, it is a lot more than a titbit. It's more like a feast."

"And what do you want in return?" asked Hutton warily.

"Two things. Firstly, my name must be kept out of it. Secondly, I want to know any new information which comes your way."

"That seems fair. I guess a beer or two might be involved as well."

"No, I don't want anything tangible that could come back to bite me. I'll settle on your word as a near approximation of a gentleman."

"Do you trust me?"

"Not one bit. I just thought we might start with the pretence of trust and worry about its loss later."

Hutton laughed out loud. He was already trying to work out what game Jack was playing.

"Okay, hit me with it. What have you got?"

"Do you know Marcus Tummel?"

"Yes, the trainer."

"That's him. Do you fancy some lurid accusations about him?"

"You know I do."

"Then settle back because you are in for a ride."

By the time Jack had finished recounting all the details about Marcus and the stable girls, he was back in York. He spared nothing in his account and added a few embellishments to spice things up. He detailed what he had seen and implied there were other intimate relationships. He said nothing about Laura's affair with Kit. The whole thing was more awkward for Marcus without it. At Jack's request, Andy Hutton would leave the girls' names out of the story. Other than that, everything else was fair game.

"What corroboration have I got for the story?" asked Hutton.

"Go and interview Marcus Tummel. Ask him where the scar on his cheek came from. He won't tell you but I will."

"Go on, I'm intrigued."

"Let's just say that someone with a whip got a bit carried away."

"What, a dominatrix?" asked Hutton eagerly.

"Oh yes, with high-heeled boots and everything. Gave him a proper thrashing. The mark on his cheek is just the tip of the iceberg. There are plenty more hidden away from view."

"I can imagine," offered Hutton in the most repulsive tone Jack had ever heard.

Jack pressed the button to end the call. As he walked back into his house, he was struggling to control his laughter.

***

Kelly had not slept. She felt like she was in a trance. Her mind was unable to shut down after her night at the casino. It had gone downhill from the moment she had got there. Once Jordan had given her the VIP chips, her whole world felt like it had fallen apart. They were gone in four spins of the wheel. The silver ball did not come close to the numbers she needed.

The croupier had stared at her impassively, unconcerned about the state she was in. It was only afterwards that her thoughts had turned to what the chips were worth. There had been nothing on them other than those three letters. 'VIP' meant exactly what it said. If you had to ask about their value, you could not afford to use them.

Those lost chips brought her back to the casino. She had to see Jordan. She was wearing the same dress as the night before and had skipped work. She had described it as a stomach bug when she phoned in to offer her excuse. It was only her second day off since she had started. There was little danger that it would be noticed.

Her parents had queried why she was not going to work. They were fobbed off with a story about being owed some time from an important investigation she had been on. They failed to notice the tiredness around her eyes. Nor did they see the dress she was wearing.

At the front desk, Kelly signed in. The whole act took place on auto-pilot. Nobody stopped her as she walked through to the tables. A friendly smile at the door confirmed that she had spent far too long in the place.

Any nervousness from the early days was now consigned to the past. She moved about without restriction. Her eyes scanned for Jordan. He would emerge as soon as he saw her like a fly to a honey pot. It felt like he was always waiting for her. And yet the one time she wanted to see him, he was nowhere to be seen.

At the bar, a new barman took her order. An Australian, with a distinctive accent, smiled nervously as if it was his first day on the job. As he served her, he shuffled from foot to foot. He called the office at Kelly's request and it yielded the desired result. When her name was offered, the call ended abruptly. The barman shrugged and pushed her drink across the bar.

"He's coming down," he stated.

"Thanks," said Kelly. She took a small sip from her glass.

Jordan Bilby appeared less than a minute later. Dressed in casual trousers and a white shirt, he looked relaxed. As soon as he laid eyes on Kelly, he smiled. For once, Kelly did not react to his presence. Her mind was still drowning in her worries. Somehow, she had to ask him the question that was troubling her.

She forced a smile towards Jordan and then stood helplessly. Kelly wanted him to take her into his arms to offer her a big hug. She needed that comfort after a torrid couple of days.

"You're becoming one of my regulars," he said.

"I know," she replied meekly, the guilt pulsing inside her.

"I reckon you'll soon be on permanent VIP status. How did you get on last night?"

"I lost," she replied, the colour draining from her face.

Jordan did not seem troubled by the statement. His shrug was accompanied by a few dismissive words. He had seen it so many times before. One more girl sinking herself in deeper was not going to ruin his day.

"It happens. I'll sort you out with some more chips." He reached into his pocket and handed them over with an intoxicating smile. "You have a go with these and I'll get myself a drink. I expect some winnings by the time I get to the table or there will be trouble."

"What sort of trouble?" asked Kelly, her face suggesting that she had seen a ghost.

"It's a joke. Go and have some fun and I'll be there in a minute."

"Oh, right, okay."

His words felt like anything but a joke to Kelly. She made her way to the nearest table. She sat down and placed her chips in front of her. Behind her, Jordan had already offered a nod to the croupier.

Jordan remained at the bar. He waited until Kelly had been given enough time to make her bets. From his vantage point, he watched her closely. He allowed himself to study how she reacted. Despite her attractiveness, the stress was starting to show.

Only when she was on the verge of losing did he move over towards her. He approached without a care in the world. Kelly was in pieces. It would be her last spin with the free chips. Her hand was shaking as she placed the chips down. She covered little with what she had left. As the wheel spun, both of them held their breath and prayed. They were wishing for two very different outcomes.

"Oh shit!" exclaimed Kelly. Her eyes closed for a moment. She was hoping that the world would be different when they reopened.

"That was not very ladylike," laughed Jordan.

"Sorry, I just lost your chips."

"They were your chips, not mine. Let's grab a table and we can have a chat over a drink."

"Just answer me one question first. How much were those chips worth?"

"Some were five thousand; the others were two," he replied. He walked away to leave Kelly to digest the numbers.

By the time she reached him, Jordan was sitting down. He was calm and enjoying the hook he had on his lady. In contrast, Kelly looked stressed. Her head was incapable of thinking clearly. She needed to find a duvet to hide under in the hope that the pain would go away.

"But I haven't got that sort of money," she said, the panic in her voice so clear.

"Stop worrying; I'll get you some more chips."

"I can't afford the ones you have given me so far."

"You might as well give it another go. Whether you are down a couple of hundred thousand or a million, what difference does it make?"

"A couple of hundred thousand!"

"Maybe a bit more. Come on, let's enjoy our drink. It will allow you to tell me more about yourself. Seeing as you owe me money, I might as well get to know you better," he laughed.

"I'm just plain Kelly; that's all," she insisted while trying to remember the back story of her undercover role.

"Well, plain Kelly, do you have any family in York?"

"I'm here on my own."

"A boyfriend?"

"I'm single."

"You must have somebody who cares for you…other than me, of course."

"No, not really. I could be gone tomorrow and nobody would ever notice."

With those precious words, Jordan sat back and tried to hide the smile that was spreading across his face.

Chapter 20

Jack eased himself out of bed. His head pounded like it was inside a drum. He only had himself to blame. There was a celebration to enjoy for dropping Marcus Tummel neck-deep into the mire. It was a lock-in at a newly opened watering hole around the corner. He had decided to steer clear of The Cellars. He feared that Andy Hutton might be in there, hoping for more details on the story. Jack need not have worried. Hutton had been busy working a late one to get his exclusive into the following day's paper.

Jack showered and put on some nearly clean clothes. Feeling hazy, he shuffled out onto the street. It was eight o'clock, still well before he was due in the station. That meant some precious time to clear his head. A brief stop at a cafe allowed him to pick up a coffee, his body not feeling up to a cooked breakfast. As he was growing older, the mornings were becoming more delicate. Ten years ago, the answer would have been a full fry-up. Now, a large cup of coffee and a gentle walk were becoming the norm.

He texted Lisa to enquire what time she would be arriving at the station. He offered her a coffee and asked whether she wanted it brought in. As soon as he sent it, his phone sprung to life. A welcome voice greeted him.

"Morning, Jack," she said. "Where are you?"

"Just heading to the station. I'll be there in ten minutes. Why?"

"It's Louth. He's on the warpath."

"What about this time?"

"Have you seen the paper?"

"No; what's in it?"

"It's probably best that you have a look and yes, I will have a coffee if you are offering to bring me one in."

"No problem, I'll see you in half an hour."

"I thought you said you were going to be ten minutes."

"That was before you gave me errands to run."

"Seriously, Jack, don't push it with Louth this morning. He's out for blood and I don't think he is overly precious about whose it is."

"In that case, he can have his own."

"Jack, I mean it. Be careful."

"Okay, I'll put a vest on and see you in thirty minutes." He pressed the phone to end the call just as Lisa's sigh came through loud and clear.

Jack's first thought was to get to a newsagent. He grabbed a copy of the local paper off the rack and took it to the counter. He smiled at the middle-aged lady behind it and offered a bland greeting in her direction.

When the paper was laid out, the full extent of the story was displayed. It was sensationalist and focused on the worst bits of what Jack had said. There were some added embellishments thrown in that not even Jack would have dared to make up.

"It's disgusting what that pig is doing to those girls," she hissed, her eyes piercing Jack with devilment. "I don't know who reads this stuff."

"I don't know either," shrugged Jack as he pushed the money over the counter.

"You want to see what they say on page five. It beggars belief that he can get away with it in this day and age. And as for the comment he made on the following page, it is disgusting."

"You're right; I really don't know who reads this stuff," smiled Jack. He tucked the paper under his arm and left.

As soon as he was clear of the shop, he sat down on a wall and began to read. It was all there; the abuse of the girls and the sordid tales of Marcus Tummel's sex life. Unnamed sources had come forward to provide support to the story, with two ex-employees tracked down to add flavour.

The coup de grace was the close-up picture of Marcus's face, with the whip mark standing proud. Then Jack's heart sank. An unnamed police source was noted as providing the evidence. It was made clear that the information had come from York. The detail offered would narrow it down to a handful of potential culprits.

Jack was fuming. His request for anonymity had been thrown back in his face. He was ready to knock Hutton out, with his anger building by the second. Common sense told him to ignore it. The impending row with Louth was his priority. He would have to play things carefully and convince the others that he was not the one who had done it.

"Hutton, you're a toad," growled Jack as he marched purposefully to the station.

By the time he got there, he had discarded the paper and collected a coffee for Lisa. He had bought another for himself, knowing that it might be his last trip out for a while. Louth was likely to put everyone on a curfew where they were not allowed out without his permission. For once, Jack felt a small amount of guilt. He knew the effect it would have on the team. Then there would be the reaction from Marcus Tummel. That sadistic bully was going to lash out towards somebody.

"Briefing room one," said Lisa as she took the coffee from him.

"Let's go and face the onslaught."

"Seriously, Jack, just keep your mouth shut," insisted Lisa. "The first one to speak today is going down the road. I'm sure of it."

They eased into the briefing room and sat down. They were the last two of a dozen or more people who entered the room. All the attendees looked on edge. Their eyes were shifting around nervously. It felt like everyone was undertaking their own investigation and trying to eliminate the suspects. Everyone knew that someone was guilty. There was no shortage of theories doing the rounds.

Jack knew that at least half of those present would have pinned it on him even if they had no evidence to back up their conclusion. So long as he kept quiet, little could be done to prove it.

Even Hutton would not offer up his name. Jack was too valuable for him to do so.

DCI Louth entered the room two minutes later. He walked quickly to the front. His face was flushed with a deep shade of red that confirmed the anger inside him. The room descended into an unusual hush, with none of the usual flippant remarks being aired. Everyone knew that a barrage of noise was coming and yet nothing could have prepared them for the outburst.

Louth took out a copy of the newspaper and stared at the gathering. After making eye contact with everybody individually, he slammed it down onto the desk. It exploded like a gunshot and forced every set of eyes to the front.

"I...want...answers," he growled softly in the last whispered words he would offer. "And I want them now!" he bellowed suddenly. His voice threatened to rattle out the windows. "One of you gave this story to these scumbags and I want to know who it was!"

The room fell completely silent. Louth looked at everyone venomously, daring somebody to speak. Eyes flitted around, with nobody prepared to utter a word. Even the more jovial officers said nothing, knowing it was not a time to throw a wisecrack into the room. Louth was primed to react to the first person who spoke. There would be no holding back his fury.

"Well?"

In the uneasy atmosphere, everyone's suspicions were bubbling away. Once out of the room, the gossip would start, with Jack the main focus of the exchanges. Until then, silence was the only possible tactic.

Jack was experienced enough to know that the heat would soon die down. He had to ride it out and wait for Louth to lose interest. The DCI needed to get his officers back on the streets. That would end the meeting long before Jack was forced to offer up the truth.

"Not even got the guts to own up," hissed Louth. "Whoever it was has until the end of the day to tell me. After that, I will consider the matter gross misconduct. Now, in case any of you hadn't noticed, we have got two bodies in the morgue and not a bloody clue who put them there. Get out!"

It was loud and aggressive and left no one in any doubt about how angry DCI Louth was.

***

Everybody walked from the room in silence. Heads were down as the attendees filed out like school children. Even once the meeting was over, nothing was said. The normal chitter-chatter was replaced by solemness. Nobody wanted to be put on Louth's radar. Their superior was searching for somebody's blood to spill on the floor.

Lisa waited until Jack had broken away from the group. She followed him towards the stairs. He slowed his pace to walk with her. Her smile was a nervous one. It told Jack the question she wanted to ask. She paused as if contemplating whether to go straight in with it. After a moment of thought, she decided it was not the right time.

"Thanks for the coffee. I didn't dare drink it in there."

"He was a bit on the fiery side this morning, wasn't he?"

"Fiery? That's one way to put it."

"He must have had a bad morning," smiled Jack.

"Or someone tipped the press off about information that only you had."

"Lisa, that is a scandalous accusation. I hope you have good evidence to back up your wild assertions," said Jack. His mocking tone was met with a scowl.

"Just answer me one question. Why?"

"If you had seen the terror on that girl's face, you would know the answer to that. I'm sorry but the bastard deserved it."

"You know Louth won't stop until he finds someone to blame, don't you?"

"To be honest, I don't care. As long as it doesn't bring others down with me, I'm not going to lose any sleep about it."

"Do you really mean that?"

"I don't want others affected."

"I meant that you don't care."

"Maybe I care a little. It still doesn't change the fact that I would do it again. He had it coming."

"I can't argue with that,"

"Plus, half of that story didn't come from me. Hutton just made it up," added Jack.

"How much did you give him?"

"That would be telling," he grinned.

"Jack, don't make me beat it out of you."

"If you are going to do that, I'll put you in touch with Marcus Tummel. It sounds like you would make a lovely couple."

Lisa went to respond only to see that Jack had already walked away.

***

Jack moved through the station, aware that heads were turning as he walked. Each of them was trying him for the crime without worrying about whether the facts met with their verdict. They were the judge, jury and executioner and were determining his guilt without the need for evidence. Such theories would be shared around the coffee machines and in the pubs after work. At least it would be done discretely until DCI Louth had calmed down.

Jack ignored them and sought out the sanctuary that he needed. An earlier invite allowed him to head to a quieter part of the station. His old colleague, Dan Millings, greeted him with a welcome that felt genuine. Even then, Jack was given a strange glance by a middle-aged woman who looked up from her desk. He scowled towards her to send a message that she should get on with her work.

"I take it you have seen the headlines," offered Dan after greeting his colleague.

"Yes, it's pretty damming for Marcus Tummel."

"And for the person who gave the press the story."

"I wouldn't like to be in their shoes," said Jack.

Dan turned and looked at his old partner. Jack was stoic and offered nothing that would allow his face to be read. He thought for a moment and then decided that he was brave enough to say what was in his mind.

"You do know that people are saying it was you, don't you?"

"It's a logical assumption to make," shrugged Jack. "I know the reporter and was the last officer to see Marcus Tummel, so I must be bang to rights. It's just a matter of time before they come and arrest me. Fortunately, I have got time for a coffee first."

"I will work on the basis that you are taking it very seriously," laughed Dan.

"Lying awake at night allows for more drinking time," grinned Jack.

Dan decided that it was best not to respond. He made a coffee and handed it across to Jack. They took it over to Dan's desk. Jack's eyes went to the items that had been set out meticulously on its surface. It looked more organised than Jack could ever imagine himself being.

As Jack cradled his cup, Dan typed away at his computer. Once he had what he was searching for, he sat back and allowed Jack to look at his screen. He linked his hands and waited for Jack to work out what he was showing him.

"Okay, that's Darren Brand," said Jack. "What am I supposed to be looking at?"

"Look at his employment record."

Jack's eyes scanned down the lengthy list. It was like a summarised CV, with all his known job details included. Except it was more than that. All his unofficial interests were added in.

Jack took a moment and then stopped. He turned to Dan with a look of shock etched across his face.

"I take it that's the entry you want me to see?" queried Jack.

"It came out of the manual records yesterday," nodded Dan.

"Why would a successful businessman want to do cash-in-hand work on the door of a casino?" mused Jack.

"Maybe the owner had something on him?" shrugged Dan.

"Or maybe he was a compulsive gambler attempting to pay off his debts?" added Jack, inviting another response from his colleague.

"What sort of man gets a job closer to the very thing that is likely to cause him a problem?"

"I would say a desperate one," said Jack. "And I know just the man to ask about it."

"I thought you might. Just make sure DCI Louth finds out before the press."

"I'll ignore that on the basis you gave me coffee and some good information," said Jack. The look he offered Dan was sent as a warning.

***

Jack walked straight out of Dan's office and drove to the casino. It felt like the right place to go when the whole case was veering towards Jordan Bilby. Dan's warning had been clear. He would need to be careful. And yet there was no sense of regret. If Marcus Tummel was being hounded by the press, it might buy the girls some time. Whether it would be enough still troubled him.

Jack wondered whether any of Hutton's insiders had been real. If they were current employees, Marcus would seek them out. He would want his pound of flesh in revenge. A chilling shudder went down Jack's spine.

His thoughts turned to the scar that Marcus would be left with. How would he explain that to Laura and the outside world? An assault? An unnamed attacker? They were stories you could only maintain for so long. Jack smiled. He would only give Marcus a small amount of respite. Then he would throw Andy Hutton another titbit. Elizabeth Moss would need to be out by then. Once she and the other girls were safe, he would give Hutton enough to ruin Marcus Tummel forever.

At the casino, Jack parked in a space reserved for the manager. A doorman went to stop him and was repelled with a flash of his warrant card. It brought a look that implied Jack was dirt. He got out of Lisa's car and walked slowly towards the building. On his way in, he faced up to the bouncer. Jack snarled at him, ignoring the ten-inch difference in height.

"The car belongs to a friend. If it is touched, I am holding you responsible."

"Yeah, right, Grandad."

"Remember, the law is on my side. I can have you in a cell just like that," he said. Jack clicked his fingers directly in the lad's face.

"Not if I ain't done nuffin', you can't."

"Bless the naivety of youth. When did guilt and evidence get in the way of us putting people away?" laughed Jack, using the stereotype to his advantage.

"Okay, I'll keep an eye on it for you."

"Good lad. I won't be long."

Jack marched through the door that was opened in his path. He nodded his head to acknowledge the politeness. A quick scan of his surroundings ended at the reception. A smart-looking lady was sitting behind it. He smiled at her and then walked over to the internal entrance. The door had been left unguarded for a moment. Not waiting for a debate, Jack pushed it open and entered the casino.

"Hey, wait, you can't go in there without signing in!" shrieked the lady, her heavy footsteps chasing behind him.

Jack ignored her and allowed the door to close behind him. He paused at the top of the stairs and gazed over at the gaming tables. Just six were in operation, all offering roulette, with no more than fifteen customers spread between them. Each one of them got a look before his attention was taken by a voice behind him.

"I said, you cannot come in here!" snapped the lady.

Jack waited until she was right beside him. Feeling her angry breath on his neck, he turned to face her. Standing tall, she had puffed herself up like a peacock. Her display was a warning. It felt like she was a bouncer and the receptionist rolled into one. Jack thought of the man watching over Lisa's car outside. He wondered whether he would take her on.

"Would you please leave, sir?" she asked, her tone a little less fierce than before.

"I'm with the police," offered Jack. He flicked up his ID without giving her time to take a proper look at it.

"I don't care who you are with. You need to sign in."

"No, I don't," insisted Jack.

"I am afraid you do or you will be leaving," she said before another voice interrupted her.

"I will deal with this one, Maggie. He's a known troublemaker, aren't you, DI Husker?"

Jack glanced across to see that Jordan Bilby had emerged from a room to the side. His ever-white smile was lighting up the room.

"Right you are, Mr Bilby," said Maggie. She scurried back towards the front desk.

"Are you looking to cause trouble again?" asked Jordan.

"Not at all. It is just a passing visit."

"I am sorry to disappoint you but there isn't much to see. This is our quietest time of the week."

"You mean when everyone's money has run out?"

"If you like," shrugged Jordan. "What is it you want? I'm happy to be sociable. However, I don't think you have come here for that purpose."

"Perceptive, as always, Mr Bilby. I thought you and I might have a little chat."

"That's fine; book an appointment. Maggie has my diary."

"Why don't we chat now?"

"It would have to be quick; I haven't got long."

"You will have as long as I need or we will do this the hard way."

"DI Husker, we can do this whichever way you want. I am not scared of you or your threats. I have got nothing to hide, so I suggest you make it quick."

Jack's eyes narrowed further. The stand-off felt like two bulls in neighbouring fields. There was venom, particularly on Jordan's side and yet he was never going to strike out. Opposite him, Jack was irritated by his sneering smugness. His thoughts turned back to the stables. He wished that he had Marcus's whip in his hand.

"Why don't I have a look around?" said Jack.

"Presumably you have come with a warrant?"

"I can get one if you want. If I go down that route, I'll turn the place upside down for the sake of it."

"Go and get one then. The only thing you'll find is what you bastards plant."

"No bodies then? Sorry, my mistake. You dump them in lakes."

"DI Husker, I have no idea what you are talking about."

"Then answer me this. How is it that your former employees keep getting found in lakes with a bullet hole in their head?"

"Maybe they can't cope with leaving?"

"Or maybe the life insurance you give your employees is too good?"

"You could be onto something there," laughed Jordan. "We do look after our staff. Perhaps we do it too well."

"But not your former ones and especially not those with a gambling problem."

"All this is a bit fanciful, isn't it? Why don't you come back when you have got some evidence and then we will do our best to help you."

"I think I might do that. Don't go anywhere. I reckon I'll be seeing you in the next couple of days," stated Jack. He wandered across the casino floor, muttered a couple of comments towards the croupiers and then turned to leave.

Jordan smiled and shook his head. The detective had the appearance of an old man who was completely lost.

Chapter 21

Kelly sat with her face in her hands. The folder of documents in front of her had not been looked at in over an hour. DCI Louth had asked her to review the financial records of everyone connected to the case. It felt like a time-filler to keep her out of the way.

With little progress made since she was given the task, her opinion had not changed. And yet her mood had. Just looking at anything related to money felt deeply troubling. It was biting into her. The losses she had racked up were occupying every moment of her life. Not just in the day. The lack of a good night's sleep was becoming a problem.

Thumbing through the documents felt like torture. Large positive numbers were a contrast to her perilous finances. She was just about managing her bank balance. Her overdraft was a couple of hundred pounds inside the limit. It was not what was on the statements that concerned her. It was the debts looming over her head. For now, Jordan Bilby was being kind about it. She had been on the earth long enough to know that would only last for so long.

Her last meeting with him had insinuated just that. His questions had become more probing and he had insisted on exchanging phone numbers. He was eager to know more about her personal life. A husband; a boyfriend; the link to a partner had been tested tentatively. It was obvious it was being done for a reason. The pressure would be applied as he backed her into a corner. The next step would be some form of sordid proposition in return for flexibility on her debts.

Her head remained in her hands. The darkness offered no respite to how she was feeling. Nobody needed to tell her that she was in trouble. Her lack of sleep and dwindling appetite were leaving her permanently tired. She had to do something to break the cycle. Her inability to focus on work would soon be found out. When her phone pinged with a text from Jordan, it confirmed that the time to act was now.

Kelly, will I be seeing you tonight? Jx

Kelly's fingers struggled to grip the phone. She read through the words, wondering whether to reply. Common sense said to ignore it and yet that would be at odds with the undercover work she was trying to complete. She had to send something. The only option was to stall.

You might do if you are lucky.
I was born lucky.
Then you will probably see me.
I can't wait. I might have a little proposition for you.

Kelly dropped the phone in horror. Her worst fears were displayed on the screen. It would be tonight when Jordan would make his move and his sordid game would step up to the next level. Kelly knew that she was in too deep to tackle him alone. She needed help. She had to speak to someone. Lisa was sitting at a desk just a few metres away and was staring intently at her screen.

Kelly eased up nervously and shuffled over towards Lisa. Her stomach churned, knowing her whole world was about to fall apart. Twice, she stopped and stared aimlessly at her superior. In a few seconds, her career would come to an end. She didn't care. Doing nothing meant the purgatory would continue and Jordan's game would be played out at her expense.

Kelly edged nearer, hoping that Lisa would look up. The DS barely noticed that she was there. Only when she was standing right beside her did she offer some words. They were said without taking her eyes away from the screen.

"How's it going, Kelly?" asked Lisa.

"Err, fine, I guess."

"Anything in those financial records?"

"Not yet; I was..."

"Did you get them for all of the casino staff?"

"I'm not sure."

"Can you check, please? I've got a couple of calls to make, so let's catch up when I'm back."

"But..."

It was too late. Lisa got up from her seat and marched out of the office, leaving Kelly feeling helpless and alone.

***

Jack left the casino and went straight back to Lisa's car. It was untouched, just as he expected it would be. It did not stop a sense of relief from flowing through him. He knew that he was pushing his luck by constantly borrowing it even if it gave him an excuse to see Lisa. They were getting on well though there would come a time when they would have to take the next step. That would mean parading themselves as an official couple, with shared accommodation and lifestyles to go with it. That could wait until they did not have the DCI on their backs and bodies turning up in lakes.

As he drove away from the casino, his phone rang. He glanced down and noted the familiar number that appeared on the screen. Jack pulled the car into a bus lane and checked that nobody was watching. A police emergency justified the infringement.

"DI Jack Husker speaking."

"Hi, Jack, it's Elizabeth Moss."

"Hi, Elizabeth. How are you?"

"Not good."

"Are you able to talk?"

"I will be able to in ten minutes if you are free. Can I call you back?"

"Yes, of course."

Jack hung up and took the opportunity to move the car. He drove a few hundred yards and parked up in a lay-by. By chance, it had a food van in it, offering the welcome opportunity to get a cup of coffee. Nothing fancy; just a cup of instant. It would do while he waited for Elizabeth Moss to call him.

It was not a long wait. By the time Jack returned to the car, his phone sprang to life. He answered it quickly and greeted Elizabeth with a tone of recognition. She spoke softly as if she was worried about being overheard. It rang alarm bells in Jack's head.

"Are you sure you are safe to talk?"

"Yes, it's fine," she whispered. "One of the other girls is asleep in the room next to me. Don't worry; she was out late last night and is dead to the world."

"Hung over?"

"She will be when she wakes up. She was in one hell of a state when she got in. I thought we had a removal firm stripping the place out when she came up the stairs."

"That sounds like my sort of night," laughed Jack.

"Mine too. I'm not sure it will be such a good day for her."

"It never is. Trust me, I have plenty of experience in that area. Now, what is it I can do for you?"

"I think we have trouble brewing."

"In what way?" asked Jack. He took a sip from his overheated coffee. It burned his lip and forced him to stifle his cry.

"You know that article in the paper about Marcus?"

"Yes, I read it."

"Things have not been right since it came out. Marcus and Laura are at each others' throats and he is blanking the stable girls. That is an obvious sign that something is wrong."

"That can't be a bad thing for the girls."

"I guess not but then Kit Grady has been sacked. There was an almighty row between Marcus and Laura and now Kit is gone."

"I guess he has just found out what everybody else knew. These things tend to come back to haunt people one way or another in the end."

"Jack, I'm scared. I need to get out of here."

"You'll be fine," Jack assured her. His mind was full of thoughts about how useful Elizabeth Moss was. She was an insider in the one place he had no other means to get access to.

"I want to leave."

"Why don't you give it a couple of days to settle down? If it doesn't, I will come and get you myself. That is a promise."

"Do you mean it?"

"Of course I do. When I give someone my word, I always keep it," he assured her. It sounded convincing even though Jack was not quite sure whether he believed it himself.

***

Jack drove slowly back to the station. It was deliberately sedate, offering him time to reflect on what Elizabeth Moss had said. The more he thought about her, the more uncertainty filled him. Was he putting the girl in danger? Marcus would be raging and was likely to lash out at anyone. Kit had already borne the brunt of that as had Laura. The only question was which of the stable girls would be next.

At the roundabout, Jack's uncertainty made him loop around in a full circle. He was tempted to drive straight over to rescue the girl from her fate. Despite the urge to do so, he resisted. No crime had been reported or officially committed. Instead, he continued on his journey. Elizabeth was more than capable of looking after herself. As the most articulate and intelligent of the girls, Jack convinced himself that she would not be targeted.

The thought of going back to the station felt unappealing. Those drab grey walls sent a shiver through him. It was too early for the pub, making it the perfect opportunity for lunch. A quick call to Lisa was met with a positive response. Her voice sounded excited at the prospect of meeting up. That offered a moment of joy away from the troubles that were brewing.

Jack drove to the restaurant and parked on a single yellow line. A note indicating police business was thrust into the window, alongside his phone number. That trick had always worked though it had never been tried in Lisa's car. He headed inside and was pleased to see there were plenty of spare tables.

"Table for one, sir?" asked the waiter. He greeted Jack before he was barely through the door.

"No, for two, please. I know, dressed like this, it is hard to believe that someone would happily have lunch with me."

A polite nod was returned and then Jack was taken to a table in the window. He sat down and accepted the menu. He ordered a filter coffee while he waited. The waiter left Jack to scan through the complexities that were written before him. All Jack wanted was a simple bowl of pasta and yet it felt like he was decoding an Enigma machine.

Not for the first time, he needed Lisa to help guide him through it. When she arrived, she appeared flustered as if she had rushed from the station. Her hair looked windswept while her hands were clamping her coat shut. Despite not looking her best, her attractiveness to Jack was never in doubt. A quick kiss was a rare moment of public affection. Both blushed when they parted and took their seats before anyone could see them.

"How was your morning?" asked Jack.

"Utter chaos. Louth is making everyone's life a misery. Every few minutes, he is barking out a new set of orders. I'll let you guess who they are blaming."

"The Tories? They take the blame for most things."

"For once, be serious, Jack. They are blaming you."

"Why would they do that?"

"Jack, it's me you are talking to. Don't play me for the idiot that you assume everyone else to be."

"Sorry, Lisa. It felt like the right thing to do at the time."

"And now?"

"I don't regret it from Marcus Tummel's point of view. He deserves it though I would accept that nobody else does."

"Is that an apology?"

"Almost. How are the rest of the team coping?"

"Since you asked, I am concerned about Kelly."

"Why?"

"She looks so withdrawn. If she didn't live with her parents, I would be worried about her not sleeping or eating. She tried to talk to me earlier but I pushed her away. I was neck-deep in errands for Louth. I should have taken the time to speak to her."

"What do you think is wrong?"

"I don't know. She might be finding the undercover work harder than she thought it would be. As soon as I get a chance, I will speak to her. What about you? What was your morning like?"

"The usual. I went to see Jordan Bilby and rattled his cage."

"And?"

"He played it pretty cool. I gave him the full works. I threatened to pull the place apart and he never even blinked."

"Which means he might be hiding nothing."

"Or is bloody good at it."

"True enough. Are you telling me that is all you did?"

"Pretty much," laughed Jack. "I did take a call from Elizabeth Moss."

"With more information?"

"It is properly kicking off over there between Marcus and Laura. Kit Grady has been sacked."

"Just another quiet morning at the stables," smiled Lisa.

"Something like that."

"How was Elizabeth?"

"A bit shaken. She will be fine."

"Tell me you are not leaving her in there."

"She is a good source of information."

Lisa's hackles rose. The relaxed look on her face turned to thunder. She stared at Jack when she realised he was telling her the truth. It felt wrong to put the young girl at risk, particularly when there were no specific leads. Lisa placed her napkin on the table and leaned forward with steely eyes.

"You have to get her out of there."

"She's fine; stop worrying."

"Jack, don't patronise me. We need to get her out of there now. If she gets hurt or worse, that's on our watch and I am not having that. It's not about our necks being on the line; it's about doing the right thing."

Jack sat back and fiddled with the collar of his shirt. Gone was the softly-spoken lady he felt affection for. In her place was an authoritative woman. What bugged him most was that Lisa was right. Elizabeth Moss deserved a way out of her troubles. It was what he had promised her. It was also the right thing to do even if he was reluctant to admit it.

"Can we talk about it over lunch?"

"There is nothing to discuss. You will go over there and get her out. Don't make me threaten to drop you in it with Louth."

"That's below the belt."

"No, it isn't. Where my boot kicks you in a minute will be. Do the right thing, Jack." Lisa's hands contorted into fists without her realising it.

"Okay, I'll do it. Can I ask for two favours first?"

"For crying out loud, Jack. How many more favours can I do for you?"

"Two, if you are asking."

"Go on then; what are they?"

"Firstly, could you decipher the menu? It's all Greek to me."

"It's Italian. What's the second?"

"Can I keep hold of your car to go and get Elizabeth? I'm not sure the bus goes past the stables."

Lisa shook her head. She was unable to comprehend the cheek of the man. She wanted to refuse but it was obvious what the response would be. She took hold of the menu and moved it upwards to block him out of her view. It was not hard to see why two ex-wives had left him or why he had the bruises to prove it.

"Yes, you can use my car," she hissed, "but only on the condition that I am ordering for you. Today, it is vegetarian lasagne and a glass of water."

"Vegetarian?"

"Yes, with real vegetables."

"That sounds good," replied Jack. "Tell them to stick a couple of sausages on the side. It's hungry work going to rescue a damsel in distress, especially in a car that struggles to do much over a hundred miles per hour."

By the time Lisa had lowered the menu to protest, Jack's smile told her that she had been hooked like a fish.

Chapter 22

It was three o'clock by the time Jack turned into the Tummels' yard. After finishing lunch, he had answered a panicked call from Elizabeth Moss. Marcus and Laura had exchanged another heated row. This time, Laura had left in a hurry, insisting the marriage was over. That had sent Marcus into a rage. Elizabeth was worried that he might direct his venom towards the stable girls.

Elizabeth's call was just the excuse that Jack needed. With Lisa's words ringing in his ears, it allowed him to backtrack on his previous advice. Armed with new information, he was insistent that he would take her away from the yard. Her first instinct had been to resist for fear of losing her independence. Common sense soon took over.

Jack had given her half an hour to pack up her things. She had to be ready when he got there. Marcus was likely to react badly when Jack marched onto his property.

With his eyes scanning around, Jack parked as close to the staff house as he could get. The whole place looked deserted. He had told Elizabeth to keep a low profile until he arrived. Someone would need to face up to Marcus and he was the man to do it.

Jack got out of the car and walked towards the building. His eyes searched for signs of Marcus or Laura. They were nowhere to be seen. His arrival had not been noticed by anyone. That gave Jack mixed feelings. A small part of him wanted another confrontation with Marcus.

He knocked on the door and entered. Calling out Elizabeth's name, he was met by the girl descending the stairs. In her arms, she carried a large holdall and a rucksack. She was struggling under the weight of two bags that threatened to overwhelm her. Jack took the heaviest and almost toppled forward with the weight.

"That's the advantage of working with horses," said Elizabeth. "You end up with arms like Popeye."

"Mine are more like Olive Oyl's," laughed Jack. "That's what you get for police work."

It broke the ice and caused Elizabeth to smile. That moment of humour was only short-lived. She was terrified. The fear was written across her face. She was scanning around for imminent danger, knowing Marcus would not be far away.

Jack made sure he led the way. He was ready for any confrontation that was coming. They got to the car and loaded the bags without anyone coming out to see them. Jack opened the passenger door and allowed Elizabeth to get inside. She eased herself in and looked up towards him. He saw the same scared girl he remembered from the past.

"Where's your car?" asked Jack, noting the absence of the red Volvo.

"In the garage. It needs a service."

"That's good. It's one less reason to come back. Have you got everything you need?"

"Yes, I think so. I feel terrible leaving the other girls here."

"I'm going to get a squad car to come over as soon as we have got you out of here. We'll call it in as a neighbour reporting a disturbance. If anything happens, they will sort it out."

"Where are you going to take me?"

"You are going home to your parents."

"Oh," she said, her face dropping noticeably. "I take it a request to sleep on your sofa for a couple of nights is not an option."

"I'm sorry, Elizabeth. I have to do the right thing. We both know that is reuniting you with your parents."

She forced a smile. It felt like it was the hardest thing she had ever done. She leaned over towards Jack and gave him a hug that he was not expecting.

"You're a good man, Jack."

"Just promise me that you won't tell anyone that. It would damage my reputation."

For the second time, Elizabeth smiled. She put on her seatbelt and took one last look across the yard. Her time at the stables had been good for her and yet it no longer felt like home. That special place was back with her parents.

Jack drove away, leaving the crumbling empire behind them. He turned out of the drive and headed towards the main road.

Jack kept an eye on the girl to his left. Her nervous fear seemed to subside the further she got from the stables.

Once onto the A64, she seemed to breathe more calmly. She sat up straighter and reached out to turn on the radio. What followed was a cacophony of noise to Jack but acceptable to the younger ears of Elizabeth. Jack allowed her to find something that she felt comfortable with.

"You don't mind, do you?" she asked when she noticed Jack screwing up his face.

"No, it's fine."

"Arctic Monkeys," she announced, raising her voice to talk over the sound.

"I'm sure it is."

"That's the band," she stated as if she was explaining it to her father. It was the first time she sensed that Jack and her father were from the same generation and not as dissimilar as they often pretended to be.

"I know. I'm not a total dinosaur."

"Sorry," she blushed in the same way as she would with her parents.

Ignoring the music, Jack drove to the Moss's house. It had been a while since he was last there, his memory directing him through the more expensive parts of York's suburbs. They were houses that he could only dream of affording, with their front gardens often a substantial plot in their own right. It was a world that Jack neither lived in nor felt very comfortable visiting.

Elizabeth guided him into the correct drive. It was a large family house that offered an immaculate appearance. Jack wondered what reception he might receive. Their last conversation had ended with him punching David Moss. The passage of time would have changed little, with a sense of bitterness still embedded in the man. Maybe by bringing back the greatest gift of all, they could finally bury the hatchet.

As he brought the car to a standstill, Elizabeth seemed to tense. Gone was the relaxed smile and in its place was a girl racked with uncertainty. The next few days would be difficult for her and they both knew it. The world she was returning to would be very different from the one she had left. Maybe it would be too tough for her and she would not stay longer than she had to.

"I'm not sure I can do this," she said.

"Do you want me to speak to your parents first?"

Elizabeth Moss nodded.

Jack left her in the car and walked to the front door. Within seconds of ringing the bell, David Moss was standing in front of him. None of the fury had left his face since they last saw one another. There was no mistaking the hatred he conveyed without a word being uttered. Jack waited for the explosion and then decided it was time the deadlock was broken.

"Hi, David; DI Jack Husker. It's been a long time."

"Not long enough in my opinion. What do you want?"

"I am pleased to say that I have something of interest to you."

"I can assure you there is nothing of worth that you can give me."

It was the type of response that Jack wanted to hear. He smiled and stepped aside to allow Elizabeth to get out of the car and walk over. The look on her father's face was memorable. The anger melted in a fraction of a second. It was a moment which made the job worth all the pain and angst he had suffered.

"Elizabeth!"

"Daddy, I'm sorry! I love you!" she called out when their eyes met for the first time.

As she said it, she ran towards him and enveloped her father in the tightest of hugs. Elizabeth broke down in tears and sobbed deeply into his chest. Holding her tight, the tears began to form in David Moss's eyes. From inside the house, Jennifer Moss heard the commotion and came out to join them. When she saw her daughter in her husband's arms, she slumped against the wall and struggled to breathe.

"Elizabeth, you're back!"

"Yes, Mummy; I'm so sorry."

Jack smiled and nodded contently. Watching the family being reunited tugged at his emotions. He returned to the car and brought Elizabeth's bags to the front door. Once they were placed down, he turned and walked back towards the car. Behind him, he heard the heavy footsteps of someone walking towards him with purpose. Jack ignored it and continued to approach the car.

"DI Husker, wait!" called David Moss. It was softer in tone than the aggressive manner he was used to.

Jack turned to face him, with one hand on the car door. David Moss was hurrying towards him, looking flustered as he moved. He appeared to be fighting his body to cover the ground quickly.

"Where are you going?" he asked.

"Back to work. These criminals don't catch themselves."

"Will you at least stay for a cup of tea? Perhaps we could call it a peace offering."

"I will be getting on my way. I think this is a time for your family to be together."

"Are you sure? We really do appreciate what you have done for us, DI Husker. I know we have had our differences but this means...well, it means the world to us."

"I'm just doing my job."

"No, you are doing far more than your job requires as I suspect you normally do. You just don't like anyone else to know."

Jack shrugged and smiled. He was uncomfortable with the plaudits he was getting and even less comfortable with what happened next. As David Moss offered a hand to thank him, Jack reached out to accept it. The hand was quickly pulled back and replaced by an all-embracing hug.

David Moss held him a little too tight and squeezed the breath from Jack's body. The larger man seemed to consume Jack's smaller stature. It was hard to fathom that this was a man he had punched on the jaw. Now the guy was trying to kill him with more kindness than he thought he had in him.

"Okay, let me breathe," said Jack, extricating himself from his grasp.

David Moss eased back in a slightly embarrassed manner. He offered some final words of thanks and allowed Jack to leave. Jack watched him hurry straight back to Elizabeth. He had done the right thing by getting her away from that bully and back into the arms of her parents. By doing so, he had lost an important source of information at the stables. It didn't matter. Something told him that was no longer the place he should be looking.

***

From the moment Lisa had walked away from her, Kelly had nowhere to turn. She needed to talk to somebody but there was nobody left in the station. Her whole world was spinning around her. It was leaving her feeling queasy. She knew the persuasive charms of Jordan Bilby would be too much for her to face alone. With the debt hanging over her, he would be able to lead her into the darkest of places.

Without Lisa, she had no idea what she would do. Those around her would be quick to judge her failings. Her parents would disapprove while DCI Louth would most likely dismiss her. She could not rely on Jack, who would be impossible to pin down. The rest of her colleagues would just find humour at her expense.

She knew the unwritten rule. No police officer should ever admit any form of weakness in the station. That meant fronting up to Jordan Bilby. Every ounce of common sense told her it was the wrong thing to do. She had no choice even though she would be offering herself up for his mercy.

Such destructive thoughts made her leave the station early. That was becoming a regular pattern and yet nobody seemed to care. The remaining financial checks could wait until the morning. It was a dull line of investigative work that had been given to her as a fill-in job. The real detective work was out on the streets and she had been excluded from it. Too junior or just not rated, it made little difference to how she was feeling.

She went home and got changed into a suitable dress to go to the casino. It was not one of her sexiest outfits. She was past caring about how she looked. As soon as she was ready, she headed to the nearest bar. She needed a drink before she faced a man who would be waiting to pounce.

Just a few hundred yards from the casino, she slumped down in a modern pub. A stool at the bar was the perfect place to order a double vodka. The contents of the glass were downed in one swift gulp. It brought looks from others around her as well as an unpleasant feeling inside her stomach. It never stopped her from ordering a second one, which was dispatched with the same lack of fuss.

"Are you okay, missie?" asked the barman, with a slight frown on his face.

"I'm fine, why?"

"Experience tells me there is normally a problem when somebody drinks like that."

"I'm just warming up for the night ahead."

"Then I would say there is definitely a problem. I'm sorry but I cannot serve you any more alcohol."

"I don't want you to. I'm done."

The barman appeared surprised by the lack of an argument. He watched Kelly slip off her stool and walk out of the bar. He swept up the glass and went about his work. Once she had left, she was soon out of his mind.

Kelly could feel the effect of the drink when she made her way into the casino. The combination of fear together with the shots she had downed were making her feel dizzy. After passing through the entrance, she walked over to the bar. Her head was spinning and that needed to stop.

She ordered a Coke, hoping that it might clear her senses. Jordan Bilby would soon be on the prowl. She needed to have her wits about her. She stared around and then took her drink. A calming sip was all she had time for before a man moved slowly up behind her.

True to form, Jordan appeared with a smile spread wide across his face. Kelly wondered whether the barman had him on call. More likely, he was watching through the cameras. That meant she needed to be careful. Anything she did would be recorded for him to rewatch later.

"It turns out that I am lucky," he smiled. Jordan greeted her with a hug and planted a kiss on her cheek.

"Maybe we both are," replied Kelly, doing her best to offer some allure.

"Come on, let's get you a proper drink and then we can have some fun."

Before Kelly could offer an objection, a signal was made to the barman. He brought over two cocktails. Kelly felt too light-headed to ask what was in them. They clinked glasses and both took a sip. The strength of the alcohol hit her immediately. With the double vodkas she had downed, it would further numb her senses.

Jordan took his time to engage Kelly in conversation. He could sense a slight slurring of her words, with Kelly beginning to lose a few inhibitions. He was not going to push things with her. There would be plenty of time for him to make a move. First, he would wait for the drink to take its full effect.

"I think I had better slow down," giggled Kelly. She placed her glass on the bar.

As Jordan smiled, Kelly puffed out her cheeks. She could feel the effects the alcohol was having on her. She could also feel her defences waning. The worry of her debts was gone. Her sense of darkness had been lifted by Jordan. There was no getting away from the attraction he offered even if she did not trust him.

"Stop worrying. What's the worst that can happen?" he replied. He handed the drink back to her and watched her finish it.

"Do you want me to answer that?"

"The answer is nothing because you are with me. Drink up; there is another one on its way." Jordan waved his hand at the barman to make sure the drink was kept flowing.

"Are you trying to get me drunk?" asked Kelly, her words becoming harder to decipher.

"What type of man do you take me for?"

"One who might take advantage of me," she replied. She slipped off her stool and stumbled into his arms. "Whoops!"

Jordan steadied her. He handed her a new drink and linked his arm through hers. It was as much to hold her up as to stay close to her. He walked slowly, ensuring Kelly remained alongside him. She needed support, not to be scared away. Any resistance she had would soon be ebbing away so long as he played his cards carefully.

"Where are you taking me?"

"I think we both know the answer to that question. It is time you and I had a little chat."

"What about?"

"That proposition I promised you. Don't worry; you will be able to say no if you don't like what I have to offer."

Jordan quickened the pace. It forced Kelly to concentrate on where she was walking. She swayed on her heels and needed his support to stop her falling. The turn into his office saw her topple. Jordan held onto her to make sure she got there unscathed. He sat her down on a chair and then slid onto the corner of the desk. It left them within inches of each other.

"How about a toast to the two of us and then we can have a chat?" he asked. He clinked the two glasses together for one final time. "Bottoms up."

He downed his drink in one swig. The act obliged Kelly to do the same. She forced it down with less ease than Jordan. It hit her like a bolt of lightning and made the whole room swirl around her.

"Wow, that was strong," she slurred, blinking away the shock in her eyes.

"I'm always a double-measure kind of guy. I reckon you might be that kind of girl as well."

"I guess."

"Would you like to hear the proposition I have got for you?"

"I'm not sure," said Kelly, her confidence wavering as she said it.

A hand reached out from Jordan. He ran his fingers through Kelly's hair. He saw her flinch though not with any great disgust. She did not find him unpleasant. That brought a smile to his face.

As he moved his hand around her head, he brushed her cheek. He traced his fingers across her and looked into Kelly's eyes. She barely moved. The nervous smile never left her face. She was struggling to offer any coherence.

"Is this about the money I owe you?"

"It is, Kelly. I always knew you were a clever young lady."

Her face went serious for a moment. She was fighting to form the words that would phrase her question. She knew what she had to ask and yet it was impossible to do so. Kelly felt the shame go through her. If it cleared her debts, she would do whatever he wanted. She just needed to be assured that there were limits to his expectations.

"What do you want me to do?" asked Kelly.

"What makes you think I want you to do anything?"

"I owe you a lot of money and I can't pay you."

"So you think you are going to have to pay me in kind, do you?"

Kelly nodded slowly and looked downwards. She felt dirty even if the feeling was softened by the effects of the drink. She was ready for Jordan to make his move and was not going to do anything to stop him.

"Do you think you are worth two hundred and seventy-two thousand pounds?"

"How much?" she asked, her head lifting suddenly in alarm.

"Two hundred and seventy-two thousand pounds. Those are your total losses."

"They can't be!" she cried out, her tears exploding in an instant.

Jordan allowed her to cry. After a period of sobbing, he lifted her chin with his hand. To take advantage of her in such a state would be easy. But why would he? She was unattractive when she cried like a wretch. It was not a time to exert himself on her when he had far greater plans for Kelly. They were plans that would see him rewarded handsomely.

"Dry your eyes, my pretty one. I have just the solution to your problems."

Chapter 23

Lisa was the first to arrive at the station. She had woken up early. It was her misfortune to do so. Her sudden appearance caught DCI Louth's attention. She still had her coat on when she was ushered into his office. It felt like he had been waiting for somebody to pass his problems on to.

"I need you to get out to Kirkham Abbey. A dog walker has turned up a body in the Derwent."

"Are there suspicious circumstances?"

"It looks like whoever it is has been shot in the back of the head."

"As in an execution?"

"It could be, so we need to act fast. Whatever you have on, drop it and get yourself over there. Take whoever you need with you but do it fast and keep the press out of it. I don't want to be standing in front of a camera on this one; not until we have some answers."

"Do you think it might be linked to the other killings?"

"It doesn't sound like it. An early assessment of that would be good."

"Okay, I'm on my way, sir. I will need to borrow a car."

"I thought you had just bought one?"

"It's a long story. The short answer is somebody else is using it."

"As in Jack?"

Lisa forced a smile and felt the redness flush through her cheeks.

"That's fine. Take whatever you need," he said.

"Thanks."

"And one final thing."

"Yes, what is it?"

"Good morning, Lisa. Sorry, I should have said that first."

"Good morning, sir."

Lisa left his office and headed downstairs. She collected a set of keys on her way out to the car park. It felt strange to feel grateful for the loan of a car when Louth was right. She had just bought one. In the time she had owned it, she had barely had the opportunity to drive it.

What made it worse was that Jack had never even offered to return it. They had enjoyed a drink together to clear the air after their tense exchange about Elizabeth Moss. He had kissed Lisa goodnight at the door to her flat and then walked home to spend the night with her car parked outside his house.

She passed Kelly Knox and PC Jenny Blake who were walking across the car park. They were chatting like two schoolgirls. Huddled together, their heads were down to keep out of the wind. Neither saw Lisa as they shuffled past nor broke stride to acknowledge her presence.

"Good morning, ladies. Have you got a minute?"

Both girls turned around. Their heads lifted to reveal two young faces. They appeared shocked at the intrusion into their world. Lisa smiled at Jenny who appeared fresh-faced while Kelly had tiredness written across her. Neither looked enthralled about the possible conversation they were about to have. It might see them volunteered for an unpleasant task.

"Morning," they both offered in unison.

"Are you alright, Kelly? You look tired."

"I didn't sleep last night."

"No doubt a lucky fella," Lisa laughed, to which Kelly forced out a smile. "I need some help, so can you jump in the car with me? Don't worry; DCI Louth has cleared it."

"But, I need to...err...I've got things to do," said Kelly.

"Not any more, you haven't. This isn't a request; it is an order, so don't expect me to ask you nicely again."

"Sorry," she mumbled contritely.

Lisa pointed towards the car that she had been given. Kelly let Jenny Blake get into the front in the hope that she might enjoy a few moments of peace. She was battling a delicate mixture of fear and a hangover. The journey in the back of a car was the last thing she needed.

When Lisa put her foot down, Kelly thought she was going to be sick and clutched her hand to her mouth. Her sole thought was on not embarrassing herself. Jenny did not feel much better. Lisa's driving was both erratic and fast. Neither dared say anything to their superior.

After a sombre drive, Lisa pulled up alongside the police van that was already in attendance. She offered a quick briefing and then got out of the car. Tape was still being put across the area by a young PC who looked like he had been dragged from his bed for the task. He appeared cold and miserable as if he would rather be anywhere else other than on the side of a river. Lisa showed her warrant card and ducked under the cordon without engaging him in conversation.

"Jenny, can you stay here with the officer? Make sure nobody and I mean nobody crosses the tape. Kelly, you are with me."

Neither girl said anything in response to the stern tone. Jenny Blake was relieved not to be the one going beyond the perimeter. She was still struggling to come to terms with anything gruesome, a part underplayed during her recruitment. Kelly had other concerns. She had heard Lisa's briefing and was wondering whether her stomach would cope with what she might see. There was a real likelihood that she would let herself down at the scene.

Ahead of her, Lisa pushed through until she got to the edge of the water. Once again, she was left wishing that she had changed her shoes. The mud was seeping up around the sides as she glanced down to where two officers were working. They were bent over a corpse and seemed untroubled by the knee-deep mud.

"Hi, I'm DS Lisa Ramsey."

"Tara Adams," said a middle-aged lady, her eyes looking up from a body. "This is Jonny Drayton, who is shadowing me."

"Hi," he offered while trying not to look out of place.

Lisa decided not to waste time by asking personal questions. Tara was not a crime scene officer she had come across before while Jonny looked very new. She saw they were working on an adult male whose body did not look too badly composed. Edging a little closer, she stared down to get a better view.

"What have we got so far?"

"White male, possibly thirty to forty years old, with the back of his head shot out," said Tara. "He hasn't been in the river long; perhaps a day or so. I reckon he has been deposited in a hurry and his body has washed down to this bend. He was found by a dog walker early this morning when he saw an arm trapped in the overhanging bushes."

"Where is the dog walker?"

"He collapsed with shock. He's been taken to hospital. I've got his details."

"Thanks. What state is the face in?"

"Pretty much intact. There is an exit wound from a bullet but it has gone out of the top of his head. That means the face is in reasonable condition...for a dead man. Do you guys need a few pictures?"

"Yes, please. We can then get the ID process started."

"Have you got a camera? You can take some with you."

"Kelly, this one is all yours," smiled Lisa. "Grab some pictures with your phone."

Reluctantly, Kelly stepped forward. She moved over to where she could take a picture. Tara removed the cover over the man's face. As Kelly looked down, she dropped her phone in shock.

There, staring up in his lifeless form, was the body of a man she had seen before.

"What's going on?" snapped Lisa.

"Sorry, I just dropped it. It won't happen again."

Kelly swept up the phone. She took the pictures and stepped back as quickly as she could. Lisa was shocked at Kelly's lack of professionalism. She made a note to follow up on it later.

"Any clues on him to give us an identity?" asked Lisa.

"None. His pockets were empty. No keys, wallet, sweets or even a tissue. It feels like somebody has cleared them."

"And you don't think he went into the river here?"

"No, " replied Tara. "From the way he was trapped in the branches, it looks like he has been caught on his way down. We have had a fair bit of rain. That will have washed him downstream. Who knows how far he has travelled?"

"Are you sure the cause of death is the gunshot wound?"

"We cannot be sure at this stage. That shot in the back of his head would kill most people. The only other thing we have picked up is he is a drinker. Even with his time in the water, there is still a hint of alcohol about him. If it wasn't for the gunshot wound, my theory would be he was drunk and fell in."

"Do you think it could be a factor?" asked Lisa.

"It can always be a factor even if it isn't the cause."

Behind her, Kelly had moved back to a safe distance. Her conversation with Jordan was going around in her head. He had been so blunt with her when he had made his offer. Despite his words, she was still struggling to understand him. Had he really meant that her life would be at stake?

A glance back towards the body made her wonder whether Spencer had received a similar offer. Had he found himself in debt and then shared the same conversation? It was information that she had to pass on but how could she? She was up to her neck in debt. Even if she resolved that problem, the DCI would want to make an example of her.

"Are we done with the pictures?" asked Kelly.

"Yes," said Lisa, offering a slightly confused look.

"I need to pop back to the car. Give me a minute."

Before Lisa could object, Kelly was gone. She marched through the mud in her haste to get away from the scene. She had a call to make before things spiralled further out of control. Lisa shook her head. Kelly's attitude was increasing her fury by the second.

Kelly's only thought was to find somewhere she could make a phone call. She saw the car and young Jenny Blake who looked oblivious to the world. The young officer alongside her seemed intent on closing the space between them. Like two lovebirds, they were snuggled together. It was probably to share warmth rather than to start a relationship.

Kelly moved away from them and walked down the road. She called Jordan on the number she had been given. He answered on the second ring while Kelly checked over her shoulder. Nobody was in earshot. It allowed her to speak without the risk of being heard.

"Good morning, Kelly," he announced as if Jordan had all the energy in the world. He sounded pleased to hear from her, with his tone as welcoming as it had been in the casino.

"It's about the conversation we had last night," she said nervously.

"I am afraid your opponent hasn't confirmed the details yet. Once they have been agreed, I will be in touch."

"I don't want to do it," she stated bluntly.

There was a pause while the words sunk in. Once they had, Jordan came back with a sharp retort.

"Kelly, it is arranged and that is all there is to it. You will get a date and you will be there, one way or the other."

"I'm not doing it."

"I don't think you have too many options. In case you have forgotten, you owe me two hundred and seventy-two thousand pounds."

"I haven't forgotten."

"Then I suggest you find a way to clear that debt."

"I didn't know what I was doing."

"Kelly, this is not difficult. You either pay me the money or you play the game."

Jordan ended the call. He left Kelly to dwell on his words. The message sent a chill through her spine. She was more scared than she had ever been in her life. She had so few options and those that were left seemed to be disappearing quickly.

***

Jack was waiting at the mortuary. He watched the vehicle arrive from the sanctuary of Lisa's car. The grubby unwashed van was transferring the body to its place of inspection. It felt like an unceremonious journey to signal the end of another life. He bowed his head to offer a small amount of respect to the deceased. And yet he was impatient to know the details of who was inside.

Two men walked around the van. They were laughing and exchanging comments between them. Happy in their work, they manhandled the body out of the back. One dropped his end of the trolley, which sent everything crashing to the floor. That brought further laughter and forced Jack out of the car.

"Show some bloody respect!" he barked.

His eyes stared at the first of the two men and then towards the floor. It only angered him more to see the lack of dignity. Neither man seemed to accept the less-than-subtle hint. They exchanged glances like two kids sniggering behind an adult's back.

"I don't think he'll complain," said one of them. "It's hand-written complaints only in this game," he added before his partner felt the need to get involved.

"Yeah, that's if they have a hand left," he laughed. "It can be a bit of a pick and mix if it's a car crash."

"In a minute, you'll be joining him in the bag, son," said Jack. His angry expression dared either of them to respond.

Jack walked forward to back up the threat. The two men did not take it overly seriously until Jack started to bristle. He edged closer to within a few feet. Looks were exchanged and then a gruff voice interrupted the debate. It was Cathy Duggan. She had heard the noise of the van and had walked out of the building in her overalls.

"I hope you boys are playing nicely," she said. Her smile disappeared when she looked down towards the floor. "If I find out that is one of my clients, it will be me you have to answer to. Get that body picked up and taken inside, now!"

Her accompanying scowl saw the two men leap into action. They recovered the body and moved it swiftly inside.

"You always had a way with men," laughed Jack.

"Only the naughty ones," she smiled. "What are you doing here?"

"That body interests me," he replied. His conversation with Lisa had sent him straight to the mortuary.

"I am afraid that you might have a bit of a wait. I have three in there before that one."

"If I ask nicely, could there be none before it?"

"I'm not allowed to do that. The arrival times are all recorded."

"Who records them?"

"I do."

"I am sure some mistakes do get made," grinned Jack.

"You would know about that better than I do. After all, you let me slip through your fingers. Come inside and I will see what I can do for you. It's about time you had something to make up for it."

Jack followed Cathy into the building. Even in her work clothes, she had an allure that he remembered fondly from the past. He had moved on and so had she. Their lives were so different to the time they had spent together. There were no regrets for either of them when they were both happy with the direction they had moved in. Cathy was now just a work colleague even if he still liked her company. She was fun to be around and there was nothing better than watching the way she turned men to jelly.

"What are you doing putting the body there?" he heard her bark. "I want that one taken straight in for examination."

Jack smiled and followed her into her inner sanctum. The two delivery men were given another set of orders before they scuttled out of Cathy's sight. Jack offered another stern look and then wondered why he bothered. No matter what he did, they would never be as scared of him as they were of Cathy Duggan.

"Men, eh?" she tutted as Jack blushed with a smile.

"I never liked them myself," replied Jack.

"Oh, I do, especially all dressed up when they watch me work."

"I think I might wait on the outside for the results."

"Oh no, Jack. If you want this one prioritised, you are coming in there with me."

"Does that mean putting all the gear on?"

"It certainly does," smiled Cathy, with a mischievous twinkle in her eyes. Jack remembered it from their dating days and the shiver it always sent through him. "Now, strip!"

Jack laughed for a moment before his eyes caught sight of hers. A moment of fear went through him when he realised that Cathy Duggan was not joking.

Chapter 24

Kelly asked Lisa to drop her off in the city. It was done under the excuse of needing to pick up a prescription. The truth was simpler. She did not want the confrontation that was coming back at the station. She had seen the look of thunder on Lisa's face when she had returned to the car. Only Jenny Blake's presence had saved her from her superior's wrath.

It had not stopped the stern glances in the rear-view mirror. After her conversation with Jordan Bilby, it was the last thing on Kelly's mind. She needed someone to help her. The more she thought about it, the more she realised it would not be someone she worked with.

Lisa had said that she would speak to her later. Kelly had smiled, knowing that she would do everything she could to avoid her. She needed to keep Lisa at a safe distance until she had found a solution. Without help, she would be summoned to a game where there could only be one winner.

Kelly walked across town until she reached the taxi office. It was a dingy place, with nothing more than a desk and a couple of spare chairs. It was manned by an overweight controller who was called Fat Sam, for no other reason than his shape. Nobody had been interested when he told them his real name was Ralph. Why would they be? The unpleasant lad with lank hair was there to do his job and nothing else.

"Sam, is Shaun in?"

"Kelly! It's been a while," he said, offering a hint that they had once been close. "What are you doing around here?" His chubby white face lit up at her presence and blossomed into a deep shade of red.

"I want to see Shaun."

"I thought you two were history?"

"We are, but I need to see him."

"Are you seeing anyone else?"

"That's none of your business."

"Then nor is Shaun's location."

"Sam, if you were the last man on this earth, I would not go out with you."

"Is that a maybe?"

"It is a no and it will always be a no."

"That's a shame," he said before calling one of his drivers. "Can you do a pick-up at the station immediately?"

"Yeah, on my way, Sam," crackled the response on the cheapest radio money could buy.

"Are you going to tell me where he is?" demanded Kelly.

"Are you going to give me your number?"

"Give it a rest," she growled to a face that was not going to offer any concessions. "Okay, location first, number second."

"No way. Do you think I am stupid?"

Kelly rolled her eyes to suggest that she did not need to offer an answer.

"Where is he, Sam?"

"Write it down and then I'll tell you," he insisted.

"You are not getting the piece of paper until you tell me," insisted Kelly.

"I still want it written down."

Kelly released a loud huff. She snatched the pad from in front of him and ripped off a sheet. She scribbled her number on it and then folded the piece of paper in half. Sam went to grab it, only for her to snatch it away. The deal had been agreed and she was not going to allow him to change it.

"He's next door in the pub. He's having his lunch."

"Is he alone?"

"Hang on; that is another question. I want the number."

Kelly threw it onto the desk and walked away. She was not going to spend longer with the repulsive man than she had to.

"Yeah, very clever!" shouted Sam. "Nine-nine-nine; aren't you the funny one? No wonder he dumped you, you stuck-up bitch!"

The words were lost on Kelly. She had marched out through the door and into the pub. She saw Shaun Farrow dining alone in the corner. As soon as she set eyes on him, she felt a sense of fear go through her. The memories of their turbulent relationship came flooding back. He was a mid-level gangster, with ambitions to rise through the ranks. That was incompatible with her role as a trainee police officer. Not that he had ever accepted that or had forgiven her for forcing the split.

"Well, that is not a face I was expecting to see," he smiled. He pushed out a chair with his foot. "Kelly Knox, looking as radiant as ever."

"Have you got a minute?"

"Take a seat and I'll order you a drink."

"I'm not staying."

"Then I am not talking. You either sit down and accept a drink or we don't talk. I don't like rushing things these days."

"Are you getting too old for it?" said Kelly, to which he shrugged in the affirmative.

Reluctantly, she eased into the chair he had offered. She watched the way he was devouring his steak and chips. It was done without fuss, just as most things had been when they had dated. Her abiding memory of Shaun had been that trouble had never been far away.

As she studied him, she noted how little he had changed. His angular face and jaw were still accompanied by a shaven head. He had a new scar above his left eye. It would be a badge of honour from one of his recent skirmishes.

"How's the steak?"

"Good. Do you want one; my treat?"

"No, thank you."

"What are you drinking?"

"Just a glass of water, please."

"Let's make that a wine."

"I'm on duty."

"Oh yeah, I forgot. What brings you here? Is it to rekindle our romance?"

Kelly blushed when she tried to avoid answering the question. She did not want to offer a refusal until after they had spoken. If that meant allowing Shaun to think he had a chance, she would play a dangerous game.

"I am after a favour."

"What sort of favour?"

"It is sort of financial. It's not money I need but breathing space."

"I think you might be more confused than I am. Can we keep it simple?"

"I need a loan deferring."

"I'm not a bank."

"It's not that sort of loan."

"Now I am intrigued."

"It's an informal debt. I need it kicking down the road."

"Kicking down the road or are you looking for it to disappear?"

"I don't think it can disappear. Can you help?"

"That depends on who you owe. Would it not be easier to pay it off?"

"It's over two hundred thousand pounds."

"Jesus, Kelly!" he spluttered. "I underestimated you. That is not the sort of money I carry around with me."

"No, but you can get your hands on it, can't you?"

"That's all speculation and rumour. Are you wired?"

"No, why?"

"This is all sounding a bit fishy. You will have to excuse me if I do not like where this conversation is going."

"I only want some space on the debt."

"And then what?"

"I don't know. I'll work something out. I know I will."

"I'm sorry, Kelly. I don't want to get involved in this. If you don't mind, I need to finish my lunch."

"Aren't you going to help me?"

"Sorry, sweetie. Look, Sam always had a soft spot for you. Why don't you pop next door and see what he can do? Maybe you could hide behind him if the debt collectors come looking for you. They would never see you there." Shaun grinned and popped a chip into his mouth.

Kelly got up and stormed away from the table. Shaun laughed and enjoyed the last piece of his steak. His eyes were on Kelly, the moody little princess he was pleased to be free of. She was never dating material but there had never been any harm in enjoying the view that she presented.

***

Jack's mobile rang while he watched Cathy Duggan go about her work. He was pleased that it gave him an excuse to slip from the room. He had seen enough to form a conclusion. The similarities to the other killings had started to come together. They would need more tests to confirm that it was the same gun. The only difference was that this victim appeared to have run away rather than stare down his attacker.

"DI Jack Husker."

"Jack, it's Andy...Andy Hutton."

"I'm not sure I should be speaking to you."

"Why not?"

"Do you know how much trouble you've put me in?"

"Hang on; you gave me the story."

"It wasn't supposed to be in enough detail to narrow the source down to one."

"Well, it was a good story," sneered Hutton. "And let's be clear; the bastard deserved it."

"True enough," said Jack.

"Did you hear that his wife has walked out?"

"Walked out or rode out on somebody else? She's hardly a saint herself."

"Tell me more, Jack," he sniggered. The sound was unpleasant even over the phone.

"That's for later. Her affairs were consensual, I think."

"We might let the readers judge that for themselves when the story breaks," he grinned.

"Let's cut to the chase, Andy. What can I do for you?"

"I think the question is, what can I do for you?"

"Okay, hit me with it."

"At least play along for a little bit. Make me feel important for a couple of minutes."

"I am not in the mood. I am in the middle of seeing a body cut open. Just tell me what it is before one of us ends up on the slab next to him. Hopefully, through old age, but it could be sooner. We're hardly adverts for a healthy lifestyle."

"That's a fine way to talk to someone who is about to do you a big favour."

"Okay, I'm sorry. I am appreciative; I just have a lot on."

"That's better. Your apology is accepted. I figured that I owed you a favour, so here is something for you. It's about that young detective you knock around with."

"You mean DS Ramsey?"

"First names, please."

"Okay, Lisa," said Jack while trying to stifle his irritation.

"Not that one. The younger one."

"Lisa is hardly an old timer."

"I guess not," he laughed. "There is a younger one though."

"Not that you can link me with before you write your filth," barked Jack.

"I mean a younger copper that you work with."

"I work with a lot of younger ladies."

"Come on, Jack, that detective one…you know, plain clothes. Sometimes, very sexy plain clothes."

"If you are talking about Kelly, you are old enough to be her father."

"Kelly?" queried Hutton. He chose to ignore Jack's accusation.

"DC Kelly Knox."

"That's her."

"What about her?"

"Does the name Shaun Farrow mean anything to you?"

"He's a small-time gangster who fancies himself a bit."

"Keep going?"

"He is a former boyfriend of Kelly's. If you print that, I will arrest you for hampering a police enquiry. That does not need to be in the public domain."

"Jack, will you stop with the threats? That's what I want to speak to you about."

"It's history, Andy. You're a couple of years too late on that one."

"Not for a clandestine meeting they were just having in the pub, I'm not."

"That's impossible. She is with DS Ramsey or Lisa, as you prefer."

"Not any more, she isn't. From where I was sitting, she was with her old flame."

"I find that hard to believe."

"It gets better, Jack. Figures into hundreds of thousands of pounds were being bandied about."

Jack laughed. "Shaun Farrow hasn't got that type of money."

"No, he hasn't. So where does that point to? I will leave that one with you," smiled Hutton.

"Are you suggesting what I think you are?"

"I am just presenting the facts as I always do."

"Is this going in your paper?"

"No. This is a gift for you by way of an apology for any trouble that I may have caused. It also makes it your turn to offer me something next time."

"How sure are you?" asked Jack.

"One hundred percent, as always. I'll be seeing you, Jack. Don't forget that follow-up story about Laura Tummel and her affairs. My readers love a good soap opera."

Andy Hutton ended the call with a slimy grin. A link between the police and Shaun Farrow was golden. He chewed his lip and nodded. For now, he would do nothing with it. With Jack on his side, that story about Laura Tummel would be priceless. She was something special. If it gave him an angle on her, he would play every bit of it to his advantage.

With alarm bells ringing in his head, Jack sent a text to Lisa. Andy Hutton was many things that he despised. Yet if he said that he had seen Kelly with Shaun Farrow, it would be factual. Hutton did not need to make that up, particularly when he had Jack in a difficult position.

Lisa, is Kelly with you?

No, I dropped her off in town. Why?

Chapter 25

Jack met Lisa back at the station. She had got there twenty minutes before Jack, which had been enough time to brief DCI Louth. He had phoned Jack and relayed the same information that Lisa had told him. By the time the three of them came together, a series of options had been discussed. Louth was bouncing up and down when they met in a meeting room.

"We have to pull her in and question her," insisted Louth.

Both Jack and Lisa stared across at one another. Neither of them felt ready to speak. It was hard to argue with Louth's logic and yet something inside them doubted that the facts were as clear as they appeared. Lisa bit her lip in thought. She turned towards her superior with a look of uncertainty.

"Let me speak to her."

"I think we should *all* speak to her," confirmed Louth.

"No," interrupted Jack. "Let Lisa have first go. If that doesn't work, we can follow up. I think she might be more open to a softer approach."

"Are you sure?" asked Louth. "I know we want to give Kelly the benefit of the doubt but this could get serious very quickly."

"Yes, I'm sure," said Lisa.

"Fine, but I want Jack outside the door. If there is anything in it, I want two of you in there from minute one."

"Thank you," said Lisa, first to Louth and then silently towards Jack.

As soon as the meeting was over, Lisa called Kelly. The phone rang off, leaving the call to go to her voicemail. Rather than leave a message, Lisa sent her a text. It was one that she hoped would not arouse suspicion.

Kelly, I need those pictures ASAP. Can you pop them into the station? Tough day, so I suggest you take the rest of the day off after that.

Both Jack and Lisa waited. Their eyes stared intently at the screen. In the silence, it felt like they were praying for the phone to spring to life. There was nothing for a minute and then it rang. Lisa looked across to Jack and raised a finger to her lips.

"Hi, Kelly. Where are you?"

"In town. I just needed some air. I'm sorry about how I reacted at the river."

"Forget about it. It was not pleasant for any of us. I just need to download those pictures and then you can call it a day."

"Can I bring them in tomorrow? Or I could try sending them."

"No, don't send them. I want the live picture files as well. How about I meet you in town? Do you fancy a drink?"

"Not really. Are you sure it can't wait?"

"I have to get them in. If I had balls, the DCI would be busting them."

Kelly giggled. The laughter was a combination of nervousness and exhaustion. Lisa's reassurance allowed her to relax for a moment.

"How about a coffee?" asked Kelly. "I'm two minutes from Starbucks on Stonegate."

"I'm on my way. Order me a latte and I'll be there. Grab a receipt and we will sneak it onto our expenses."

Lisa picked up her coat and ran towards the door. Jack went after her and tried to keep up. He was soon left trailing behind as he struggled to get some air into his lungs. It allowed Lisa to get to the driver's seat first even if it was not her own car. That was parked on the other side of the car park and had long since been forgotten.

"Come on, old man, keep up."

"Have you heard the expression, it's a marathon, not a sprint?" Jack gasped.

"Only from old people," replied Lisa. "Now, belt up, literally."

Jack slipped the seatbelt into the slot. It clicked into place, offering some unwelcome pressure on his chest. He needed air and the restriction didn't help. For the first time, Lisa looked across with genuine concern.

"Seriously, Jack, are you alright?"

"I'm not built for running any more."

"Were you ever?"

"Not really."

"That sounds like I might have to put you on an exercise programme."

"I can think of one we could do together," he grinned.

"That sounds fun. Your place or mine?"

"Yours is warmer. Now step on it before Kelly scarpers quicker than either of us can move."

Lisa floored the accelerator and sent Jack jolting back into his seat. The wheels spun on the way out of the car park. As Jack recovered his balance, Lisa took a hard right. It swung Jack into Lisa's lap and left him sprawled across her. She barely noticed until Jack scrabbled to get upright. A left and a right turn sent him tumbling back towards her.

"At least wait until we are home before you jump me," she laughed as one final turn sent Jack crashing against the passenger door.

"If I had wanted bruises, I would have gone to see my ex-wife," sighed Jack.

"I'll dump the car here and go on ahead. Give me five minutes and I'll call you," said Lisa.

"Do you think she will stay that long?"

"Probably not. Better make it two."

Lisa leapt from the car while Jack scribbled out a note for the dashboard. Parked up on a pavement, he wondered whether it would hold much sway with the warden. He did not care. A ticket would be passed off as a police emergency. As Jack watched Lisa disappear, he counted down the seconds before he would follow. Lisa had said five and then two minutes. He would struggle to wait more than one.

***

Kelly was sitting quietly at a corner table. She was tucked away in case Lisa wanted to talk. In front of her, two lattes were untouched. Her phone sat between them, containing the pictures that Lisa had requested. From the moment Kelly had spoken to Lisa, she had rehearsed her story. She needed Lisa to understand her problems but first, she needed her to listen.

Lisa walked through the door and looked around for her colleague. The coffee shop was deserted except for Kelly. It took a moment for Lisa to spot her. Kelly rose briefly and signalled her over. Lisa smiled as she approached. The naivety of the young DC meant that she was trapped.

"I need one of these," huffed Lisa, without picking up her drink. "This has been a seriously grim day."

"Sorry about earlier. I don't know what came over me."

"I told you to forget about it. It happens to all of us. Have you got those pictures?"

"They are on there," said Kelly. Her finger beckoned towards her phone. "Do you want me to have a go at sending them to you?"

"There will be too much to send them all. I've got my laptop in the car. I can download them. Just fire across a couple to get started with."

Kelly picked up her phone and offered the indication that she was trying to send them. She grimaced a couple of times and then frowned. She held the phone up above the table to see if that might make a difference. Throughout the elaborate act, nothing was sent to Lisa.

"I think they have gone through," lied Kelly. "Fingers crossed, they should be coming your way."

"Great; I'll get the guys working on an ID. We can download the rest when we have finished. A guy of that age can't go missing without a few people noticing that he is gone."

"I suppose," sighed Kelly. "How's the coffee?"

"I haven't tried it yet. I'll let it cool first. I think we might be here for a while."

Kelly's face dropped with disappointment. She no longer felt able to talk to Lisa. She bought herself some time by taking a sip of her drink. It was done under the watchful stare of her superior.

"Ouch, that's hot," she commented.

"I told you to leave it for a few minutes," laughed Lisa.

"You're probably right," admitted Kelly.

Lisa watched Kelly place her latte back down. She played the role of being as distracted as Kelly was. A glance at her phone was to play for time before the first question was asked. She knew that when she pressed her colleague for information, things were going to move quickly.

"So, Kelly, how are things with you generally?"

"Fine, I guess."

"How is the surveillance on Jordan Bilby going? We haven't spoken about that for a while."

"Not as exciting as I thought it might be."

"It rarely is. That's something you learn through experience."

"I guess," shrugged Kelly.

"Have you let him get in your knickers yet?" asked Lisa bluntly.

Kelly spluttered and knocked the table when she recoiled back. Her coffee sloshed over the rim of the cup like a child spilling their drink. Kelly picked up a napkin and dabbed at the mess. Only when she had cleaned up the evidence did she look at Lisa and offer a frown.

"What type of question is that?"

"The type a colleague might ask someone who has been evasive since they got the assignment."

"I have not slept with Jordan Bilby!" she snapped.

"But you would like to."

"He is kind of hot but I am supposed to have him under surveillance, not sleep with him." Her voice was a little too loud for their surroundings.

"Now that we are clear on that, tell me about Shaun Farrow."

"What is this, an interrogation?"

"It's a simple question about Shaun Farrow."

"He is a criminal who I knew back in the day."

"To date?"

"Yes, a couple of times. When I joined the police, it was never going to work, so I ended it."

"Why did you go to see him today?"

"Who says I did?"

"Someone who saw you when I dropped you off."

"You mean, Jack?"

"Jack was at the mortuary waiting for that body we looked at. It doesn't matter who saw you. Why were you going to see Shaun Farrow?"

"He wanted to see me."

"Why?"

"You tell me. You're the one with the information."

"Don't get clever with me, Kelly. You will answer my questions or I will leave it to more senior people to ask them. Why were you visiting Shaun Farrow? He has got nothing to do with this case before you try that one."

"He was looking to rekindle our relationship."

"How sweet. I don't believe you."

"He only wanted someone inside the police to provide information, so I told him to naff off."

"I still don't believe you."

"It's the truth. Give me one good reason why I would want to see Shaun Farrow. I told you; I dumped him."

"How about I give you hundreds of thousands of reasons and then you fill in the blanks?"

Lisa's words were the catalyst for the floodgates to open. Kelly could no longer hold back the tears, not with her emotions so close to the surface. It all came out in one long stream of sorrow. Her diatribe of jumbled words made little sense. As she spoke, it was interspersed with deep uncontrollable sobbing.

Lisa bided her time. While her colleague continued to cry, Jack walked in through the front door. Kelly barely noticed, such was the upset coursing through her. Jack approached the table and stood alongside Lisa.

"Have I called at a bad time?" he whispered. The hint of a smile from Lisa told him that she had made some progress.

For the next hour, Kelly took Jack and Lisa through the full details of her relationship with Jordan Bilby. She recounted how she had got to know him and the pulse of excitement she had felt. She had expected him to make his move on her. Then came the winnings, the dresses and that feeling of being something special. It was followed by the darkness of her spiralling losses.

It shocked Lisa to hear the figures that Kelly claimed were her debts to Jordan. Jack was less surprised. He had seen Jordan Bilby's type before. He preyed on vulnerable people and tossed them away when he had enjoyed his moment of fun. In so many ways, he was just like Marcus Tummel. Jack would take as much delight in bringing him down as he had with Marcus.

The statement about Spencer was the most shocking. Kelly offered her recollection of seeing him being thrown out of the casino. Lisa was furious. Why had Kelly not mentioned that at the river? Every piece of information was needed.

It was Jack who calmed her down. They needed to keep the flow of information coming from Kelly. There would be another time for anger and to cross-examine Kelly's morals. That opportunity would come once all the information had been extracted. For now, they had to keep her talking.

As Kelly continued, Jack and Lisa began to look more horrified. Kelly told them about her drunken conversation with Jordan and the proposition he had made to her. Like Kelly, they had expected the punchline to be some form of sordid act in lieu of her debts. Kelly was attractive. A man taking advantage of her vulnerability would come as no surprise.

"Let's get this straight," confirmed Jack. "Are you saying that Jordan Bilby wants you to play some form of game to clear your debts?"

"It is for more than just my debts. There will be a million pounds on the table."

"That's a pretty big table," said Lisa. It was never meant to sound as flippant as it came out.

"What happens if you lose?" asked Jack. The question made Kelly cry.

"I take it you are not walking out of there," said Lisa.

Kelly shook her head and then dropped her face into her hands.

"Did he actually say that you would be killed?" asked Jack.

"Not in as many words. He just said that one way or another, one of us would make a killing."

"So who is your opponent?"

"I don't know. I just got told it was a high-roller and that I would be called with a time and a place for the game when they were ready."

"It has got to be Jordan," said Lisa.

"No, he's a fixer," replied Jack. "There will be somebody rich on the end of this who is playing for kicks. I would guess it will be somebody with plenty of money to burn and who has a sadistic streak, particularly with the ladies."

"Have you got someone in mind?"

"Not necessarily but I know somebody who fits the profile perfectly."

Chapter 26

Jack, Lisa and Kelly travelled back to the station together. Again, Lisa drove, this time with more care and attention. Jack sat in the back, allowing him to keep an eye on Kelly. There was no need. She was too busy sobbing to do anything stupid.

For the majority of the time, that was the only noise to interrupt the silence. There was little anyone could say after such an intense session in the coffee shop. To make light of it with idle chit-chat would be wrong. Saying nothing was hardly a better solution.

The eeriness was broken by a call on Jack's phone. It put some welcome noise into the car. Jack did not recognise the number. He used it to offer some relief in the sombre atmosphere.

"I think I am about to be sold insurance," said Jack. He stared down at the screen, wondering whether to answer.

"I get them," added Lisa, keen to offer something back. "They always want to sell me breakdown cover. Mind you, that's better than that idiot who always calls on a Sunday afternoon to sell me a conservatory."

"What's wrong with that?" asked Kelly.

"I live in a first-floor flat," Lisa replied, as Jack took the phone to his ear.

"DI Jack Husker; can I help you?"

The tone was blunt and was offered with maximum offence. It caught Lisa's attention and had her glancing in the rear-view mirror. Something had provoked Jack's reaction. That amount of irritation would normally be reserved for an ex-wife.

Jack listened to the upper-class voice of Marcus Tummel. His manner was slightly more contrite than when they had last spoken. His usual arrogance was suppressed by the need for information. That was something that Jack was not going to offer. It soon returned Marcus to his usual self.

"Look, DI Husker, if you are not concerned about one of my stable girls going missing, that is your lookout. Just don't come crying to me if she turns up as another of your unsolved murders, which, quite frankly, there seems to be a lot of."

"A stable girl, you say?"

"Yes, she has gone missing."

"Can I ask where you last left her? Was she sobbing in a secluded barn or was she in the marital bed?"

"I beg your pardon?"

"It's just that I heard it might be a little empty these days."

"I could report you for that, you arrogant swine!"

"And then how would I find your stable girl? I wouldn't want to leave you short for the weekend."

Lisa smiled. She had worked out who Jack was speaking to. She listened intently and tried to catch some of Marcus's words.

She leaned back to cut out the noise in the background. She did not have to make much effort to hear Marcus's anger.

"Are you going to help me or not?"

"I would love to. Which one of your girls has gone missing?"

"It's Elizabeth."

"Elizabeth? Do I know an Elizabeth?"

"You should do. Elizabeth Moss is the daughter of the councillor in York."

"Oh, that Elizabeth."

"Do you want some details about her?"

"No need, Mr Tummel. I know where she is."

"You do?"

"Yes."

"Where is she?"

"She is far enough away for you to keep your lecherous hands off her. Enjoy your day."

He ended the call and winked towards the rear-view mirror. Lisa shook her head. Suddenly, the day had taken a turn for the better. Marcus Tummel would be fuming. His mood was unlikely to improve in the near future.

***

DCI Louth was waiting impatiently at the station. He paced up and down and then settled into a chair. He tapped a pen on his desk and continually checked his phone for updates. It was Jack who had told him they were on their way.

When the three detectives arrived, they were ushered into a room. Louth allowed them to sit down and closed the door behind them. He had cleared his diary and his phone had been redirected to messages for as long as the meeting needed. Louth had been briefed with enough details to make him understand the importance. He was angry and yet concerned at the same time.

The lack of any conversation was troubling. Jack had not even hinted at wanting a coffee. Louth studied the group. It was a slow and deliberate move. His eyes went from Jack to Lisa and then to Kelly. It was an unnerving moment even for the most experienced in the room. Unable to hold out, Lisa decided to break the silence.

"If you will allow me to summarise where we are up to, it appears that we have a lead for the killings. As you know, DC Knox has been undercover in the casino. As part of her work, she has been invited to a high-stakes gambling event. We don't know all the details about it or how we got to this position. However, we believe that she would need to put her life on the line to participate."

"Her life?" queried Louth.

"Yes, it would appear so."

"That is ridiculous. Who on earth would take part in a game like that?"

"Someone who is very desperate," offered Jack. "Perhaps, someone who is up to their neck in debt."

Jack glanced at Kelly who flushed red with shame.

"Who else will be at this game?"

"We don't know," admitted Lisa.

"Where is it being held?"

"We don't know that either, sir."

"Right, we need to find out."

"All DC Knox has been told is that she will be given a time and a location by Jordan Bilby."

"Is Jordan her opponent?"

"We don't think so," said Jack. "We think it will be one of his high-rollers. DC Knox saw a back room full of such people."

"Bloody hell, Jack. That's a pretty sick individual."

"I know. Money does some strange things to people."

Jack's words only made Kelly feel worse.

"With your permission, sir, we would like to run a sting operation," offered Lisa.

"A sting operation!" blurted out DCI Louth. "We are talking about life and death here."

"We would like to draw out the suspect."

"We cannot use one of our officers as bait," stated Louth.

"Sir, I don't like to use the term 'bait'," said Lisa. "If DC Knox is willing, we would like her to set up the meeting. We will then raid that meeting and arrest those who are present."

Kelly Knox shuddered at the use of her name. Not just at being name-checked while present but more at the formality of her title. She had been proud to be made a detective. Now, it was hers to lose. There had been no suggestions of repercussions but they would come. When the truth came out, her role within the police would be over.

"I'm not sure this is a good idea," said DCI Louth. He stared over in Kelly's direction.

She offered nothing other than a look of fear. There was no winning in her eyes. Her fate was to be decided between Jordan Bilby and police standards. Neither would offer her a future. Everybody in the room knew that even if they were not prepared to say it.

"This is the break we need," insisted Lisa. "We know that Jordan Bilby is some form of fixer in this. We just don't know who he is fixing for."

"This has danger written all over it. I am not putting any of my team in that position."

The room fell silent. The words of Louth were contemplated by all. He was right. The danger of the situation was at the forefront of everybody's minds. Nobody needed that explaining to them.

Jack took a moment to study Louth's face. He knew it was a risk that he would take. He would put himself in the firing line to get a result. And yet with Kelly, it was different. It was not a call he could make on behalf of a youngster who had her whole life ahead of her.

"I want to do it," said Kelly. "I got us into this mess. It is only right that I help solve the problem."

She was barely able to look at the others when she said the words. It was unconvincing. The tone suggested that it was said through expectation rather than a willingness to get the job done. Inside, she was in turmoil. Her thoughts had turned to the conversation she would need to have with her parents. For too long, she had kept them at arm's length. Now things were getting tough, she needed their support.

"We cannot ask you to do it," said Louth. "We will find another way."

"No!" she barked. Her assertiveness caught the audience by surprise. It was sharp and bordering on rudeness. Louth frowned, to which Kelly blushed. She scanned the room, hoping that someone would back her up. When they didn't, she was forced into an apology. "I'm sorry; I didn't mean to be rude. All I am saying is that I am happy to do it."

Louth was in no mood to make things more difficult for her. "It's fine. Apology accepted. I know you are under pressure and we will sort this mess out. I am sure there is a complex story to come out. Whatever it is, you will get my full support."

"Thank you," said Kelly even if she didn't believe his words.

"Why don't we get DC Knox to set up the meeting and then we can take over?" asked Lisa.

"It won't work," interrupted Jack. "If she doesn't show up, they will have an exit plan. What case are we going to bring if we raid a casino and find a gambling table and some cash? She will have to go in there."

"That's a fair point. Do you think it will be at the casino?" asked Louth.

"I don't know. I suspect the initial meeting point will be close by. Where they go from there, who knows? They must have somewhere very private."

"So what are you suggesting?" asked Louth.

"I think we need to get a time and a place and then we decide. We can't be any worse off for knowing that."

"Famous last words," nodded Lisa.

"Jack is right," said Louth. "How easily can we find out that information?"

"I can text Jordan right now," offered Kelly.

"Then do it."

Have we got the game sorted yet? I need to get this over with. Kx

Kelly showed the text to the three detectives to seek approval. They nodded to accept what she had written. She sent it and watched everyone hold their breath. At first, there was nothing. Then a call came through from a number she did not recognise.

"You had better answer that," said Louth.

"Hi, it's Kelly."

"It's Jordan. I haven't got long. Come to the back of the casino tonight at ten o'clock. It's the solid door to the left of the first one you come to."

"What's the game?"

"Texas Hold'em. You do know how to play, don't you?"

"Of course I do."

"I will see you at ten. Bye."

Kelly put the phone down and turned to the group. She had one burning question in her mind.

"What is Texas Hold'em?"

CHAPTER 27

AFTER SEVERAL HOURS OF meticulous planning, every detective knew their role. Jack had played his trump card by lining up an unknown face to help them. Dan Millings was to be the man on the inside. Dan had leapt at the role being offered. It was an opportunity to go back into the field and be on the sharp end of the action. He had listened to the warnings about not doing anything without backup. A fake identity had been produced, including a card that would match a name Kelly insisted was on the entry database. She was adamant that it would never be checked.

Jack and Lisa were ready with the team to raid the building. Nearly twenty officers were on hand, all prepared to do their job. They had been kept in one area of the station for most of the afternoon. Nothing was going to leak out. Louth had made sure of it. He was still sore from the story about Marcus Tummel coming from his station. It would not happen again. Nobody was going to be sneaking out of the room with their phone when Kelly's life was at stake.

Kelly was ready to play the crucial role. After an afternoon of uncertainty and regret, it was Lisa who had accompanied her home. Never left alone for one moment, she had gone back to collect some suitable attire for the evening. After offering some initial reluctance, she had selected a tight mini-dress. It was the one which had been paid for out of her initial winnings. Lisa did not need to know that. Kelly had held it up in front of her body and looked into the mirror nervously. Her heart was racing at the thought of what might happen.

"Are you sure you are going to be able to wear that? Remember, you have to wear a wire."

"I have to. Jordan will be expecting me in something like this."

"I'm not sure I want to know any more."

"It's not something I am proud of."

They had left it at that and had driven back to join the others at the station. Kelly was pleased the visit home had taken place while her parents were out. It would have been hard enough if she was there alone. To have to explain Lisa's presence would have been a step too far.

There was silence on the journey back. Kelly could not say anything when her heart was pounding inside her chest. She knew what she was getting herself into. Her account of what had happened had only scratched the surface of the truth. Would DCI Louth still support her when it all came out?

Once back at the station, Kelly was taken into the main room. It was Lisa's insistence that she should only get ready when she had to. Her thoughts were on that dress. She did not want Kelly to parade herself in front of the uniforms. It would be a meat market once the lecherous fantasies started going through the officers' heads. She was better getting changed just before she put on a coat to head to the casino.

"Do we need to go through the details again?" asked Louth.

Everyone shook their heads. They had gone through their roles and knew what they had to do. Dan was already in place on the inside. He had texted to confirm that the casino was quiet. Jordan Bilby had made a brief appearance. Dan had sat with a glass of Coke and studied him. The man seemed to check everything before he disappeared into the office.

At nine-thirty, Kelly was ready. She had eased into her dress under Lisa's guidance. Kelly wanted her there to offer some reassurance. It was Lisa who slipped the wire down her front. The tightness of the dress made it difficult to conceal the smallest item. With little time for dignity, Lisa reached through the dress and pulled it through. Kelly squirmed against the obvious intrusion.

"I'm sorry," said Lisa. "There isn't an easy way to do this."

"It's fine. It's a bit like a drunken grope."

"Thanks. I'll work on my technique."

"I'm sorry. It's just…well…I haven't got much on under this dress."

"Trust me, I have worked that out. I'm impressed that you managed to get anything under it."

"Do you think the wire will show?"

"Not if it is left alone. Whatever happens, you must avoid physical contact. One touch and it will be obvious."

"I'll do my best not to get touched up," smiled Kelly.

"That might be difficult in this dress."

Kelly blushed a deep shade of red. She remembered how she had happily worn it when she wanted to attract Jordan's attention on a previous visit. It shamed her to even think about where the events had taken her. Now, she was just a piece of eye candy. She was there to be looked at. It felt like it was the lowest she could sink to and yet something told her there was still further to go.

Once Kelly was ready, Lisa wrapped a coat around her. There was a moment of uncertainty and then they walked into the main room. All eyes were on Kelly who clutched the coat tightly around her. Nobody was going to get sight of her until it was necessary.

A final reminder was offered by Louth before they left. It did nothing to reassure Kelly. When she went in there, she would be on her own. Lisa could see her troubled state and gripped her arm tightly.

"Come on, you can do this," she insisted.

"I hope you are right," sighed Kelly. "Can we do one last check that I have got everything?"

Kelly held out her bag. Inside were all the things a girl could be expected to take on a night out. Added to it was a pepper spray. She knew that she would be searched on the way in. The spray was something she could argue that she carried for personal safety. Any police accoutrements had been removed.

"We'll get the technical guys to test the wire outside," insisted Lisa. "Otherwise, you'll never get out of here."

Kelly forced a smile. Maybe that was not the worst outcome on offer.

After the checks, Lisa accompanied Kelly to an unmarked car outside the station. They got in and waited for the uniforms to be loaded into two vans behind them. Kelly sat in silence, with Lisa beside her. It would be a sombre journey to the casino.

***

They arrived just before ten o'clock. Lisa looked across and waited for confirmation that the vans were in position. When she was told they were, she turned towards Kelly.

"Are you ready?"

"I suppose."

"Don't do anything I wouldn't do," said Lisa. Her attempt at humour was lost on her colleague.

Kelly got out and pulled her coat tight across her. She made her way to the back door of the casino. Lisa was straight on the radio. Her message was loud and clear.

"She's going in," said Lisa. "Everybody on standby, please."

The two vans were packed full of officers. Each of them was primed for a command to send them in. An excited tension filled the air. It was the type of tension that only a raid could bring. Some lived for that moment of adrenalin.

Kelly walked tentatively. She was shaking, not that Jordan would expect anything else. She passed the back door of the casino and walked on a few paces. Once she was standing by the solid metal door, she knocked twice. There was a pause before she heard a bolt clicking. The heavy metal barrier was pushed open.

It left her staring into a dark corridor, with a small room off to the side. As her eyes started to adjust to the change in light, she recognised the face of Jordan Bilby. For once, he looked less assured. There was a hint of nerves about his manner. He held out his hand to beckon Kelly into the side room. He followed her into a space that was no more than six feet by six feet. Inside, there was a small table, a cupboard and four bare walls. The place was devoid of anything to make it homely.

"Welcome, Kelly. You are a lucky girl. I don't normally offer a meet and greet service. I guess that is the advantage of being a VIP," he grinned.

"What are we doing in here?" asked Kelly.

"This is where you leave your personal items," replied Jordan.

"Where is the game?"

"Down the corridor."

"Is that the back room behind your office that you showed me?"

"No, that is the official back room. This one is a little more discrete. It keeps the riff-raff away. Why don't you take off your coat and leave your bag on the table?"

It sounded sinister. His normally charismatic tone was replaced by a flat instruction. It felt like he was stripping Kelly of anything that would identify her. Already, the thought of standing there in her dress filled her with dread. He repulsed her. Her stomach churned in his presence. Kelly struggled to understand how she had ever harboured any feelings for him.

"How does this work?"

"Your opponent is waiting. I suggest we move things along."

"What are the rules of the game?"

"I told you; Texas Hold'em."

"You might like to give me a clue about pot sizes and starting blinds. How do they increase? It makes quite a difference to how I play," offered Kelly. She rattled off all the terminology she had been briefed with.

Her forthrightness startled Jordan. His shifty nature was a direct response to the barrage of questions. He wondered how much Kelly needed to know. If she walked out, he was in trouble. His paymaster was never the most forgiving of people.

"Your opponent will explain the rules to you in detail. I don't think you will find them very different to any other poker game, other than the stakes you are playing for. Now, if you don't mind, take off your coat and put your bag on the table. It is time to play cards."

Kelly felt the pulse of nervousness go through her. She knew the backup team were listening. They were waiting to spring when she gave the instruction. So far, she had got nothing from Jordan that would incriminate him. Her efforts to probe had fallen short.

"Are you sure you can't tell me anything more?" asked Kelly.

"As I said, your opponent will explain everything," said Jordan. He offered his hand to take her coat.

Kelly placed her bag down and slipped her coat from her shoulders. It allowed Jordan to stare directly at her. At least his hands were occupied though it was not for long. He placed her coat on the table and turned to eye Kelly's figure.

"I have always liked that dress," he smiled.

"I know. That's why I wore it."

He moved closer than she would have liked. Jordan's hand went behind her to cup one of her buttocks. He gave it a sly squeeze, which caused Kelly's body to stiffen against his touch. Frozen in fear from the assault, she stood silently while Jordan went to work.

He smiled at her lack of reaction. Growing in confidence, he began to run his hand up her back. Her thoughts turned to the wire she was concealing and how close he was to feeling it. Kelly felt a surge of panic. She had to do something or the operation would be blown.

"What are you doing?" she forced out, the words a strain to deliver.

He smiled and moved his face closer to hers. He whispered softly in her ear.

"I am under strict instructions to make sure that I search you thoroughly before you go in. We also might not see each other again, so we should make the most of this moment."

"Do you really think I could hide anything under this dress?"

"That is what I intend to find out," he replied. His hand began to slide from her back towards her chest.

"Touch the front and I will gouge your eyes out," she growled. Her eyes were fiery in their resolve.

"Okay, calm down; message understood," he replied. Jordan stepped away and raised his hands in appeasement. "You had better go in and good luck. It is a shame we did not get to know each other a little better."

As Kelly walked away, a hard slap to her bottom sent her forward. The sound echoed around the empty space. Her head swivelled to shoot a scowl back in the direction of Jordan's smug face. She could have happily ripped his head off and then kicked it down the corridor. That anger only seemed to excite him. He offered a smile and blew a patronising kiss towards her.

Chapter 28

Jack's eyes scanned the officers behind him. They were poised to make their move. Testosterone-fuelled, they looked primed to go in. They were like an over-eager body of scouts. He could sense the excitement in them. Their training had prepared them for the moment ahead. It was not unlike how Jack felt when a major crime had been committed.

"Hold your positions," he commanded.

He feared that they would make their move too early. It was a fine balance between protecting Kelly and making sure they got the evidence they needed. One shot was all they would get at it. Jack feared that Kelly's opponent also intended to deliver no more than that.

In the second van, DCI Louth was just as ready. Lisa was outside as the runner between them. Dressed in jeans and a jumper, she was wrapped up against the elements. She was considered the one least likely to arouse suspicion. Dan was in contact with her and confirmed repeatedly that nothing was going on in the public area.

They had surveyed the plans of the site before the mission. Kelly was in an unmarked area. It was neither an old outbuilding nor a developed yard. Their survey of the place had shown no signs of a habitable building. The wire was their only link to her and it had already confirmed the presence of Jordan Bilby.

They had listened carefully to the exchange between them. The tension had grown when Jordan was making his move. Louth had questioned whether they should go in, only for Jack to tell him to hold his nerve. It made for uncomfortable listening and yet Jack had every faith in the young lady. Kelly could handle the situation and would cry out if she needed assistance. If Jordan pushed his luck any further, he might be the one who needed their help.

Lisa slipped into Jack's van to get an update. Jack chose to offer a sanitised version of the events on the inside. Lisa would be in a difficult position if she thought Kelly might be under pressure. Jack assured her that she was doing well. The tracker in her handbag meant they knew where Kelly was in the building. The only concern was that Jordan had separated Kelly from her bag.

***

Inside the dark space, Kelly walked nervously down the corridor. She was still spitting with fury. How dare the man touch her like that? His hand had been invasive and had gone so close to the wire. She would take great pleasure in seeing him being arrested.

He had ruined her career. Worse still, he had taken liberties with her.

She struggled to know how she had ever found him alluring. Her repulsion overtook her nerves for a moment. That soon changed. Her movement down the corridor brought her back to the present. The darkness felt like it was closing in on her. All she could see was the door ahead of her.

She looked back briefly. In the gloomy light, she could make out the figure of Jordan. He was watching her. It was best not to react when a support team was ready to strike. Kelly took hold of the metal handle and squeezed it in her hand. When it turned, it opened up a secretive world behind it.

As she peered inside, she could see a seated figure. Sitting at a cloth-covered table, her opponent had eased back away from the light which shone down from above. It was impossible to make out the details of their form. Kelly noted the narrow shoulders and the hair which appeared to cascade down beyond their neck.

Kelly allowed the door to close behind her. The clang of it shutting sent a jolt of panic through her. Unable to settle, she shuffled over to the table. It was then that she saw the bundles of cash along with a gun to the side. A shudder went through her. Her legs were threatening to give way under the strain.

She knew that the gun was there to scare her. With Jack and Lisa poised outside, she had nothing to fear. But what if things got out of hand? The instructions had been clear. The game must not be allowed to start. The officers would move in long before it did. Kelly's only task was to find a safe position while they stormed the room. In such a small space, that was impossible. There was nowhere to go other than to face down her opponent.

"It's Ms Knox, isn't it? May I call you Kelly?"

The voice shocked her. Instead of the harsh masculine tone that she was expecting, the softer sound of a woman was speaking to her. Kelly looked directly at the figure and saw the cruel smile of a lady staring back at her. In her forties and distinctly attractive, it took Kelly a moment to recognise her. When she did, she recoiled in horror.

Laura Tummel was staring directly at her, with the same leering eyes that Jordan had offered before. It was all she could do not to blurt out her name. Kelly tried to avoid offering any clues that she knew her.

"Kelly is fine."

"Please take a seat, Kelly."

"Thanks," she said quietly.

"And what do you do for a living, Kelly?" Laura asked. Her questioning put Kelly on edge.

"I am between jobs at the moment."

"And boyfriends?"

"I'm between them at the moment as well. It has been a long while on that front," she added. It was an attempt to portray herself as being alone.

"I find that hard to believe with a pretty girl like you."

"I am just on a bad run."

"Which brings us here, I guess."

"I guess so," sighed Kelly.

"Jordan tells me that you are a pretty impressive gambler, so I am expecting a tough game. Have the rules been explained to you?"

"Not all of them. What is the blind structure?"

"How about I do a full recap? We are playing heads-up Texas Hold'em with half-million stacks. Starting blinds are five and ten thousand. The blinds will double every ten hands. We will play until one of us is eliminated. If you win, there is a million pounds for you to take. Most of it is in the case over there. The rest is on the table. Something tells me a lady like you would not find it difficult to spend that amount of money."

"And if I lose?"

"Do you really want me to spell that out to you?"

"I would like to know how long I have got," said Kelly, solely for the benefit of the listeners.

"About as long as it takes for me to pick up the gun and shoot you in the head."

Kelly went pale. She shivered at the bluntness of the words. Her reaction was not lost on her opponent. Laura savoured every second of her flinching. It was delightful to see Kelly squirming in her seat. The girl was stunning and crying out to take that bullet. If she could watch her suffer, the feeling would only get better.

A wave of sadistic pleasure rippled through Laura. A second surge accompanied the thrill of watching the attractive young girl screw up her face. It was such a waste and yet that was part of the pleasure. It was a satisfaction that nothing else could give her. Sex with Marcus was good and it was even better with Kit. Nothing could compare to the feeling of ending someone's life.

"How can I be sure that I will get the money if I win?" asked Kelly.

"You simply pick up the case and walk out of here. It's up to you whether you want to bother with the few thousand that is on the table."

"Will we ever see each other again?" confirmed Kelly.

"That is up to you. I think we both know that I will see you again in a few months," laughed Laura.

"What do you mean?"

"Come on, Kelly, we both know the phrase. Once a gambler, always a gambler. That money will be lost within weeks. You will be back in here begging Jordan for another shot, if you will excuse the pun."

"I won't!" snapped Kelly, in a desperate bid to convince herself.

"We both know that you will, which is a shame. With a body like yours, there is so much more you could achieve with it."

"You mean like you have?" she growled back.

Laura recoiled at the sudden change in tone. She looked deep into Kelly's eyes, almost interrogating her with her stare. She was no longer such an innocent young thing. For the first time, Laura felt discomfort.

"What do you know about me?" she asked. She placed her hand over the gun ahead of Kelly answering.

Kelly could feel panic surging through her. She glanced towards the door and saw there was no handle on the inside. There were no exits to get out. She was stuck in the room with Laura. It put her in immediate danger, which would leave Jack and the team with no time to strike. She had to control the situation.

She took a breath and turned towards Laura. Her hands were linked together to calm them. Once the trembling stopped, she picked up a chip and played with it between her fingers. Despite her training, she had no idea of its value.

"I just figured that if you could afford to play for a million pounds, you must have done pretty well for yourself. Come on, let's play cards. I am feeling lucky tonight."

Her response did nothing to settle Laura even though her hand did lift from the weapon. Not all the way but far enough to take away the immediate risk. Kelly was on a countdown, knowing that she had sent the signal. Those carefully chosen words were her call for the building to be stormed. It would bring the raiding teams from the vans and end the charade that she was playing.

***

Except, there was silence. Contact had been lost when the door to the concealed room had been closed. It had stirred Jack into action. He was demanding that the technical team regain the connection. They were adamant that the problem was not at their end, with tempers fraying by the second. First, Jack and then DCI Louth erupted.

"Right, we're going in," demanded Jack.

"Hang on," said Louth. "Just give them a moment to see if they can re-establish the connection."

"No way. I'm not leaving Kelly in there alone."

"One minute; that is all I'm asking.

"Kelly could be dead by then," snarled Jack.

"Then she shouldn't be in there. Mike, what can you do for us?"

Mike Walters stared at the equipment. His place on the team was solely down to his ability to make communications happen. He had formed a reputation in the force as someone useful to know. He was at his best when locked in a room with equipment surrounding him on all four sides. A surveillance van was just about perfect for him other than the people cluttering the space around him.

"I might have something," said Mike while manipulating the dials with a dexterity a piano player would have been proud of.

There was a crackle and then nothing. A moment of annoyance was ended by the sound of a faint whisper. It was impossible to make out the conversation, other than two voices having some form of an exchange.

"That could be anybody," said Jack. "For all we know, it might be the neighbours discussing a shopping list."

"It's definitely the same source," insisted Mike. "It's just very faint. They must be in a room with some form of lining to dampen the signal."

"Can you amplify the voices or not?" asked Jack.

"I think so but it will take time."

"Time is not a luxury we have."

***

Kelly watched Laura complete the dealing formalities. She was already past the point that she wanted to get to. She shifted nervously in her seat. Twice, she had got up and wandered around in her frantic state. It made no sense that it was still quiet. Her signal had been clear. By now, the building should have been filled with officers. She patted her chest under the guise of clearing her throat. The only purpose was to make sure the wire was still in place. When she got up for a third time, Laura Tummel lost her patience.

"Please will you sit down?" said Laura. The cards and the blind bets were in place. All she needed was for her opponent to play.

For Kelly, the whole game felt alien. Her knowledge was limited to the small amount of tuition the force could provide. Just one member of the team seemed to know the rules and his instructions had made no sense. She needed rescuing and that needed to happen right now.

"For the last time, Kelly, you need to sit down. If you don't, I will consider the game over." Laura reached towards the gun to confirm her next move.

"Sorry, I am just nervous," replied Kelly. She slid back into her seat and stared over the table at her opponent.

"You might be but you agreed to play the game. Shall we start?"

Kelly remembered Louth's instruction that under no circumstances was she to begin the game. And yet what was she supposed to do when Laura Tummel had her at gunpoint? She thought for a moment and flexed her hands as if readying herself for the skirmish ahead. Laura had already bent up the corners of the two cards in front of her and was staring in Kelly's direction.

"Okay, let's play cards. I am feeling lucky tonight," said Kelly, hoping her repeated signal would force some action. She reached forward to look at what she had been dealt.

"You already said that. How about less chatter and more poker?" growled Laura whose eyes had narrowed down to offer a spiteful stare.

Kelly peered at her cards. A four of spades was paired up with an eight of clubs. They were two cards that she would be expected to discard. And yet, on the small blind, she could try to stay in without much commitment. It would allow her to stretch out the game and buy herself some time.

"I'll check," she stated. Kelly pushed enough chips in to even up the bet that had been made.

"Excuse me?" queried Laura.

"I said, I'll check."

"You mean, you'll call."

"Check, call, it all means the same thing," said Kelly hastily, dismissing the technicality that Laura was noting.

"It doesn't, but whatever. I'll raise you thirty-thousand," she declared. Laura counted out the necessary chips and pushed them forward.

The speed with which she acted caught Kelly off-guard. It was designed to bully her. Kelly's reaction was flustered. She pushed her cards into the centre of the table. In the absence of any words, Laura scowled again. Her eyes tore into her opponent.

"Oh, yes, I'll fold," declared Kelly belatedly. A moment of uncertainty went through her as she tried to remember the words from the briefing.

Laura swept up the chips and the cards. She shuffled and dealt the next hand. She pushed her small blind into the centre and moved the dealer's button. A glance at Kelly was followed by a shake of her head. Rather than wait for her opponent to act, she dragged the big blind in from Kelly's pile of chips. As they both looked at their cards, Laura tested the water with a bet. It was purely for information, with little in her hand to back up her move.

"I'll raise thirty-thousand."

Kelly took one look at her cards and announced that she was folding. She never even considered making a bet. Laura thought for a moment and then claimed the pot.

Her efficiency soon had the next hand in play. This time, she studied Kelly. Something felt wrong. The girl did not appear to care about the cards. It put Laura on edge. There was a lack of tension in the room and that made the game difficult to enjoy.

"Call," announced Kelly immediately. She took the opportunity to align her terminology after taking a peek at her cards. The five thousand she needed was pushed to the centre of the table without even looking at her opponent.

Again, Laura raised. This time, it was only ten thousand, offering a cheap opportunity to see the next three cards. Kelly took another look at her hand. She shook her head and pushed her cards to the centre of the table.

"I'll fold."

"Do you understand the game you are playing?" snarled Laura.

"I'm just waiting for the right cards," replied Kelly.

"You might be dead by then. This is head-to-head, you know."

"You don't need to remind me."

On the fourth hand, Kelly folded again to Laura's raise. The move ignited the fury inside her. Laura was raging that her pair of kings had not been seen even though her bet was small. She stood up and towered over Kelly. Her eyes were full of fire and it was threatening to explode at any moment. She was ready to kill her. She would blow Kelly's brains out just to rid herself of the frustration that was engulfing her body.

"Right, that's it! What's your game?"

"I told you; I'm waiting for good cards. It's my life and I will play it my way."

"And what is wrong with these cards?" snapped Laura. She turned over Kelly's discarded cards.

"It's a three and a seven and you are not allowed to do that," insisted Kelly. "That means you have to forfeit the game."

It forced Laura back into her seat. Her eyes opened wide and her mouth dropped open. In a daze, her face blushed red with shame. She had crossed a line and regretted the act the moment she had picked up the cards. In front of her, Kelly was leaning over the table aggressively. She was determined to seize her opportunity to take the moral high ground. Laura shook her head against the withering stare and then walked away from the table.

The gun was forgotten, with Kelly's eyes moving towards it. Laura's focus had been taken away by her breach of etiquette. To Kelly, it felt odd to have somebody with such high morals in poker and yet with so little regard for life itself.

***

"All backup, move in, now! Go go go!" called out Jack. He was unprepared to wait any longer. There had been no discussion with DCI Louth before he made the call. With his fear for Kelly spurring him on, he signalled for twenty armed men to run for the door.

Jack chased behind them, with Lisa following a few paces back. It caught Louth out and left him sitting alone in the van. He jumped up and went after the group. He did not want to miss being a set of boots on the ground. It was his team. He would make sure that he was in there with them, especially if there were arrests to be made.

The back door was smashed open. The battering ram took three attempts to force the bolts from their housing. A startled Jordan Bilby was met by an army of officers. He was forced into the small room where the cuffs were slapped on his wrists. His protestations were lost in the melee.

The rest of the manpower went charging down the corridor with their flashlights pointing from the front of their guns. Their target was the door at the end of the corridor. They smashed it open to send the raiding party into the room with great noise. It was like a herd of animals stampeding through the forest.

"Police, get on the floor!"

Inside, Kelly was standing with both hands on the gun. The barrel was aimed at a terrified Laura Tummel whose back was pressed against the wall. Her hands were high above her head and her eyes were wide open with fear. Kelly was shaking uncontrollably and had her finger pressed on the trigger. She had already decided that she would finish it.

Kelly moved towards Laura and traced the gun up her until it was pressed hard into her forehead. Her hatred for the woman went through her. For the first time in days, Kelly allowed herself to smile. She looked Laura in the eye and increased the pressure on the trigger.

"Drop the weapon!" came the command. A hand went up to hold back the other officers outside the room.

Kelly never moved. She continued to savour the terror on Laura Tummel's face. It was one thing neither she nor Jordan Bilby could take away from her. Her life and her career were over. They had cost her everything. Now the bitch was going to die.

"I said, drop the weapon!"

Kelly pushed the gun forward with enough force to make Laura wince. She was driving it into her forehead to make sure she did not move. Behind her, Jack pushed through to the front and beckoned the armed officer to lower his weapon. In the hush of the room, the officer eased back as far as he could.

"Kelly, put the gun down," said Jack. "It's over."

"Not yet, it isn't. I'm going to kill her."

"Kelly, put the gun down," urged Jack. He inched towards her. "She isn't worth it."

"Jack, I'm sorry. This is going to end now," insisted Kelly.

"Kelly, please," urged Jack. "Don't ruin your life because of her."

Kelly glanced over her shoulder and smiled. She shook her head and then turned back to Laura. She edged closer as the grin spread further across her face. There would be no backing down. Laura Tummel was going to die.

"Kelly, don't waste your life. You'll go to prison."

"I don't care," she snarled. "I'm going to kill her."

"Think of your family," insisted Jack.

Kelly took a deep breath. For the first time, her hold on the gun weakened. Her parents flashed into her mind. No matter her hatred for Laura, she could not do that to them.

"Please, put the gun down," offered Jack. As he said it, he reached up and eased it from her hand. He passed it back towards the officer behind him and allowed himself a small exhale of breath.

"DI Husker, I never thought I would say I was pleased to see you," said Laura Tummel. "I hope you are going to arrest this girl for kidnapping me and for attempted murder. She probably killed those other people as well."

Jack shook his head at Laura. He had little energy left to argue with her.

"Don't waste your breath," he sighed. He looked back towards the officers. "You can cuff her and I bet that isn't the first time a man has said that to her."

Laura Tummel lunged in Jack's direction. Two officers stepped in and restrained her futile resistance. Jack had already turned to Kelly who had disappeared into Lisa's arms. There were no tears though they both knew it would only be a matter of time before they came.

"You did well," Jack said. "Very well."

"Did you get Jordan?" asked Kelly.

"Yes, he's in the other room."

"Can I see him?" she asked suddenly.

"Why?"

"I just want to say something to him."

"Kelly, that is not a good idea," said Lisa.

"Please."

"Just leave it," urged Lisa.

"This might be the last time I can speak to him as a police officer, so it would mean a lot to me," offered Kelly.

"Okay," said Lisa, "Just don't do anything stupid."

"You can come with me if you want."

"We will."

They walked down the corridor towards the small room where Jordan Bilby was being held. Behind them, Laura Tummel was cuffed and ready to be escorted to the van. Kelly turned and came face to face with Jordan. His hands were secured behind his back while two officers held him by the shoulders.

The sickening grin that Jordan always offered appeared on his face. He smiled at Kelly and savoured his last moment of control. Before he could say anything, Kelly lunged forward and cracked her palm across his face. It was like an explosion and it left her hand imprinted on his cheek.

"That's for thinking you could play with me like a toy," she snarled.

The sudden act of violence did nothing to remove the smile from his face. Jordan's eyes drifted down her as he mentally stripped Kelly of her dress. He leered at her and nodded to confirm what he was thinking. Kelly slapped him for a second time. It was just as brutal and sent his head jerking to one side.

"That's for putting your disgusting hands on me."

Jordan flexed his jaw to ride out the hurt. After a momentary pause to regather his thoughts, he straightened his head. Despite a small trickle of blood that ran from his lip, he maintained his smug appearance. His eyes were back on Kelly. He stared deep into her eyes. She was his and there was nothing she could do to deny it.

"We could have been good together," he grinned. "You and I, like two insatiable lovers."

Kelly's reaction was instant. She kicked out and struck him between the legs with her right foot. He sunk to his knees and released a sickening sound. For the first time, the smile was gone from Jordan Bilby's face.

"And that is for slapping my bottom, you piece of shit."

A wounded whimper slipped from his mouth. It was pathetic and brought a smirk from the officers. They had released him when he fell and left him on his knees before her. It allowed Kelly to bend down and lift Jordan's head by the chin. Their faces were inches apart when she spoke.

"If you ever touch me again, I will kill you," she whispered. "Do you understand?"

"Yes," he gasped before Kelly marched from the room followed by Lisa.

Jack was left with the two officers on either side of Jordan. Both had enjoyed watching Kelly put on a show. They stood in silence, unsure what they were supposed to do next. Neither was going to help Jordan unless they were given a direct order.

"There are a few beers in it for you lads if you didn't see that," said Jack as he offered them a knowing nod.

"Rest assured, DI Husker, we saw nothing. Our sole focus was on saving that lady's arse."

"That I can believe," laughed Jack. He looked at Jordan and twitched suddenly to leave the lad flinching at his feet.

Chapter 29

The briefing at the station went on longer than Jack would have liked. Though DCI Louth was satisfied with the outcome, he had warned that there would be a series of investigations to follow. The operation had threatened to go badly wrong. Kelly had been put in a dangerous position. Questions would be asked as to why she was allowed to go undercover so early in her career.

Such negative thoughts were tempered with the knowledge that both Jordan Bilby and Laura Tummel were locked up in the cells. Already, they were blaming each other, like two lovers going through a separation. The case against Laura would be easy. The only question was whether they could pin the murders on Jordan as well.

There was also some breaking news. Marcus Tummel had been arrested and was on his way to the station. Both Becky Rose and Pippa Jones had agreed to provide statements. The only question was whether it could be classed as rape. He would be interviewed in the morning after being left to stew in the cells overnight. A man like him could wait. After what he had done to the stable girls, there would be no concessions made for his comfort.

Jack had already told Louth that he would be questioning the man himself. He would also be the one to provide Marcus with the full lurid details of what Laura had done. The affairs would be dropped into the conversation shortly before they were offered up to Andy Hutton. In so many ways, the day could not get better.

Kelly had been taken away for a medical check. There would be a counsellor assigned to her, knowing that she was at risk of doing something she might regret. It worried both Jack and Lisa that the girl had got herself into so much trouble. It was hard to imagine a way back when the full facts came out.

Lisa leaned over towards Jack. Her question was one that she knew the answer to. She still needed to ask it just to make herself feel better and to share some of the burden she was carrying.

"Do you think Kelly will be alright?" asked Lisa.

"I hope so," shrugged Jack. "We all made plenty of mistakes when we were younger."

"I am surprised that you can remember that long ago."

"Cheeky."

"Seriously; what do you think will happen to her?"

"I don't know. Police standards will have a field day with both her and us. I think Louth will take a lot of the flak. That's for another day. At least we got her out of there safely."

"True enough. Do you think she will lose her job?"

"I hope not. She has the makings of a good detective. I would like to think there will be sympathy for what she has gone through."

"Police standards and sympathy," laughed Lisa. "That's a new one on me."

When Louth's speech finally came to an end, he told everyone to go home. It was late and they all needed sleep. A briefing would be held at eight o'clock. It was no time to take the foot off the pedal, not if the result was to be delivered. He wanted reports on his desk in the morning and he would not accept any excuses.

"Let's get off," said Lisa. "I don't need to spend another minute at work today."

"Any chance of a lift home?" asked Jack. He handed the car keys back to Lisa.

"No chance," she replied. "You can give me a lift home."

"But it's your car?"

"You might as well keep hold of the keys. That way I have an excuse to summon you at any time. It also gives me a designated driver to go out with."

"Come on then, I'll drop you off," said Jack.

"Or you could just stay at mine. That way we could see more of each other. I think we probably need to get beyond a few snatched moments together, don't you?"

Jack smiled and looked around the room. For once, he did not care what anyone else was thinking. He took hold of Lisa's hand and marched confidently out of the room. They were a couple. It left everyone, including Louth, to stare open-mouthed in their direction.

"Something tells me that things are never going to be the same," smiled Lisa.

"Maybe that is for the better," offered Jack as he squeezed Lisa's hand even tighter.

Acknowledgements

Just to say thanks to all those who helped in the publication of this book. All contributions, no matter how small, were greatly appreciated.

Available Now

Death Sketches

A UNIVERSITY STUDENT IS found hanging from a butcher's hook in the Shambles. Her body has been stripped and her bloodied form sketched by her killer. When she is found, it is the marks on her body that catch the detectives' attention. They are not there by accident but have been carved meticulously into her body.

DI Jack Husker is the detective tasked with finding the macabre killer before another student goes missing. He must put aside his own problems and the distractions from his past. Will he solve the case before the killer strikes again or will more of the brutal artwork be found across the city?

Set in the beautiful city of York, this is DI Jack Husker's debut outing as he tries to solve the toughest case of his career.

"Now my beautiful sculpture, please be quiet. I need silence for my work."

Death Sketches

Chapter 1

He pushed her forcibly up the stairs. Her slow, stumbling steps in the narrow staircase hindered her progress. Around her, she sensed an old building, its distinctive damp smell hanging in the air. She could see no part of it, the hastily tied blindfold masking her main sense and yet he offered her no concession for her lack of progress.

She tripped on the fourth step, her tied hands unable to break the fall. The tread of the stair above it cut into her shin. It felt broken. Numbness filled her leg. Her loud cry was met with a heavy grab of her shirt, dragging her back to her feet. She stumbled again, her leg unable to take the weight put on it. She needed a moment to rest but he had no compassion. Why should he? It was her weakness and he despised it.

Once more, he lifted her. His strong arm wrapped around her to prevent her from falling for a second time. There was barely room for the two of them in the stairwell. Still, he expected her to move forward. Her sobbing grew louder but it would do her no good. He was immune to emotion and unable to comprehend why anyone would plead. Pleading was what you did if you were hurt and he had barely started.

"Get up!"

She recognised the voice. No matter how hard she concentrated, she could not place it. She wanted to rip off the blindfold to reveal her tormentor though he had tied her well. Too well.

"Please, who are you?"

There was nothing.

She could sense they were near the top of the stairs. The climb had exhausted her. Blood was running down her leg and her body felt weak. She was never good with such things, prone to fainting at the tiniest sign of a scratch. Mummy had always said she should be braver. For once, she was thankful for the blindfold.

A lock. She heard him fumbling with a lock and a key. She memorised the time it took for him to turn it and the sound it made. An old building, a narrow staircase and a heavy-sounding lock. There would be blood on the fifth or sixth step, her blood, and then there was the familiar voice. They were all things she could tell the police about her abductor. The modern policemen would find him from the smallest detail. They were good at things like that. All she had to do was get through her ordeal and try to be brave.

He opened the door to a distinctive thud. The door needed a push, perhaps out of shape for the frame. Again, more evidence, more information to find the place, a damp corner somewhere in the middle of the city.

She sensed light as it opened, the sun streaming into the room to hit her face. A shove to her back pushed her to the wooden floor, bruising her knee. Why did he have to be so rough? She would do as she was told. It was her best hope. Then she would reason with him and he had to listen.

The door closed behind her. The turning key sounded more sinister from the inside. He was locking them in, trapping the two of them in the room. Her mind raced, her breathing more erratic than ever.

"What do you want?"

Again nothing, just footsteps walking across the room. His weight on the wooden floor vibrated through her body. How could he be so calm?

"Please, just let me go. I'll do anything."

Silence.

Suddenly, the room plunged into darkness. The curtains were pulled across the window with force. He flicked the switch to her side, providing a dim light by which he could see. Beneath the blindfold, there was just darkness and a sense of desperation in her thoughts. She was truly alone.

For the first time in her life, she prayed. She prayed she was back in Durham in the comforting presence of her parents and her dog. In front of the warm fire in their large house, she would be safe. From her position on the rug, she could see the top of the cathedral and the university where her parents had wanted her to go. Instead, she had chosen York, as much to exert her independence than for education. Now, she wished she had followed their path.

"Please, I'll scream."

A single strike to her head forced her to drift out of consciousness. The sweet taste of blood in her mouth was her last memory as she slipped away from the world.

***

She was the obvious choice. He had watched her carefully over those past few weeks. Indeed, he had studied her shape and she was perfect. Perfect in almost every dimension and he could change those parts where she was not. Why did she have to threaten to scream? Why could she not play along like the good girl he thought she was? Did they all have to be that way?

He walked around her lifeless body, watching her, studying every inch of her form. She was beautiful and at peace with the world. It was his favourite moment and he had prepared for it. He had followed her so many times. Now, he could get as close as he wanted. He could stare at her, touch her and taste her. She would taste so sweet when he ran his tongue across her face. He knew she would.

"Why did you scream? We were getting on so well, weren't we?"

She never answered.

It irritated him. Why did she ignore him? She had been so keen to talk when they climbed the stairs. Yet now, she was silent. It made no sense. Nothing ever did.

"Get up!"

Still, she ignored him, defiantly. For how long? They never ignored him for long.

"I said, get up!"

He hated rejection. It had been the watchword of his life. First, his father and then his mother. He would show them both and they would be proud. He would make them proud.

He dragged her to her feet. She felt limp. If she would not stand up for him, he would make her do it. Then he would sketch her.

"Take off your clothes."

She defied him again, ignoring his commands as if to spite him. He had tried hard to be friendly. He hooked her hands onto the large metal hook in the beam above her head. So convenient and perfect to hold her in place. He would strip her and he would not be nice. Oh no, he had tried that and she had ignored him. He had brought knives and he would use them. He would cut her clothes from her and if he hurt her, it was her fault. Not his. She had brought it upon herself.

Carefully, he laid the three knives on the floor. Each so different, they demanded to be examined. Just the way they glinted in the light, offering her reflection to him. All spotless, they had been cleaned well, making it a difficult choice between the three. He had his favourite; the one that always made the first cut. He smiled and held it up, feeling the adrenalin pumping through him. It was time and he could wait no longer.

The act did not take long. The sharpened knife sliced the clothes from her body in seconds. He wished he had taken more time and savoured it but he had work to do. He had no wish for delays and she would not help him. And now she looked perfect. Just as he had imagined she would. Her beauty was screaming at him in the most artistic of ways.

With a smile on his face, he moved away from her body and stood behind his easel. The position was perfect, the single bulb illuminating her naked figure. He needed to work and get every last detail right. It had to be just as he wanted if his work was to be admired.

"Now my beautiful sculpture, please be quiet. I need silence for my work."

Printed in Great Britain
by Amazon